Cast of Cha

Lady Lupin Lorrimer Hastings. Not your average vicar's wife, she's young, pretty, scatterbrained, and terribly kindhearted. Everybody seems anxious to tell her their life stories.

Diana Turner. Lupin's great friend, a children's book writer who has turned her inheritance, Orchard House, into a country hotel.

The Guests

Paul Ramsden. Diana's cousin, a cynical young artist. His share of the inheritance enabled him to give up the engineering job he hated.

Lavinia Dyson-Drake. An egotistical novelist and a friend of Paul's, whose only concern is that the manuscript to her new book is missing.

Ruth and Charles Rennie. A young couple. Married less than a year, they seem happy only when quarreling bitterly with one another.

Mrs. Mydleton. A sweetfaced but domineering widow.

Grizel Mydleton. Her spineless daughter, who has her own dreams.

Mrs. Smythe. A proper vicar's wife, greatly feared by Lady Lupin.

Arthur Smythe. Her chinless son. His mother fancies him to be a poet, but all he really wants is a chance to work on motorcars.

Colonel Robert James. Invalided out of the army, he is kind and sensible but seems to Lupin to be too much of a ladies' man.

Other Characters

Bert Gower. A garageman. Although an ardent socialist, he is a great admirer of Lady Lupin. He has a small daughter, **Rosie**, whom Miss Dyson-Drake ran over in her motorcar, and a fond wife, **Betty.**

Mr. Borden. A detective, engaged by Colonel James to sort things out. He's well aware that Lupin's prattlings often contain shrewd insights into human nature.

Plus assorted servants, police, firemen, tradespeople, and so forth.

Books by Joan Coggin

The Lady Lupin Quartet

Who Killed the Curate? (1944)
The Mystery of Orchard House (1946)
Why Did She Die? (1947)
Dancing with Death (1947)

Girls' Books

Betty of Turner House (1935)
Catherine Goes to School (1945)
Jane Runs Away from School (1946)
Catherine, Head of House (1947)
Audrey, a New Girl (1948)
Three New Girls (1949)

The Mystery at Orchard House

A Lady Lupin Mystery

by Joan Coggin

The Rue Morgue Press
Boulder, Colorado

The Mystery at Orchard House

FIRST AMERICAN EDITION

ISBN: 0-915230-54-2

The editors thank William F. Deeck
and Katherine Hall Page
for bringing the Lady Lupin
mysteries to their attention.

PRINTED IN THE UNITED STATES OF AMERICA

About Joan Coggin

In *Who Killed the Curate?* (1944), we were introduced to the lovely Lady Lupin Lorrimer, a 21-year-old earl's daughter who unexpectedly married 43-year-old Andrew Hastings, vicar of St. Mark's parish in Glanville in Sussex. Totally unprepared for the duties incumbent upon a clergyman's wife (she often confused Jews with Jesuits), somehow Lupin managed to soldier on, gladly abandoning her previous life of parties and indolence to be with her soulmate. As scatterbrained as she was, Lupin's tender heart and genuine concern for others won over even those parishioners who thought her too young and too pretty to be a vicar's wife, and her unconventional thought processes still pointed the way to identifying the murderer in this debut mystery.

The Mystery of Orchard House (1946) takes up her story over two years later, again in some indefinite period shortly before World War II. Lupin now has a two-year-old son, Peter, but a recent bout of influenza has forced her to leave him in the care of her husband and her old nanny while she takes a rest cure in the country at the hotel run by her good friend Diana Turner, a children's book writer. There's little rest in store for her, unfortunately, and once again Lupin's peculiar talent for getting at the truth, however circuitous a route she might take, comes in handy when the eccentric guests at Orchard House are plagued by a series of thefts and an attempted murder.

The final two books in the series, *Why Did She Die?* (1946) and *Dancing with Death* (1947), are set just after World War II. The first and fourth are the more clearly identifiable as traditional detective stories, although all four fit comfortably in the genre. All were originally published by Hurst & Blackett, a relatively obscure and long-since defunct London publishing house, in what must have been fiendishly small print runs, as they are extraordinarily difficult to find on the used-book market. None was ever published in the United States.

In addition to her four mysteries, Coggin, using the pseudonym Joanna Lloyd, wrote six girls' books set at the imaginary Shaftesbury School and based on Coggin's own school years at Wycombe Abbey. These stories are as charmingly told as Coggin's mysteries, and indeed the young Catherine, who figures in several of these books, bears a remarkable resemblance to Lady Lupin, although unlike Lupin, there's no doubt that Catherine has a first-class mind..

Born in Lemsford, Hertfordshire, in 1898, Coggin was the granddaughter on her mother's side of Edward Lloyd, founder of *Lloyd's Weekly London Newspaper*, which no doubt is why she used Lloyd as a pseudonym for her schoolgirl books. Her mother died when Coggin was eight and the family moved to Eastbourne, one of the easternmost towns in Britain, where she was to make her home for the rest of her life and which was clearly the model for Glanville.

After she was graduated from Wycombe Abbey in 1916 in the middle of World War I, Coggin worked as a nurse at an Eastbourne hospital. Although she suffered from a mild form of epilepsy, Coggin did not let it inhibit her lifestyle. After the war, she returned to those activities expected of a young woman of her class and upbringing—the social round of bridge, tennis, golf and books. She also worked with the blind.

In the 1930s, she turned to writing, producing her first girls' book, *Betty of Turner House*, in 1935. With the exception of that book Coggin's writing career was limited to a five-year period between 1944 and 1949, during which she produced nine books. For the last thirty years of her life she apparently did no more writing. She died in 1980 at the age of 82.

Her contribution to crime fiction was slight but memorable. Lupin, probably the first clergyman's wife to take up crime-solving as a hobby, may remind readers of Gracie Allen of Burns and Allen. She's certainly the spiritual godmother of the Pauline Collins character in the very funny BBC comedy series *No, Honestly* from a few years ago. The Collins character came many years later, of course, and although Coggin may well have been familiar with Gracie Allen's routines, there is little doubt that Lady Lupin sprang fullblown from Coggin's own imagination. She's that rarity in cozy crime fiction—in spite of her many eccentricities she seems more real than most of the people we encounter in real life. Or maybe that's just wishful thinking.

Tom & Enid Schantz
Boulder, Colorado
December 2001

CHAPTER 1

"THIS is absolutely perfect, Di, exactly what I have been longing for. I just want to do absolutely nothing for a bit." Lady Lupin Hastings looked round the big bed-sitting room and through the window at the apple orchard, glowing in the afternoon sun, with a sigh of satisfaction. "I foresee a fortnight of absolute peace and quiet in front of me, and I shall go back to Glanville as fat as a pig."

When pretty Lupin Lorrimer, at twenty-one, married the forty-year-old vicar of Glanville, there were plenty of people to prophesy disaster, for Lupin had spent her life hitherto almost entirely in the search of amusement. However, the pessimists had been wrong. She had been married now for over three years, had a two-year-old son, was still devoted to her husband and popular with his parishioners. She could not be called an efficient clergyman's wife, but was always ready to plunge into any activity that was going on, and her natural gaiety and good humor made a parish bazaar or a temperance meeting an occasion for pleasure for most of the people concerned, although the original purpose of the gathering became frequently somewhat obscured.

Lupin was seldom sick or sorry, but after her husband, her small boy, all her servants and most of the parishioners had gone down with influenza, she succumbed herself and had actually been sent away for a rest cure, a thing that had never happened to her before in her entire life.

Her great friend, Diana Turner, had lately been left a lovely old manor house in Kent, called Orchard House. Unfortunately, she had not enough money to enable her to live in it, so she had turned it into a guest house and it was here that Lupin had come to recuperate. She hated leaving her husband and her boy, Peter, who had just reached what was surely the most fascinating age in the world, but as she looked at the apple blossom and at the daffodils in the long grass, and as she realized that no Sunday-school teacher would come in to ask her advice about the catechism, no widow to ask help in filling in a government form for a pension, and no member of the Temperance Society to ask her support with the town council in the banning of the sale of intoxicating liquors, she heaved a great sigh of relief.

The last thought reminded her that it was time for a little refreshment. After a conference with Diana on the subject, her maid, Staines—who had accompanied her here, as she had accompanied her from Lorrimer Castle to Glanville Vicarage, and as she always would accompany her wherever she went and however much she might disapprove of her destination—was sent in search of it.

"I am afraid Staines is a bit hurt with you," remarked Lupin.

"I thought she seemed a bit chilly. I suppose she does not like me keeping this 'pub.' Funny. She was quite friendly when I was suspected of murder."

"Murder is one thing, earning your living is another. Staines is not exactly what you would call a socialist, you know."

"So I gathered. Oh, good, here it is," as Staines returned with a couple of glasses of sherry. "Now, do tell me all about Glanville," begged Diana as Staines left the room, for Diana had lived there many years and still took a keen interest in all its inhabitants.

"It was going on beautifully until everyone was taken ill. Since then I haven't really seen many people. Parishioners kept on arriving on the doorstep and begging me to leave it all to them, so of course I did. They were mostly taken ill the next day, so whatever it was got left altogether, but I don't expect it did any harm. Most difficulties solve themselves if left long enough. Oh, there was one excitement—the Brownes' house caught fire. The guide captain rang up all her guides to come to help put it out, but by the time they had put on their uniforms and she had inspected their nails and sent them home to put on stockings, the fire brigade had put it out, and the Brownes said it was just their luck because if they had got the insurance money he could have retired. Anyway, there was a photograph of 'valiant girl guides, with their leader,' in the local paper the next Saturday, only it had got rather mixed up with the next one which was the opening of the Magdalene

Hostel for unmarried mothers. Which reminds me of one of my bricks. They asked me to open a bazaar for it and, of course, I got all mixed up and thought it was for the Mothers' Union and I said I hoped they would go on having heaps more babies as big families were so much nicer than small ones, which they are, aren't they? I do hope that Peter will soon have heaps more brothers and sisters. Well, as you see, I really am getting most awfully parochial. Even Miss Gibson, the Sunday-school superintendent, is beginning to unbend to me a bit. You know, to start with, I think she thought Andrew had made a mistake in marrying me, but anyway she sent me some oranges when I was ill and a little book entitled *What a Mother Can Do for Her Child.* I must read it sometime, it would be nice to know. Oh, and the guides sent me a beautiful illuminated text about smiling and singing under all difficulties. Not a very easy thing to do when you are being busy with the basin! I did try it once, but the nurse said: 'Is the pain very bad, dear?' which was rather damping. Then the Parochial Church Council sent me some lovely flowers and a card attached, 'With deepest sympathy,' which I thought a little premature. I must say, however, everyone has been most frightfully kind. Now, do tell me all about you."

"Well, Aunt Lucy died and left me this place. It was a great surprise to me as I had never thought of such a thing. I took for granted that she would leave it to my cousin, Paul Ramsden. He had always spent his holidays here when he was a boy as his parents were in India and she was devoted to him. He was a dear little boy; I used to see quite a lot of him though, of course, I am years older than he is. As a matter of fact, he is a dear now but he has rather strange ideas. He is an artist, but he admires everything that most people think hideous. Everything that we admire is obvious and not worth looking at! Beauty is something one should search for in unexpected surroundings, so he tells me. I don't pretend to understand it myself. He has no use for anything old and he has never made any secret of his opinions. I suppose Aunt Lucy was afraid he would do something frightful to this place, give it a blue roof or cut down the cherry trees and plant petrol pumps or something ghastly. I must say I see her point. I should have hated to see it spoilt. I've always been very fond of it, though I didn't really want her to leave it to me. I don't like to sell it, as she obviously left it to me because she didn't want it altered, but naturally she left Paul most of her money, so I couldn't very well afford to live here in the ordinary way. Hence the P.G.s and the loss of Staines's esteem. Never mind, one day

I will write a bestseller and then I shall be able to live in it as a lady should! Paul has been awfully decent and found several of the guests for me. He is a bit weird but I hope you'll like him. Of course, as I said, he is years younger than I am, and looks on me as a terrible example of the last generation, but he is quite kind to me."

"But aren't the guests a frightful nuisance? I mean, do you get any time for writing your books?" For Diana was well known as a writer of children's stories and had a couple of detective novels to her credit as well.

"Yes," said Diana, sipping her sherry. "I found it difficult to fit it in at first, but now I have everything going I can usually manage an hour or two each day. The people aren't much trouble on the whole. There is one woman who has changed her room three times, and there is a husband and wife who quarrel all the time. They are friends of Paul's and I sometimes wish he hadn't persuaded them to come here, but he meant well and they don't haggle about the bills. And then there is another friend of his, a ghastly female who is always wanting to talk about literature. She said to me the other day, 'We must have a long, long talk some time.' So I have to spend my time dodging her. Oh, and there is rather a dreadful youth with no chin who writes poetry."

"Oh, I'm used to them," said Lupin, "only they are usually in the YMCA or the Scouts and they have Adam's-apples. I have often wondered why chins and religion seem so incompatible."

"His father is a clergyman."

"Oh, dear, is he here?"

"No, but his wife is, a Mrs. Smythe."

"You don't mean to say you've let me in for meeting a real clergyman's wife. She'll find out the first minute that I am phony."

"Why? Aren't you a clergyman's wife? I always had the impression that you and Andrew had been married for three years. What a shock!"

"It's all right, I've got my lines—at least I did have once, though I don't know where they are now. But you know yourself that I am a very poor kind of clergyman's wife. Even after all these years I get mixed over the CMS and SPCK and SSU. Of course, they are used to me in Glanville but if I ever have to go to anything outside the parish, for clergy wives, everyone looks at me as if I had leprosy."

Diana looked at her friend critically. She had not changed much during the last three years. She was thinner, but her hair was just as golden and her eyes still had that childish, friendly look that had enchanted Diana and many others on first seeing her.

"No, I am afraid you don't look very much like a clergyman's wife," she said. "You will be as out of it when Mrs. Smythe starts about societies for keeping girls pure as I am when Miss Dyson-Drake starts about the rhythm of literature. Well, I mustn't stay here gossiping with you, I am one of the world's workers. By the way, do you remember Nanny? She was with me at Glanville, in fact, she has always been with me."

"Yes, rather, is she here?"

"Of course, running the whole place, so I don't really need to do anything."

"What luck! She and Staines were always rather buddies, so she will talk her round. I've got my old nanny for Peter. Everyone said I ought to have someone from a training college or something, but I knew she would try to train his mind or something frightful. I don't expect for a minute that he has a mind and I want him to have a happy childhood, not taught handicrafts, nor Morris dancing, nor self-expression."

"I agree with you. Dinner is at a quarter to eight, don't look too conspicuous the first evening." For try as Lupin might nothing would ever make her clothes look at all parochial. "Goodbye for the present."

"Goodbye. Oh, there you are, Staines! I think I had better have a bath."

"I have turned it on, my lady."

"Oh, good! I say, what do you think I had better wear? Miss Turner doesn't want me to look too gay, if you know what I mean."

"I should think your gray would be suitable for the occasion, my lady."

"The gray! Yes, of course. Just the thing! Everyone will see that I am a clergyman's wife at once and behave accordingly." But somehow when she had put on the gray she did not look like that at all. It was such a delicious shade of gray, and the material was so soft and filmy and Lupin looked so young and pretty that everyone gazed at her as Diana led her to the table reserved for them in the corner of the dining room. Lupin was hungry after her journey and thoroughly enjoyed her dinner, but the first pangs of hunger satisfied she looked round at the other diners with interest.

The quarrelsome couple were seated quite near and Lupin guessed them at once. She was not very clever, but when she heard the man say,

"My dear girl, if you cannot open your mouth without showing your utter ignorance of the matter, it would be better if you kept quiet," she guessed that they were the ones, and when the girl replied, "If I knew as little as you did on every subject except your moldy science, I should certainly keep quiet in front of strangers. And if you only knew how everybody laughed at you behind your back you would not be so pleased with yourself," she was certain of it. It was a pity they were so disagreeable because they were both rather nice-looking in their way. He had brown, wavy hair that would not lie flat however much he brushed it, and the sort of face that Lupin thought would light up if he smiled. His wife was distinctly pretty, although it was a pity her mouth drooped as it did at the corners and that her clothes were all just wrong. Lupin learned from Diana afterwards that she hailed from one of the London suburbs and had a hankering after bohemia and that her husband was a science lecturer at London University.

A little farther down the room was a very sweet-looking woman with white hair, dressed in black velvet, and with her a rather pretty, faded-looking daughter, probably still in her early thirties but looking more.

"That is the one who keeps changing her room," said Diana, following Lupin's eyes.

"Oh, is it? She looks nice," replied Lupin, surprised.

"Oh, she is pleasant enough, but she expects everyone to spend their time waiting on her. I am rather sorry for the daughter, Grizel. She is not allowed to call her soul her own, I believe. That is my literary friend," and she turned her head slightly towards the corner where a weird female with a lot of hair and many floating scarves talked across the room to a young man at the opposite table.

"To me," this woman said in a loud and dominating voice, "all material is imaginary. The food we have just eaten has no real substance. One eats it and forgets it. It is our thoughts that give us nourishment."

"I wish, in that case," said Diana, in a low voice, "that she would not wolf down so much of it at every meal. She has the biggest appetite in the place."

"I like food," said the young man. "To me, a well-grilled steak surrounded by crisp, golden-brown onions is a pleasant picture."

"That is my cousin," said Diana. "I told you about him, didn't I?"

"What, the artist? He looks quite normal."

"Yes, he rather prides himself on not looking like an artist, in the same way that he prides himself on preferring gasworks to cathedrals and steaks to flowers. But he is a nice boy, though I rather wish he had not brought his lady friend here. I am sure her bill does not cover what she eats and I am afraid she may drive away the others. Mrs. Mydleton, the pretty, tiresome woman, has complained about her once or twice, so has Mrs. Smythe, the clergyman's wife."

"Which is she? Oh, I know," as her eyes fell on a middle-aged woman with a purposeful expression and a garnet brooch, talking to a young man whom Lupin at once pictured in the clothes of a scoutmaster. "Yes, she is a genuine one, I can see. I shall avoid her like the plague. Surely that weird woman in the scarves is years older than your cousin."

"Oh, yes, I'm sure it's quite platonic, but she is a nuisance, all the same."

A middle-aged man came in and spoke to Diana on his way to his own table. "I am sorry I am so late, but my car conked out on me five miles from home. I hope you have left me a lot to eat because I am very hungry."

"Miss Dyson-Drake has announced to us all that the food she has just eaten had no substance. I hope you will be luckier. Lupin, may I introduce Colonel James. Lady Lupin Hastings."

"How do you do? Isn't this weather marvelous? I hope it will stay like this all the time you are here," and he walked on to his own table, waving to the young married couple as he sat down.

Coffee was served in a large drawing room overlooking the garden. The sun was setting and a golden light lay over everything. Lupin was not artistic, but she would have summed up her feelings on looking out of the window as "everything being rather decent."

"Does not this fill your soul, Miss Turner?" inquired the literary Miss Dyson-Drake, stopping at their table. "What more do we mortals want, when we can have our whole being soothed, inspired, and awakened by a scene like this?"

Lupin avoided Diana's eye, having already heard how much more Miss Dyson-Drake did require to keep her going. Diana's cousin now joined their group. "Obvious," he remarked in a rather tired voice. "Anyone can admire a sunset. It takes the eye of an artist to appreciate a row of tenement houses or a fishmonger's shop."

"Talking of fishmongers," said Diana, "I must go and speak to the cook."

Lupin looked after her rather despairingly and was just about to follow her out of the room when Miss Dyson-Drake turned to her again. "What a pity she wastes her time over such mundane matters, she will never be an artist."

Lupin thought it would be a poor lookout for the guests if Diana ignored all mundane matters, but contented herself with saying, "I don't think she wants to be an artist. She writes books, you know."

"And can't a writer be an artist? Do you consider the painter in words falls below the standard of the painter in color?"

"Oh, no, rather not! I think it is awfully clever to write books and Diana's are awfully good. Did you read *Murder in the Basement?"*

"No, I may do so one day, if I feel the need to relax. But I have never felt she had any message for me."

"Crime," said Paul with a shudder, "too, too obvious!"

"I don't agree with you," said Miss Dyson-Drake. "I have read some very powerful books about crime. Of course, I am not interested in the tracing of the criminal, as in the ordinary detective story, but in the psychology of the subject. Some of the Russian writers have much to say on this matter. Of course, they are realists. I don't think our own writers approach the subject from the right angle."

"The Anglo-Saxon has no sense of rhythm," agreed Paul.

"Well, I must go and find my friend," said Lupin, getting up.

"Friendship is a very beautiful thing," said Miss Dyson-Drake. "Much is made in books of love and crime but little is said about friendship."

"I don't see that you could say much," objected Lupin. "Either you are friends or you are not. It wouldn't make much of a story, would it?" In her hurry to get away she nearly collided with the chinless young man who was carrying a card table across the room to Mrs. Mydleton, the sweet-looking woman in black velvet. Lupin was just thinking what a moldy lot of men the hotel contained and how Andrew need not have any fears of her flirting with any of them, when she noticed that the faded-looking girl called Grizel was quite pink and flustered as the young man arranged the table in front of her mother.

"Thank you, Arthur," said the latter. "But you should not have bothered. Why did you not ring for one of the servants?"

"Oh, it's quite all right, Mrs. Mydleton. It's as light as a feather. Do you think while you are playing your patience, Grizel and I might have a walk round the garden? It's such a lovely evening."

"I think Grizel would find it too chilly. Just shuffle the cards for me, dear."

"Oh, no, Mother, it isn't a bit cold and it's such a lovely sunset."

"Is it? I might come with you, perhaps, but then I should have to change my shoes. We had better leave it till another evening."

Lupin had passed out of earshot by this time, but she felt sorry for the daughter who seemed to like the chinless young man and who would evidently have enjoyed looking at the sunset with him. Paul Ramsden was just walking out of the French windows with the pretty little Mrs. Rennie. She had lost her peevish look and was listening to her companion with frank admiration. She was probably learning how inferior an apple orchard was to a fish shop. Lupin was nearly at the door when the clergyman's wife accosted her.

"Forgive me for introducing myself, but I saw from the visitor's book that you lived in a vicarage and as I am a vicar's wife myself, I hoped you might be connected with a clergyman's family. My name is Mrs. Smythe."

"How do you do?" said Lupin in a resigned voice. "Yes, as a matter of fact my husband is a clergyman. It is nice here, isn't it?"

"Yes and no. The place is quite comfortable and not expensive, I must say that for it, and, of course, Miss Turner is a lady, which makes such a difference, doesn't it? But I call that cousin of hers a most extraordinary young man. You never know what he is going to say next, and as for that Miss Dyson-Drake! She is a terrible woman. They are both thorough bohemians, if you ask me, although I must say Mr. Ramsden looks quite normal. But her clothes! And Mr. and Mrs. Rennie, I can't say I care for them at all. In fact Mrs. Mydleton and her daughter were the only people from here that I saw in church on Sunday. So I am delighted you have come. We must have some nice talks, mustn't we? I shall enjoy hearing all about your parish. One feels lost out of one's own element, don't you think?" As she spoke she looked rather keenly at Lupin, who did not look very much like a vicar's wife. Her hair, her frock, her complexion, and her nails were all against her.

"Yes, we must have a nice talk tomorrow," said Lupin. "I am afraid I must go now or Miss Turner will be wondering what has happened to me." She wandered into the hall and asked George, a friendly-looking individual who acted as porter and general factotum, where she would be likely to find Miss Turner.

"I expect she's up in her office, my lady. Shall I show you the way?" and he led her along several passages and up and down several small flights of stairs. As they passed one door, it opened and Mr. Rennie dashed out, nearly knocking Lupin down. Instead of apologizing, he gave her a look of concentrated fury and darted back into his room. Lupin felt Mrs. Smythe was not far out in her estimate of the other guests; they were not an attractive lot. However, it was lovely seeing Diana again, it was a gorgeous place, and she need not worry about the other people.

"Oh, there you are!" said Diana. "There was a minor tragedy about the fish."

"Well, I wish you had taken me with you. I got caught by the vicar's wife and I would rather have been mixed up with the fish—not that I know much about fish, but I am better at it than I am on the Girls' Friendly Society and the Young Men's Christian Association. We are going to have a heart-to-heart talk tomorrow. She is longing to hear all about my parish. A nice figure I'll cut when she asks me what the children learn in Sunday School! Oh, they do know about Joseph and his brethren, because I told them that the day I had to take a class, and I always think it is such a nice story, but even then one of the boys asked me why Joseph got put into prison, and I had to say, 'you can go home now,' because I didn't like to tell them about Potiphar's wife. I am sure Mrs. Smythe has heaps of clubs for pure girls, good wives, and bad husbands, but I don't think we have anything except the Girl Guides, of course, and a boys' football club, oh, and some people play whist on Thursdays. I don't know who they are but they all take sugar in their tea."

"Well, I shouldn't bother your head about them now. You have come here to forget. I never thought of Mrs. Smythe having the nerve to introduce herself before you had been in the place a couple of hours. She was all over Mrs. Mydleton and Grizel before you came. They will get a rest, anyway. I live in dread of her finding out that I am a clergyman's daughter. It is bad enough Miss Dyson-Drake having found out that I write."

"I don't do that, anyway, so the literary ones will leave me alone, I hope. I suppose I had better go, and get a good night's rest in preparation for tomorrow. Good night, my dear."

Diana insisted on seeing her to her room, as the passages were rather confusing and Staines was awaiting her with a glass of hot milk. At last she was alone, with the curtains drawn back and the windows wide open. She settled down with a sigh of relief into her comfortable bed. She had had a great many disturbed nights lately, and it was lovely to look forward to ten hours' undisturbed sleep.

CHAPTER 2

LUPIN was just dozing off when there was a knock at the door. She opened her eyes and switched on the light. Grizel Mydleton stood in the doorway.

"I am so sorry to disturb you," she said, "but I thought I saw a light."

"I have only just turned it out. Is anything the matter?" Lupin wondered why Miss Mydleton had chosen a mauve dressing gown, as it was the last color she should ever have worn.

"It's only…I wondered whether you had any sal volatile. Mother isn't very well, in fact she has had one of her attacks, and Burton, that's our maid, hadn't realized that the bottle was empty and we don't quite know what to do, and as I thought I saw a light under the door I thought you wouldn't mind…"

"I'm afraid that I haven't any sal volatile, but I've got some brandy, if that's any good."

"Oh, I don't know…thank you so much…perhaps she would… sometimes it does her good…she has a weak heart, I shouldn't have left her," and Grizel stood wringing her hands, while Lupin got out of bed and hunted up the brandy flask.

She must have been quite pretty when she was a girl, thought Lupin compassionately. In fact she'd be all right now if she'd make up a bit, wear something that didn't clash with her face, and do something with her hair. She hospitably proffered a toothglass. "I'd have a spot yourself if I were you," she remarked. "You look a bit done up."

Rather to her surprise, her visitor poured herself out a liberal portion and gulped it down neat. "Oh, thank you," she said. "You are kind. As a matter of fact I am in great trouble and I'd like to confide in you sometime."

Oh, goodness! thought Lupin. I might as well have stayed at home. At least, people don't come into my bedroom there with their confidences. Aloud she said, "Rather. I expect I shall be seeing you tomorrow or some time. Hadn't you better pop along to your mother with that brandy? I mean, if she's having a heart attack she may— I mean, perhaps a little brandy will do her good."

"Yes, I must fly. I should never forgive myself if anything were to happen to her. Grizel tore herself away reluctantly and Lupin lay down again, switched off the light, gave a sigh of relief and was soon asleep.

She was awakened again within half an hour by the door being flung wide open. As the windows were also open and quite a strong wind had got up, the papers on the writing table were blown across the room and a vase of daffodils fell over with a crash. She switched on the light, supposing that it was Miss Mydleton returning with the brandy flask, but found herself staring into the furious face of the young married woman, Mrs. Rennie.

"Oh, God!" exclaimed the intruder. "I thought this room was empty."

"Well, it isn't," replied Lupin, rather feebly.

"So I see," was the retort. "Do you know where there is an empty room?"

"No, I am afraid I don't. I only arrived this evening."

"Well, I must sleep somewhere."

"Haven't you a room of your own?" asked Lupin, rather puzzled.

"A room of my own! Aren't you married?"

"Er, yes," said Lupin. She was feeling very sleepy and didn't quite know what she was saying, but she felt that she was on firm ground here. "Yes, I've been married for three years."

"Three years! Ye gods! I've only been married for six months but it feels like six years. In fact it feels like six hundred years. How ever have you stuck it out?"

"I like it," said Lupin.

"Like it! You wouldn't if you were married to my husband."

"No, I don't expect I should. I mean, I'm sure he's very nice."

"Nice! He is a fiend in human form. I simply loathe him. I have a very affectionate nature." By this time she had seated herself on the end of Lupin's bed and was fixing her with smouldering dark eyes. Rather like the Ancient Mariner, thought Lupin, although, of course, his eye was blue and glittering.

"If I loved a man," went on Mrs. Rennie, "I should love him forever. I am passionately faithful. I only want to love and serve, but I must have understanding in return. Mine is a very complex nature. I am highly strung and terribly sensitive. A word is worse than a blow to me."

"Oh is it? I always feel that:

'Sticks and stones
Can hurt my bones,
But talking
Cannot hurt me.' "

"You are very different from me," Mrs. Rennie said. "You are one of the simple souls who do not demand much from life. You love your husband, in your own way, and you have no wish for a larger, fuller existence. I thought I loved Charles once but I realize now I was mistaken. I was young. Six months may not sound long but I have grown up in those six months, more than you have in your three years of happy, humdrum married life. I may not look old, but I am old, older than many a woman of eighty."

"Older than the rocks on which she sat," murmured Lupin, who was falling asleep. She had a habit of remembering sentences or phrases that she had heard, although she seldom knew from whence they came.

"The Mona Lisa!" exclaimed Mrs. Rennie, delightedly. "Is that of whom I remind you? How clever of you! I have often thought she must have been rather like me."

"Is that the one I meant? I know someone sat on some rocks and was older than they were, but I can't remember who it was. I always thought that it must have been dangerous for an old woman like that to go sitting about on wet rocks."

"The whole thing is, what am I to do now?" declared Mrs. Rennie, ignoring Lupin's ramblings.

Lupin knew the answer to that one. "I should go to bed if I were you," she said "As a matter of fact, I was half thinking of turning in myself. I have had rather a long day and I haven't been very grand lately. Influenza, you know."

"But where?"

"At Glanville, that's where I live. My husband is the vicar. We were all ill. I am really quite all right again but I'm by way of having a sort of rest cure."

"Where am I to sleep?"

"To sleep? Oh, haven't you got a bedroom?"

"Yes, but my husband is in it."

"Oh, I see; yes, of course, he would be, they usually are, husbands, I mean."

"Nothing would induce me to sleep in the same room as that man. I should feel that I was committing a far greater sin than I should be if I slept with a man I loved, even if he were not my husband. In fact, I really disapprove of marriage. I should never have married if I had known what it meant."

"I thought everyone knew nowadays," murmured Lupin. "They always seem to be lecturing or writing books about it. 'Straight talks to young people, and the facts of life made plain, etc.' "

"I wasn't taking about that."

"Oh, I'm glad," replied Lupin, dropping off to sleep.

She awoke to find that Mrs. Rennie had gone, but her place had been taken by Miss Dyson-Drake, who stood in the doorway looking like Lady Macbeth. For a moment Lupin did not realize that a change had taken place. "I'm afraid I've only got one bed," she said, "but if my bathroom is any good to you—"

"It has gone," declared Miss Dyson-Drake.

"What, the bathroom?" asked Lupin, wondering if she were asleep or awake. "How do you mean, gone?"

"I left it in my bedroom while I took a moonlight stroll with Paul Ramsden, and when I came back it had gone."

"I expect it will turn up," said Lupin optimistically, wondering what it was that had gone. "I dare say it's underneath something. I lost ten pounds once and—"

"Ten pounds! What is ten pounds? Do you think I should care if I lost ten pounds? Or fifty pounds? Or a hundred pounds for the matter of that? I have lost my work, my life, my child."

Lupin woke up thoroughly at that last word. "Your child, did you say your child? I hadn't grasped it. I'll come at once," and she jumped out of bed, slipped into a blue satin dressing gown and hurried to the door. "We had better find Diana, Miss Turner, you know. I wonder where she sleeps, I never thought of asking her." She was on the landing by now and she knocked at the nearest door. Charles Rennie came out in pajamas and ruffled hair. "So you have come to your senses at last, have you?" he said. "Oh, I'm sorry."

"It's quite all right, but the most awful thing has happened. Miss ...er...Mrs...er...well, she has lost her child. We had better get up a search party. Some of us could go all over the house, and some over the garden, and someone had better ring up the police." She banged on a few more doors and Arthur Smythe appeared fully dressed and offered to go out into the grounds.

Mrs. Smythe also emerged, neatly clad in a dressing gown suitable to a vicar's wife, but Lupin was too much agitated at the moment to feel her own inferiority in that direction. She thanked Arthur fervently and enlisted Mrs. Smythe's help in searching the house. Mrs. Smythe, although sorry about the child, was glad to have an opportunity for using her powers of organization.

"Wrap up warmly," she said to Arthur. "You know that you are subject to colds."

"I'll come with you," volunteered Charles Rennie.

Suddenly Mrs. Rennie appeared on the scene. "Where are you going, Charles?" she cried, as her husband made for the staircase, shrugging on an overcoat as he went. She rushed to him and caught him by the arm. "Oh, Charles, don't go," she cried. "I didn't mean it," and she threw her arms round his neck.

"That's all right, darling. I won't be long, but there seems to be a child missing and Smythe and I are just going to have a look round the grounds. I'll be back in two ticks." And he patted her shoulder, obviously divided between pleasure at the reconciliation and embarrassment at having so many witnesses.

"Now we women had better explore the inside of the house," said Mrs. Smythe. "Lady Lupin, will you come with me to the top story and perhaps, Mrs. Rennie, you and Miss Dyson-Drake will do the first floor, and you might call up Miss Turner while you are there."

Paul Ramsden joined the party in a very charming négligé of blue velvet, and the middle-aged man who had come in late for dinner arrived in a serviceable Jaeger dressing gown. "Anything up?" he inquired.

"Yes," replied Mrs. Smythe, who had taken charge of the proceedings. "Lady Lupin's child has disappeared."

"Not my child," explained Lupin. "He is safe at home, at least, I hope he is. It's Miss…er …Mrs. Dyson…"

"I didn't know you had a child, Lavinia," said Paul.

"I haven't, replied Miss Dyson-Drake. "But," she added bravely, "if I had, I shouldn't be ashamed of it."

"Whose child is missing?" asked Mrs. Rennie.

"I don't know," said Lupin in a bewildered tone of voice. "I…I understood Miss Dyson-Drake to say that her child had disappeared so I thought I had better wake everybody up."

"Well, you have certainly done that," remarked Diana, who had materialized among her guests.

Grizel appeared at the far end of the corridor. "Oh, please, Miss Turner," she said, "could you ask people to be a little quieter. Mother has just woken up, she says that there is a dreadful noise, and that she will never get off again."

"Well, tell her that a child has just been kidnapped," said Lupin, "and she will understand our being a bit agitated."

"A child kidnapped!" cried Grizel, in a voice of horror. "We must keep it from mother."

"But what child has been kidnapped?" asked Diana. "There is no child in the house, so far as I know."

"I am sure you said your child had disappeared," said Lupin reproachfully to Miss Dyson-Drake.

"I couldn't have done as I have no child. I was talking of my manuscript."

"Oh, your manuscript! I thought you said 'child,' and I was so upset. I don't know what I should do if anything happened to Peter."

"I'll go and tell Charles," said Mrs. Rennie.

"Tell him it is a manuscript he has got to look for, not a child," remarked Diana dryly.

"And please tell Arthur to come in at once. He's not strong and I should never have let him go out at this time of night if I hadn't thought it was the case of a poor, lost child," said Mrs. Smythe.

"I'll come with you," said Colonel James, following Mrs. Rennie down the stairs.

"Have you really lost your manuscript, Lavinia?" asked Paul Ramsden.

"Yes, fifty pages of typescript. I left it lying on my writing table when I came down to dinner, and when I came back it was gone."

"Shall I come back to your room with you, Miss Dyson-Drake?" asked Diana.

"Oh, please, Miss Turner, will you come to mother?" begged Grizel, returning from her mother's room. "She is in a terrible state and says that I am keeping something from her."

"And are you?" inquired Diana.

"I know what I think," announced Miss Dyson-Drake. "But it is too soon to speak. I need proof."

"Well, I think perhaps I'll go to bed," said Lupin. "All's well that ends well. Good night, everyone."

"But has it ended well?" asked Diana. "That is the question."

CHAPTER 3

LUPIN was not among those earliest downstairs the next morning. In fact, Staines brought up her breakfast to her and found her still asleep. "Oh, Staines, I had a frightful night," she remarked when she was at length awakened.

"So I gathered from Miss Turner, my lady. She suggested that you should have your breakfast upstairs."

"And a good idea of hers, too. I had scarcely got into bed before someone came in to say that her mother was having a fit and could I lend her some sal volatile. In the end she went away with the brandy, and by the way, Staines, you'd better get some more, we'll never see that again and it was in my silver flask, too. Then someone else came in to say that she couldn't sleep with her husband and what had she better do, then she disappeared, I don't know where, and still another woman took her place and said that she'd lost her child. Naturally I was upset about that. Suppose it had been Peter! So I tried to organize a search party and would you believe it, in the middle, after I had woken everyone up and sent them out into the grounds, the child turned out to be some moldy old manuscript and I might just as well have stayed in bed. So far as that goes I might just as well have stayed at Glanville. At least one is safe in bed there."

"You had better lock the door tonight, my lady."

"That's a good idea, but I expect they'll climb up the waterspout and get in at the window. One good thing is that those married ones seem to have made it up. They had a regular closeup on the stairs when he was going out to look for the child. I wonder if the manuscript has turned up yet."

"I don't think so, my lady. I understand that the writing lady is most upset about it."

"Well, I suppose it would be a bit sickening if one took all the trouble to write something and then went and lost it. Which reminds me, by the way, I was writing a letter to Mr. Hastings last night and I don't remember what I did with it."

"I posted it, my lady."

"Oh, good idea! Well, I suppose I may as well get up. I do hope Miss Dyson-Drake finds her manuscript before tonight. After all, it must be somewhere."

"I think she suspects someone of having stolen it, my lady. There are a lot of writing ladies and gentlemen in this hotel."

"Oh, and she thinks that one of them has nabbed it, does she, and is going to pass it off as one of their own? But why did she hit on me? Does she think that I'm a writing Johnny?"

"She may do, as you are a friend of Miss Turner's, my lady. Or she may merely have mistaken the room."

Lupin found her way to Diana's sitting room, there to find Miss Dyson-Drake, breathing threatenings and slaughters. She was standing in a commanding position by the fireplace. She had discarded her flowing garments of the night before and was clad in a pair of red corduroy slacks and a green pullover. She was further adorned with a single eyeglass and a green bandeau.

"If it is not found by twelve noon, I go to my solicitor," she was saying to Diana as Lupin strolled in.

"Oh, good morning, Miss Dyson-Drake. Haven't you found your manuscript yet? What rotten luck!"

"It is somewhere in this hotel, of that I am convinced," replied Miss Dyson-Drake.

"Well, that's all to the good then, isn't it? I mean, it can't be far off, can it?"

"It's not far off," was the cryptic reply.

There was a gentle tap at the door and Mrs. Mydleton entered, followed by an embarrassed-looking Grizel. "May I have a few words with you, Miss Turner?"

"Yes, of course. Won't you sit down?"

"Well, shall we go and have a look for the old manuscript?" suggested Lupin tactfully to Miss Dyson-Drake.

"It is no good looking for it. But I have said all I have to say on that head for the moment."

Well, that is something to be thankful for, anyway, thought Lupin, as she shepherded her from the room. As she shut the door, she overheard the gentle, plaintive voice of Mrs. Mydleton.

"I came here because I was told the place was quiet. My nerves are in a terrible state and my heart is in a very precarious condition. The least agitation may prove fatal. Not that I mind for myself. What have I to live for? But I have to think of Grizel, poor child! I dread to think of what it will mean to her when the parting comes! So I try to husband my strength that I may live a few more years for her sake. But last night just as I had for once dropped off to sleep for a few minutes, I was awakened by shrieks and shouts. I naturally thought the house was on fire."

"It was all most unfortunate," agreed Diana. "I am afraid Miss Dyson-Drake is rather temperamental."

"Temperamental! She is merely a selfish, unbalanced woman who, just because she calls herself an author, thinks she can do what she likes and has no thought and no regard for others. Selfishness is a fault that I cannot condone in anyone."

"I quite agree with you," said Diana. "It does seem, however, that Miss Dyson-Drake's manuscript has disappeared. She woke up my friend, Lupin Hastings, to tell her about it, I don't know why, and she got the impression that a child was missing, and I think she is rather to blame for waking people up."

"If a child had been missing it would have been a different matter," conceded Mrs. Mydleton. "Your friend, Lady Lupin, seems a very sweet young woman and would naturally be concerned for a child. But I see no reason for waking anybody up to tell them about a manuscript. Surely Miss Dyson-Drake could have waited till the morning. I don't want to be disagreeable or to make difficulties, but I am afraid if it happens again I shall have to leave, sorry as I shall be to do so."

In the meanwhile Lupin followed Miss Dyson-Drake downstairs. The hall door was open and the air was full of the mingled scents of a summer morning. Paul Ramsden and Mrs. Rennie were standing outside in the sunshine. To Lupin's relief Miss Dyson-Drake joined them. Murmuring something about writing a letter, she left them only to be greeted by Mrs. Smythe.

"Good morning, Lady Lupin. I hope you are none the worse for the adventures of last night."

"I am afraid it was all my fault," apologized Lupin. "You see, I thought Miss Drake said her child was missing. If I had known it was only her manuscript, I shouldn't have taken any notice."

"And such a manuscript, too!" exclaimed Mrs. Smythe. "I think it is a good thing that it is lost. Unless, of course, it has fallen into the hands of some innocent person."

"I don't see how it could very well," objected Lupin. "I mean, things don't exactly fall into one s hands, do they? And if someone has stolen it, they can't very well be innocent."

"There is something in what you say, but I shouldn't be at all surprised if someone, who had a great horror of anything of that sort, had taken it upon themselves to destroy it."

"Anything of what sort?" wondered Lupin. "I expect she means it's improper. I wonder if she has destroyed it herself?"

"Not that it would be right," continued Mrs. Smythe, "to wilfully destroy another person's property. All the same, think of the harm an impure book can do."

Lupin thought without much success. "I don't think I've ever read an impure book," she said. "Of course, we did Shakespeare at school, but the rude bits were all taken out first. Does Miss Dyson-Drake write impure books?"

"I got her last one out of the library," said Mrs. Smythe, "but I only read one chapter. I longed to burn it, but, of course, it wasn't my property and I should have had to pay for it. But I put it away in a locked drawer until I could get down to the town to return it."

"And you say this one is as bad?"

"I can't say. I haven't actually seen the manuscript, but I can guess what it is like. It is not that I am not interested in literature. We have a literary circle in our parish, and my son Arthur writes poetry. He has had several things printed in our parish magazine and in the county gazette. You must get him to show you some of them. Personally, I would rather read a poem about a snowdrop or a skylark than a novel about a water-closet. But I dare say I am old-fashioned."

Lupin was just wondering how Miss Dyson-Drake had managed to make a whole novel on such a subject when Mrs. Mydleton came into the hall, followed by Grizel. She smiled graciously at Mrs. Smythe, who introduced Lupin. "Grizel, I think I shall have an egg beaten up in a glass of sherry. I feel very faint. Such a terrible night!"

"I was afraid that you would be disturbed," Mrs. Smythe said. "That terrible Miss Dyson-Drake woke up poor Lady Lupin to tell her that her manuscript had been lost. As I say, if it is anything like her last book, it is a good thing it has been lost. In any case, she might have waited till the morning before she started making such a fuss and waking people up in the middle of the night. Poor Lady Lupin has come here for a rest cure."

"Most inconsiderate! She must know what an invalid I am, but people who have never suffered themselves have no sympathy for others. Sometimes I feel thankful for all I have suffered, as it has made me able to help others. What a terrible fault selfishness is!"

"Isn't it? I thought Grizel and Arthur were going to play golf this morning."

"Yes, I believe they were. But I was feeling too ill to spare Grizel."

"Perhaps this afternoon?"

"No, no, I can't be left today. Grizel wouldn't want to leave me, I'm sure. After all, she may not have me much longer."

Grizel returned with the sherry in time to hear the last remark. Her pale blue eyes filled with tears and her hand shook so much that she spilled some of the sherry.

"Really, darling, if you can't carry a glass of sherry without spilling it, you had better get someone else to do it for you. Ah, good morning, Colonel James."

"Good morning, Mrs. Mydleton, how are you today?"

"Not at all well, I'm sorry to say. I was awake all last night, and when I did get to sleep I was awakened by a terrible noise. I have just been complaining to Miss Turner about it."

"Poor Miss Turner is very worried about it all."

"Yes, I am sure she is. I know she is anxious for me to be comfortable. I have no complaint to make against her on that score. But she must keep the place quieter. I do not want to leave, but I must have undisturbed nights. She should not allow people to stay in the hotel unless they know how to behave."

"Has the manuscript been found, do you know?" asked Mrs. Smythe.

"I am afraid not. Miss Dyson-Drake talks of calling in the police."

"The police! Well, I shall really have to leave if that happens. I could not mix myself up with anything of that kind."

"She has probably hidden it herself," said Mrs. Smythe, "and thinks that if she makes enough fuss about it, it will bring her name before the public. Not that I want to say anything unkind about anybody."

"Well, I think I shall go for a little stroll before lunch," remarked Lupin, reflecting that Mrs. Smythe seemed to do a good deal that she didn't want. Perhaps she did it as a Lenten penance!

"I am afraid you were disturbed last night, too," said Colonel James. "Miss Turner tells me that you have only just got over influenza and have come here for a rest cure."

"A terrible thing, influenza," broke in Mrs. Mydleton. "I nearly died from it last year and the doctor says he can't answer for me if I get it again."

Lupin made her escape and walked out into the orchard. The trees were thick with blossom and the daffodils grew in the long grass beneath. It was very lovely and very peaceful and Lupin would have been quite happy if only Andrew had been there. She wondered how he was getting on without her, and Peter, too. Of course, he would be quite all right with Nanny, but he would have loved the garden. There were such a lot of places to hide in and he would look adorable staggering about on his fat legs in the long grass.

"Oh, Lady Lupin, do you mind if I walk a little way with you?" Grizel caught up with her. "Colonel James is with Mummy, so I…er…I mean I do hope you didn't mind me bursting in on you like that last night. I must give you back your brandy. I was so grateful. I'll tell Mummy's maid to give it to yours. Will that be all right?"

"Oh, absolutely! Wasn't it a funny thing about that manuscript? I could have sworn she said 'child' or I shouldn't have got out of bed."

"Are you fond of children?"

"Well, I've got one of my own, you know, and I shouldn't like anything to happen to him so, of course, I felt for her when I thought she'd lost hers."

"I adore children."

"Oh, do you?" Lupin felt vaguely embarrassed.

"I should love to have a child of my own, it must be too wonderful."

"I expect you will have some one day, when you are married, I mean, of course."

"I never will get married. I couldn't leave Mummy."

"Oh, I don't know. Doesn't it say something in the Bible about leaving your father and mother and cleaving to your husband?"

"I was engaged once and then Daddy died, and my fiancé wanted me to go to India, but, of course, I couldn't leave Mummy and so we broke it off. That was ten years ago."

"Haven't you ever heard from him again?"

"No, he married someone else."

"Oh, what a pity!" said Lupin. "Still, you will probably marry someone else, too."

"What's the good? I could never get married. I am never even allowed to stay anywhere alone. I was going to Devonshire with a friend last summer but Mummy had one of her attacks and I had to put it off. I can hardly even get away long enough for a game of golf."

"Is she really very ill?"

"I don't know. The doctor says there is nothing really wrong with her heart, but her nerves are so bad. If she's upset it brings on palpitations at once. I Just slipped out for five minutes last night to look at the sunset. She was talking to Mrs. Smythe and I didn't think she would miss me, but, of course, she did and I had an awful time with her."

"If her heart is really all right and, after all, the doctor wouldn't tell you it was if it wasn't, I should assert myself a bit. I mean, play golf sometimes and get married if you want to and that sort of thing. She has got a maid, hasn't she?"

"Oh, yes. Barker has been with her for years and is really better with her than I am when she is ill. But all the same, I couldn't leave her. Of course, I am devoted to her and I don't really want to leave her, but I do sometimes feel that I should like a life of my own. I did try to paint a bit once, but Mummy would show my efforts to everyone and it made me feel a fool. Oh, I oughtn't to talk like this, but even if I try to knit myself a jumper she keeps making suggestions all thc time. I can never do anything on my own. I have started several times working at girls' clubs and children's day nurseries, but Mummy was always taken ill just as I was setting off, and, of course, the people thought I was unreliable, and so I was, but it wasn't my fault. I loved the work and would have stuck to it if I had been allowed to, but in any case we never stay put long enough for me to take up anything properly. We are always moving about from place to place."

"Like the Wandering Jew. It must be a bit tiring but I have a feeling that you'll have a home of your own before long, and then you will be glad enough of a change from housekeeping."

Grizel smiled rather wanly. "I don't believe I would. I should simply love a little house of my own. I'd rather like to do my own cooking and everything myself. But it is no good thinking about it and I am really very lucky as it is. Mummy is awfully sweet. Please don't think I am grumbling."

Mrs. Mydleton was unusually gracious when they returned to the house, Grizel rather breathless for fear she had been missed. She considered Lady Lupin a nice friend for Grizel and was quite pleased to see them walking about together. As a matter of fact, she had just been struck by an idea. She was quite capable of ideas if they had any bearing on her own comfort. Her brain was not an inactive one, she used it a good deal to further her own well-being. She had known Colonel James for some years. It was he who had first suggested Orchard House to her as a really quiet place where she might enjoy a much-needed holiday, but it was not until this morning that this brilliant plan had come into her head. Why should he not marry Grizel? He was of good family and quite comfortably off. They would, of course, all live together and as he would naturally be responsible for Grizel, Mrs. Mydleton would be spared a great deal of expense.

Colonel James had a nice little place in Somerset, not far from her own old home, as well as his flat in London. Grizel would not want to be in town much. She and her mother would be very happy together in the country, looking up all their old friends, while her husband's business compelled him to stay in London. It was a pity about the business. Mrs. Mydleton had never been connected with business and she was sorry that her future son-in-law had been invalided out of the army, the army being a natural mode of life for anyone related to herself. However, for Mrs. Mydleton was capable of looking at both sides of a question, perhaps the business brought in more money than the army would have done, which was an advantage. She did not know what the business was and she was not interested, but she was satisfied, by all she had heard, that he had a good income.

All I care for is Grizel's happiness, she told herself. It was really quite time that she married. A spinster daughter was something of a reproach, and an agreeable, well-to-do son-in-law would be a pleasant addition to her *ménage.* There would be quite a lot of little things he would be able to do for her. He had very likely had some view of this in his mind when he had first suggested that she and Grizel should come to Orchard House. He obviously only needed a little encouragement and she would give it to him. It was a pity poor Grizel was so shy and awkward, but it was a lucky thing that she had a mother to think and to act for her.

"Ah, there you are, my darling," she said aloud. "I wondered when we should see you again. I know what you girls are like once you get together. Have you been discussing hats, I wonder, or hairdressing, or what? Perhaps we had better not ask," she added archly to Colonel James.

As they were all walking through the hall, Colonel James found an opportunity to remark to Lupin, "You are a brick to let that girl talk to you. She has a pretty thin time and needs a friend badly."

"Oh, good!" replied Lupin. "I like her awfully. But she does seem a bit depressed, as you say."

I wonder if he's in love with her, she thought to herself. If I were the girl I should certainly prefer him to the Adam's-apple young man. Well, I hope she will marry one of them soon and get away from her mother and have heaps of children.

CHAPTER 4

LUPIN lay down all the afternoon. She was feeling very tired after her disturbed night but awoke feeling much better, and going downstairs, ordered herself some tea on the terrace where she found a delicious spot in the sun and out of the wind. The scones and cream were good and everything seemed to be very pleasant. After tea she would write to Andrew.

"Ah, Lady Lupin, there you are! I have been looking for you everywhere," and Miss Dyson-Drake threw herself into a chair at Lupin's side and screwed her eyeglass into her eye.

"Oh, have you?" replied Lupin, wondering why. Surely they couldn't have much in common! "I have been having a bit of a rest."

"Have you any ideas?"

Lupin blinked. She was never much of a one for ideas, and when she did have them they weren't very good ones. For instance, there had been that idea of a Pierrot show for the Communicants' Guild. Well, that hadn't been a very good idea, not really. Then she had thought of bribing the children with doughnuts to come to Sunday school. Two of them had been sick, but they had certainly had a record attendance for three Sundays, and she still secretly thought that it had been rather a brainwave, but, of course, Andrew knew best. Still, it had been an idea, whether good or bad. "I do sometimes get an idea," she said guardedly.

"Good girl!" said Miss Dyson-Drake approvingly. "I thought you might. Now look here, we'll go for a drive in my car and you shall tell me what you think."

"I am afraid I must write to my husband," replied Lupin.

"Oh, we'll be back in heaps of time for that. The post doesn't go out till eight o'clock. Besides, this is a case of life and death."

When Lupin found herself sitting beside Miss Dyson-Drake in her raffish-looking car, she decided it was more likely to be a case of death than life. Miss Dyson-Drake was obviously one of those drivers who had got her driving license before testing came in, and her ideas of passing other vehicles, taking a corner, and negotiating a flock of sheep were sketchy in the extreme.

"Now the thing to bear in mind is this," she said, going round the bend on the wrong side of the road and thus compelling a cyclist to dismount in the ditch.

"Oh, dear," said Lupin. "Oughtn't we to stop or something?"

"It's not the work of an ordinary thief. My handbag lay on the table with several pounds in it and my jewel case was unlocked. I am careless in such matters."

"I am afraid I am, too," said Lupin. "Lucky for you he didn't notice them!"

"Money and jewelry mean nothing to me. If they had been taken I should not have complained."

"Wouldn't you?" asked Lupin, wishing that the road did not wind quite so much and that Miss Dyson-Drake would keep her eyes on it.

"No, but my work is my heart's blood."

There will be a good deal of blood about soon, thought Lupin as she saw a large omnibus bearing down upon them.

Miss Dyson-Drake took both hands off the wheel. "I live for my work," she announced.

"Well, you won't much longer," replied Lupin, shutting her eyes and wondering who would run the Mothers' Union. When she opened them again, she found that the car was halfway up the bank and that the driver and conductor of the omnibus had joined their party while most of the passengers stood in an interested throng just behind them.

"I shall report you to the police, madam. You have no right to drive about the countryside endangering the lives of innocent people."

"I should think not, indeed."

"She was on the wrong side of the road, I can witness to that."

"It's a wonder we're not all dead. When I saw the car coming straight at us I said to myself, there will be an accident, and so there was."

"Shime, isn't it? Stop it, Reg, you're not hurt."

"I was thrown right off my seat when he drew up so quick."

"My heart was in my mouth."

"It just shows, doesn't it?"

"Is anybody killed, Mum?"

"Never you mind. He's such a boy for questions. Just on our way to see his auntie we were. It will be a proper shock to her when I tell her of the accident."

"Amazing the people who drive cars nowadays! It oughtn't to be allowed."

"That's right."

"May I tell Auntie about the accident, Mum?"

"Eat your chocolate and be quiet, Reg. Doing well at school, he is. The teacher says he's ever so bright."

"The bus driver's not to blame—wonderful the way he drew up."

"Gives one a turn, doesn't it?"

"The young lady looks bad."

"No wonder, poor thing, it's no thanks to her mother that she's not dead."

"What's she saying?"

"Her heart is broken."

"Well, no wonder, if she's killed her own daughter."

"Is she dead?"

Lupin finished opening her eyes and gazed at the bus driver with a friendly smile. She agreed with what he had been saying about Miss Dyson-Drake's driving. When Lupin smiled there were very few people who could refrain from smiling back, and the driver was not one of them.

"Well," he said, "I won't mention it this time, madam, but you did ought to be more careful."

Miss Dyson-Drake was in the middle of an impassioned harangue about her bleeding heart and her life's work thrown away, not to mention her stillborn child, which part Lupin hoped the audience wouldn't hear.

"The young lady's come round."

"Lovely, isn't she? Wonder if she's on the pictures!"

"What's her mother saying?"

"Lost her child, poor thing!"

"But she's not dead, sitting up and smiling, she is. Isn't she sweet?"

"Perhaps it's another one that's dead!"

"Poor thing, no wonder her heart is bleeding, I don't know what I'd do if I lost my Reg."

"What's the lady saying, Mum?"

"Isn't he cute? Takes in everything, he does."

"Well, I am glad the young lady is all right."

"Take your seats, ladies and gentlemen, everything is all right."

"All's well that ends well."

"May I have a drink, Mum?"

"Stop it, Reg. You'll soon be at Auntie's now."

"How can I think of the rules of the road at a time like this?" demanded Miss Dyson-Drake.

"Well, mum, it's advisable to think of them when you are driving, if you don't want to end up in Queer Street. You don't want to kill the young lady, do you? I should drive your mother home if I were you, miss."

The unpleasantness had now somehow turned into a feast of reason and a flow of soul. With the help of their two foes the car was righted and Miss Dyson-Drake and Lupin were on the road once more, driving rapidly in an unknown direction. Miss Dyson-Drake was still driving, having ignored Lupin's suggestion of taking the wheel.

"No," went on Miss Dyson-Drake, as if there had been no interruption, "Paul and I are sure that it is the work of a specialist."

Lupin, still shaken, wondered what on earth she was talking about, but luckily Miss Dyson-Drake never needed any encouragement to go on talking. "At first we thought it was mere jealousy, that someone who had not had much success themselves grudged me my fame and was determined that this last and greatest work should be stillborn."

"Really?"

"As if success meant anything to me! So long as I can give of my best to the world, so long as my message is carried and my torch upheld, I care nothing for personal fame."

"Absolutely!"

They were approaching a level-crossing and the gates were closed. As Miss Dyson-Drake seemed oblivious of this fact, the car would crash through the gates at the same time as the London express. Lupin was sure that it would be the London express, although she had no reason for this belief. What were those lines she had learned at school?

> "To every man upon this earth
> Death cometh soon or late."

She had never realized before how true this was,

"Jealousy is a thing I cannot understand. What is one but a vehicle?" At this moment, by some good fortune, she seemed to notice the train and put the brakes on, crashing the gears as she did so. Lupin was shot violently from her seat, only to fall back again with a jerk. There was a good deal of furious hooting and what Lupin took to be bad language behind them, then the gates opened, the car leaped forward, and they were rushing madly once more down the main road. "But I have had another idea, something more devilish than mere jealousy is at work. This hotel is, as you know, full of writers."

"Is it?"

"Miss Turner, Arthur Smythe, and Charles Rennie, besides myself. Those are the only ones I am certain of, but some, if not all of the others may be writers, too, or at any rate, the friends of writers."

"So they may."

"The idea, don't you see, is to take my plot and to incorporate it into their own commonplace work."

"But would it fit in?"

"They will make it fit in. You must remember that we are probably dealing with someone fiendishly clever."

"If they are so clever, couldn't they have written the thing, or something like it to start with, instead of going to all the trouble of filching yours?"

Miss Dyson-Drake looked offended. She turned a corner on two wheels and drove a mad course down a winding lane, scattering a brood of ducks who were taking their evening walk that way.

"I don't mean as good as yours, of course," said Lupin hastily. "But they might have written something, if you know what I mean."

"They might write something. They do write something, but mere cleverness does not produce a masterpiece. You must have genius for that and the divine fire. Those I have," she added modestly.

"How nice," said Lupin. "Perhaps we ought to be turning back now. It must be getting late."

"What we have got to do," went on Miss Dyson-Drake, "is to take the writers separately and find out which of them is the most likely to have stolen my plot."

"How are you going to do that?" asked Lupin. "I think if we took that turning to the right—"

"You must obtain their confidence. Talk to them and get them to discuss their work with you. Miss Turner is your friend, you will find no difficulty there. Then there are Charles Rennie and Arthur Smythe—you must get to know them really well. Men like talking to a pretty woman. I can't think why it is, but I've often noticed it. You could easily establish relations with them."

It didn't sound a very good scheme to Lupin. After all, it was hardly the thing for a clergyman's wife to go about establishing relations with strange men, whatever that might mean, and it wasn't even as if they were attractive strange men, either. And anyhow, she had come away for a rest cure.

"I don't see how I could do that very well," she said. "Besides, I don't know what your plot is."

"That is why I have brought you out here, to tell you," replied Miss Dyson-Drake.

Lupin felt that as they had already driven half-round England, narrowly escaping death several times, she had been a long time divulging the reason for the drive. "I am afraid I really must be getting home. I really ought to write to my husband before dinner."

"A man falls in love with a woman's brain."

"Oh!"

"What do you think he does?"

Lupin could not imagine. She had had several men in love with her, but none of them had fallen in love with her brain, for the simple reason that she had not got one. "I can't think," she said. "Does he marry her?"

"No, for she is sexually repulsive to him."

"How awkward!"

"It is a difficult situation, for his love is all-devouring. He can neither eat nor sleep. His desire is killing him. What is he to do?"

Lupin could only repeat, "What?"

"The woman has a friend to whom she is devoted. They live together and have sworn never to part. So the man marries the friend and thus he can live in the same house as his beloved."

Lupin felt a little giddy. "What a queer idea!" she said.

"The proposal is a strong piece of writing, perhaps the best I have ever done. He is utterly honest and will not descend to any subterfuge. 'Rainbow,' he says, for the friend's name is Rainbow, 'will you marry me? I do not love you, it is Lalage that I love, but I am willing to spend my nights with you if I can spend my days with her. You may have my body but she will have my soul.' "

"Oh, dear," said Lupin. "It's getting a bit chilly, I think, we really ought to be going back, if you don't mind."

"Now Rainbow knows that Nicolas is in love with Lalage, so she accepts him, thinking to bring happiness to her friend, but alas! Lalage is not big enough and in spite of her splendid brain she has a mean soul. She knows that Nicolas loves her brain, but she wants him to love her body, too, so one night she creeps upstairs and stabs her lover and her friend as they are lying in bed together."

"Yes, I see. I mean, of course, it was a bit trying for her, but er… I wonder what the time is?"

"Miss Turner writes detective stories, I believe. What a marvelous denouement it would be for her!"

"Oh, it's not a bit like one of hers. Look out!"

A child was standing in the middle of the road. Miss Dyson-Drake saw her too late and pulled to the left. The offside wing caught the child and she lay on the ground.

Lupin knelt beside her in agony. Why on earth hadn't she insisted on driving the car herself, so that the woman could have done her talking without hurting anybody. The child's little face was white and her eyes were closed. Lupin felt her pulse. She was alive! The road which had been so empty now seemed full of people. A man was shouting angrily, but Lupin could not blame him, she could only blame herself. A woman was crying. A hostile crowd was closing in on them when suddenly a voice which she thought she knew said, "Where is the nearest doctor?"

"Thank heavens!" It was Colonel James.

Mrs. Rennie was with him and she didn't improve matters by calling out, "Oh, it's dead, take me away."

"She isn't dead," said Lupin.

"No thanks to you, she isn't," said the man. "I'll have you up for murder. Rich people running over poor people's children!"

Lupin felt the scene was familiar somehow, but she couldn't quite think why. Later she remembered it was something like the beginning of *A Tale of Two Cities*, when the Marquis St. Evremond runs over the child in his coach.

"This lady wasn't driving the car," explained Colonel James. "Now do you know where the nearest doctor is?"

"The hospital is not more than a mile away," said the father.

"Very well, then, we had better drive straight there."

"May I come?" asked Lupin.

"Yes, you and the little girl's mother had better sit together at the back and the child can lie on your knees."

They got in together at the back and the father lifted the child tenderly and laid him on their knees before taking his place in front with Colonel James. Miss Dyson-Drake took Mrs. Rennie back in her car.

"She really is alive," said Lupin. "I can feel her pulse."

"Are you sure, miss? If only she'd open her eyes!"

"She will soon, I'm sure she will." They were both crying, but Lupin tried to be encouraging.

"She's our only one. If she were to be taken it would kill me. You'll know what it is one day, miss, when you have one of your own."

"I have," gulped Lupin. "He's about the same age as yours."

"Never! Our Rosie was two in March."

"My Peter was two in February. I thought Rosie looked about the same age."

"She's sharp for her age. The words she says! And walk ! We'd just stopped to speak to a lady friend and she slipped her hand and darted across the road before I could say knife."

"They will, won't they?"

"My husband fair dotes on her. It will kill him if anything happens."

Lupin suddenly squeezed the mother's hand. "Look," she said. Rosie had opened a pair of wondering blue eyes and looked at her mother. Then she closed them again. But it was enough to cheer the miserable party in the car. They drove up to the hospital, and Rosie was taken away from a sobbing Mrs. Gower and an angry Mr. Gower and wheeled off to be examined.

Lupin and Mrs. Gower sat together on a sofa in the waiting room, hand-in-hand, discussing their children and their husband's ailments. Lupin came out poorly, for Andrew was disgracefully free from ailments. She did her best with his late attack of influenza but had to admit that he had nothing chronic. At last a rather fierce-looking sister came into the room. Her face relaxed as she approached Mrs. Gower, and she gave her quite a nice smile.

"It is only a slight case of concussion," she said. "The doctor wants her to stay here for the night, but you may come and see her for a few minutes."

"Oh, my dear," said Lupin, giving Mrs. Gower a hug before she followed the sister from the room. She hurried to the window where Mr. Gower and Colonel James paced up and down, smoking their pipes in silence. "It's all right," she said. "It really is all right. Slight concussion!" She wrung Mr. Gower's hand, and at last found herself sitting beside Colonel James in his car. Luckily he did not speak to her and she sat quietly in a stupor of thankfulness with the tears running down her face.

"Thanks most frightfully," she said, as they drove up to Orchard House. "I'm sorry to have been such a fool, but it might have been Peter."

CHAPTER 5

DIANA was looking out for Lupin and hurried her up to her sitting room and gave her some sherry, for which she was very thankful. The afternoon had been a nightmare and although she had awakened from it now and all was well, the effects of it, coming so soon after her illness, made her feel very shaky.

"I am sorry, my dear. I was busy at teatime or I would have kept an eye on you and prevented that Dyson-Drake woman getting you into her clutches. I ought to know by this time that if there is a chance of your getting caught by a bore, you will be."

"Oh, by the way," said Lupin, sitting up straight, "you know the manuscript that Miss Dyson-Drake said she had lost last night?"

"I do seem to have heard of it."

"Well, have you incorporated her plot into one of your novels? She asked me to find out."

Diana began to laugh. "Do you know what the plot was?" she asked.

"Yes. A man fell in love with a woman, so he married her great friend and they all killed each other in bed."

"Well, I am writing a children's story at the moment." She picked up a typewritten sheet. " 'There was a special glade in the wood,' " she read out, " 'that Peter and Pamela looked on as their own, and it was there that all their most exciting adventures took place. As Cavaliers they hid behind the trees and laughed silently as they heard the Roundheads blundering past. As airmen they sat high up on a branch of an oak, and flew the Atlantic and soared over Mount Everest. At other times, as themselves sitting among the pine needles, they went to boarding-school where Peter scored a century at a critical moment in an important match, and Pamela bowled out ten men in two overs.'—No, I don't see much scope there for either love interest or crime."

"But, then, you do write detective stories, too."

"Oh, yes! I might use the plot now I know it."

"Oh, dear! I oughtn't to have told you. But Miss Dyson-Drake seemed to think I might be able to worm it subtly out of you. Whether you had stolen the manuscript or not, I mean."

"I don't know that subtlety is your strong suit, my dear. But you needn't worry, I never write about beds, Colonel James doesn't like it."

"Colonel James! Whatever has he got to do with it?"

"He is my publisher."

"Why is he a colonel, then?"

"He was invalided out of the army and went into partnership with his brother."

"Oh, I see. He is rather nice, but I don't know why he was driving with Mrs. Rennie this afternoon. I hoped he was in love with that poor Mydleton girl."

"Well, even if he is, there is no reason why he shouldn't take Mrs. Rennie for a drive," replied Diana rather sharply.

As Lupin walked along the corridor to her own room, Charles Rennie came rushing down it and nearly knocked her over. "I say, I'm most frightfully sorry," he exclaimed. "I wasn't thinking what I was doing."

Lupin was quite surprised to hear what a nice voice he had when he was being pleasant. "Don't mind me," she replied wearily. "After driving with Miss Dyson-Drake, nothing could upset me.

His bad-tempered face crinkled up into rather an attractive grin. "Lord, no! I shouldn't think it would. But I say," and his face grew grave again. "Didn't you have an accident? I heard she had run over a child. What really happened?"

Lupin shuddered. "It was too frightful," she said. "She didn't actually run over her, but she knocked her down and I was afraid— Well, it was pretty awful. But the doctor says it's only slight concussion, thank goodness! And she will soon be all right again. I must say I do feel sorry for Miss Dyson-Drake, she must feel dreadful."

"How frightful! Poor little kid! What a mercy it's no worse!"

He is really rather nice, thought Lupin. What a pity he's usually in a rage! "Oh, by the way," she said aloud, turning back with her hand on the handle of her own door. "Miss Dyson-Drake asked me to ask you if you had taken her manuscript."

He stared at her. "Why on earth should I?" he asked.

"Well, you write books, don't you? She thought you might have incorporated—is that the right word?—her plot into one of your books."

He burst into a shout of laughter and leaned back against the banisters. "What was it about?" he asked. "Don't tell me if you'd rather not."

"I'd much rather not, if you don't mind," she replied. "It's a bit—er, you know."

"What is the joke?" asked Ruth Rennie, coming out of her bedroom.

"Miss Dyson-Drake thinks I've stolen her manuscript and have incorporated it into one of my own books."

Mrs. Rennie collapsed on to the top stair and began to laugh uncontrollably. Lupin, who was still feeling rather weak after her shattering afternoon, and felt as if she might start crying again at any moment, joined in the laughter almost hysterically.

"He writes scientific books," gurgled Mrs. Rennie.

"Miss Dyson-Drake's plot is a bit—er—" spluttered her husband.

"Well, it might cheer your books up a bit," remarked Ruth. "They are frightfully dull," she explained to Lupin.

"Miss Dyson-Drake's doesn't sound exactly dull," admitted Lupin.

"Do tell us about it," begged Ruth.

"Well, a man falls in love with a woman's brain."

The Rennies laughed more than ever.

"Of course, you might bring that in," went on Lupin. "I mean, you could make the woman very scientific."

"Oh, yes," agreed Charles. "I could write it in the form of a dialogue between the man and the woman, bringing in a little love interest now and then to brighten things up. How does it end?"

"That is the part that is rather awkward," said Lupin.

"Perhaps you could tell Ruth in private"Charles suggested, "and she could tell me later. I foresee a tremendous success in front of me. Instruction combined with glamor—the public ought to lap it up. It might even be filmed one day!"

"I don't know that I could really tell anyone, because apart from it being rather dubious, I couldn't make head or tail of it," admitted Lupin.

"Nor could you of his books," said Ruth. "So it ought to fit in beautifully."

"It is a pity we haven't got the manuscript," sighed Charles. "We might have stolen it if only we had thought of it in time, but I am afraid someone else has got in first."

Grizel Mydleton came along the corridor, gave them all a scared look and scuttled into her bedroom. "She looks guilty enough," said Ruth Rennie. "I wonder if she stole it."

"Why should she?" asked Lupin. "Does she write books?"

"No, but she might steal it and give it to Arthur Smythe to incorporate into one of his."

"I don't see how it would fit into a poem about a snowdrop," said Lupin doubtfully.

This remark sent the Rennies into renewed shrieks of laughter, but on seeing Miss Dyson-Drake coming up the stairs with Paul Ramsden, they hurried into their bedroom.

Miss Dyson-Drake looked pale and haggard and, as she approached, Lupin heard her say to Paul, "It's no good, my dear, I couldn't eat a thing."

Lupin's conscience smote her. Poor Miss Dyson-Drake! She must have been through a frightful time. I ought to have told her the minute I came in, she told herself. But I suppose I thought Colonel James would. At least, I don't believe I thought about it at all. She pulled herself together and went forward eagerly. "It's all right," she said.

"What do you mean? Have you found it?"

"The doctor says it is only a slight concussion."

"What are you talking about?"

"The child, the little girl, Rosie."

"Oh, that, yes. Colonel James told me there was nothing much wrong. I never thought there was. After all, I hardly touched her. Children shouldn't be allowed loose about the place. For a moment I thought you meant that my manuscript had been found."

"The manuscript! Oh, yes. No, it hasn't been actually found yet. But neither Miss Turner nor Mr. Rennie have got it, so that's two who haven't."

"How do you know?"

"They told me. It wouldn't fit into their books, anyway. I'll tackle Mr. Smythe after dinner. I doubt it fitting into his, either, but, of course, you never know. I must go and dress."

"Oh, Staines," she said, as she shut her own door behind her, "have you heard? It was too awful. I really thought for a moment that we'd killed her."

"It must have been a terrible shock, my lady. But I hear the little girl is doing nicely."

"Yes, thank goodness! But I'll ring up the hospital again after dinner and I'll have to ring up Mr. Hastings, too, because I've missed the post. This place is worse than Glanville. One never has a moment and I thought I was going to have a rest cure."

"If you'll forgive my saying so, my lady, I don't think that Mr. Hastings would care for you driving about the place with that Miss Dyson-Drake, a dangerous driver, I understand. Some of these writing ladies are very eccentric."

"You must say Miss Turner is a very safe driver, Staines. You remember that time she drove you to see your mother in hospital, just before Peter was born."

"Miss Turner was always a very nice lady and her books are fit for anybody to read, very different from some! But I must say I wonder at her mixing herself up with this hotel business. It's not a lady's work."

"You are dreadfully old-fashioned, Staines."

"It is a good thing some of us are, my lady. There are enough of the other sort about. My poor mother would turn in her grave if she were alive now."

Lupin thought for a moment. "I don't quite see how she could. I mean she wouldn't be in her grave if she were alive, would she? What is Mrs. Mydleton's maid like? A congenial spirit?"

"She is a very nice person, my lady. She has been with Mrs. Mydleton for fifteen years, she does not believe in changing about every week."

"Evidently not! I'd better have my bath."

"Yes, my lady. It is quite ready. Will you wear your blue?"

"I expect so, if you say so, Staines."

After dinner Lupin found herself roped in for a game of bridge with the Mydletons and Colonel James. Grizel was looking very wretched. Lupin wondered what was distressing her now. Very likely it was indigestion. One often thought people were suffering from unrequited love and it turned out to be "suffering from the stomach something chronic," like poor Mr. Gower, as his wife had confided to her this afternoon. Still, if there were anything between her and Colonel James, as she had rather fancied this morning, she wouldn't have liked him driving Mrs. Rennie about the countryside this evening, opportune as it had been for Lupin. Last night Lupin had half thought she seemed rather fluttered by Arthur Smythe, but perhaps that was just because he seemed keen on her. She would hardly take poor, chinless Arthur very seriously, but the colonel was distinctly nice. "Double two hearts," she said out and then wondered what on earth had made her say it.

"Two no trumps," said Colonel James, much to Lupin's relief.

Yes, she thought, he is nice, and nice-looking in a plain sort of way. I think he is rather keen on Grizel; he speaks to her in a different sort of voice. Perhaps Mrs. Rennie inveigled him into taking her for a drive. After all, I didn't invite her into my bedroom last night, but she came. Oh, there she is with Paul Ramsden, I dare say she likes men. I do myself, if it comes to that.

Colonel James was dealing. "I rang up the hospital," he said. "The child seems to be going on all right."

"Thank goodness," said Lupin.

"Don't speak of it," begged Mrs. Mydleton. "I can't bear to think of it," and looking at her cards she succeeded in banishing the matter from her thoughts.

Lupin found it difficult to concentrate on the game tonight. Usually she was fond of bridge, although she was but a very average player, but this evening she found her thoughts wandering badly. She lived again the awful moment when the car seemed to be making straight for the child. Suppose, while she was away from home, Peter went wandering into the street and got run over! It was very unlikely that such a thing should happen while Nanny was in charge, but one never knew, and Peter was getting rather independent. She had spoken to Andrew on the telephone just before dinner, but the next time her hand was down she hurried to Diana's office. "Do you mind if I ring up Andrew again?" she asked. She got on fairly quickly. "Oh, darling, is that you? Oh, sorry, Sara, I want the vicar."

"Is anything the matter?" asked Andrew anxiously.

"No, not a bit, but you know that child I told you about, the one that got run over?"

"Yes, dear, I hope she is not worse."

"No, she's going on very well."

"I am so glad."

"But it did just strike me that Peter might get run over while I was away. You won't let him wander about alone in the streets or anything, will you?"

"No, darling, you can feel quite happy about him. Can you see Nanny letting him wander about alone in the streets?"

"No, of course not, but I thought I'd just mention it. Good night, darling."

"Good night, my precious. Don't worry, you are supposed to be having a rest cure, you know."

"Yes, so I am. As a matter of fact I am playing bridge at the moment."

"Well, play nicely. Bless you, my darling."

"Bless you, Andrew. You know, Peter might slip his hand out of Nanny's and dart into the road."

"Not out of Nanny's, darling."

"Are you sure? I love you—bother, there's the three minutes and he hadn't time to say if he loved me or not."

"I think he must, or he would have left you long ago. You must be a great trial to him," replied Diana.

"I know, but he's a clergyman, so he can't leave me."

"So he is. He'd have had to murder you."

"1 am so sorry," said Lupin, as she hurried back to the bridge table, "but I had to ring up. That child, you know."

"Were you ringing up the hospital?" asked Mrs. Mydleton.

"No, only it suddenly came over me how awful it would be if my child got run over while I was away, so I just rang up my husband to tell him not to let him."

"Two diamonds," said Mrs. Mydleton.

Grizel got up with a murmured apology next time she was dummy, but as the one time Mrs. Mydleton's mind was fully occupied was when she was playing bridge, she never noticed that Grizel had gone, and it was not until she arrived back at the end of the hand, very pink and flustered, that her mother remarked on her absence.

"Where have you been, darling?" she asked, rather tactlessly, Lupin thought.

"I went upstairs to change my stockings," she said. "I had just realized that one of mine had a ladder in it."

Mrs. Mydleton raised her eyebrows. "Really, darling," she expostulated. "Do you mean that you put on a stocking with a ladder in it?"

"No, it had only just gone," replied Grizel. "I stooped down to pick up a card that I had dropped, and it went."

"Be thankful that you are not a vicar's wife," said Lupin, plunging in to her aid, although a sillier story, worse told, she had never heard. "Whenever I kneel down, phut, a ladder comes, and, of course, I have to kneel a great deal. Not that I don't like it, but it is hard on one's stockings."

"I don't believe Grizel will ever be a vicar's wife," said Colonel James, smiling at Grizel. Grizel went very red and looked down at the cards she was shuffling.

I wonder if they are actually engaged, thought Lupin. I can't quite see why they need be so coy about it. Then a sudden thought struck her: Grizel had stolen the manuscript for him! He was a publisher and naturally if he could get a manuscript for nothing it would be all to the good. All along Grizel had been the obvious thief, her guilty conscience was written large on her countenance. But it had been difficult to ascribe a motive to her. Mrs. Rennie's remark about Arthur Smythe could not be taken seriously; no one would commit a crime for someone with no chin and an Adam's-apple. But Colonel James was definitely attractive, or would be to anyone who was not married to Andrew. "Oh, one no trump," she said aloud.

"Two hearts," purred Mrs. Mydleton. She was positively benign. Lupin suspected her of being in the plot, too. Her look when it fell on Colonel James was distinctly possessive.

The rubber came to an end. Colonel James brought Mrs. Mydleton and Lupin some whisky and soda and Grizel some lemonade. Mrs. Smythe sauntered up. "Did you have a good game?" she asked. "I'm sure I should love bridge, but it is difficult in my position, don't you think so, Lady Lupin?'

"I find it difficult in any position," agreed Lupin. "I went three hearts just now, thinking that I had got seven, and three of them turned out to be diamonds. But I have been so agitated all day, what with that poor little girl being run over, and Miss Dyson-Drake's manuscript being sto— lost, I mean."

"You would be quite a good player with more practice," said Mrs. Mydleton kindly, mellower than ever after her whisky. "You read your cards well. Do you play much?"

"No, one never seems to have time to do anything much when one is a vicar's wife, does one, Mrs. Smythe? I mean, people do keep popping in so. I never realized how much trouble there was in the world before I married, what with children's boots and husband's insides, and landlords, and lodgers, and the ones who haven't got husbands and children are always losing their faith like poor Miss Dyson-Drake and her manuscript—"

"I often tell my husband that clergymen's wives in the Church of England are nothing more nor less than unpaid curates," remarked Mrs. Smythe with the air of one making an original remark. "But don't imagine I think there is anything wrong in a game of cards. I am very fond of whist myself. We have a weekly whist drive for our young people. I think it is a splendid thing and helps to keep the lads out of the public houses."

"I wonder why whist is so much more religious than bridge," mused Lupin. "I think on the whole bridge would keep me out of the public houses more. Whist does go on so, and you never lay two hands, which is what I really enjoy, though I am afraid I rather messed it up tonight." She broke off, feeling Mrs. Smythe's eye fixed on her whisky and soda. "I like darts, too," she added rather inconsequently.

CHAPTER 6

"OH, Staines, I never turned all night. That was a good idea of yours, locking the door."

"Did anyone try to come in, my lady?"

"Not that I know of, but I was so busy sleeping I shouldn't have noticed if they had. I dreamed I was at a parochial council meeting, in a pair of step-ins and a biretta, and the bishop accused me of eating the manuscript of his sermon. I suppose I was thinking of poor Miss Dyson-Drake's manuscript. Have you heard any more about that, Staines?"

"No, my lady, except that Barker tells me her mistress is very upset about it."

"Why on earth? Surely no one suspects her? What would she do with it?" Then Lupin suddenly remembered her suspicions of the night before: was Mrs. Mydleton mixed up in it, and was her conscience now smiting her? Or had she guessed that Grizel had got it?

"She is afraid that if there has been one burglary, there may be another and that someone may make an attempt to steal her jewels."

"From what I have seen of them, I should hardly think they'd bother, but I don't want to be catty." She took off her own pearls and rings and put them on the dressing table. "I'd better have my bath, I feel quite bobbish this morning. I do hope that Rosie had a good night.

"The little girl? Indeed, I hope so, my lady. I understand that Miss Mydleton had to sleep in her mother's room last night. She was feeling nervous after hearing of one child being kidnapped and of another being run over yesterday afternoon."

"Did she think someone was going to kidnap Miss Mydleton? After all, she's not exactly a child and anyway, no child was kidnapped, it was only a manuscript."

"I know, my lady. Mrs. Mydleton's maid tried to explain the situation to her mistress, but it was no use, she had got the idea into her head that there was danger about and it brought on one of her attacks."

"Poor Miss Mydleton! What ghastly lives some people do lead, Staines. I suppose I am frightfully lucky, Mummy being such a lamb, I mean."

"Everyone respects the countess, my lady."

"Do they?" replied Lupin, surprised. "I never thought of respecting her, the darling! I mean, she's not a bit like Mrs. Smythe, is she?"

"Mrs. Smythe? No, indeed, my lady!"

"But *she* is the sort of person people respect, you know. What I call rather uncomfortable. No one could feel uncomfortable for a minute with Mummy, but I always feel awkward when I am talking to Mrs. Smythe. I feel at any moment that she may ask some leading question and that one's whole guilty past will lie before her like an open book. Not that I *have* a guilty past, but I feel as if I had when I am talking to her. She reminds me of a mistress we had at school; when I had some sweets hidden in my stocking drawer, I was sure she knew. I know Mrs. Smythe suspects me of not being a real clergyman's wife, but I am, Staines, I really am—as you know, having been at my wedding."

"Yes, my lady, and a very pretty wedding it was. I am putting out your cherry-colored jersey suit."

"Good idea. It is a gorgeous day, isn't it? How lovely to feel I have nothing to do but enjoy myself all day long." And Lupin went into the bathroom.

She knew that Diana liked to get through her hotel business in the morning so that she would be free to write later in the day, so when she had finished her breakfast she wandered into the garden, meaning to write her deferred letter to Andrew. She found a deck chair and seated herself beneath a cherry tree. How lovely and fresh everything smelled! April was certainly the loveliest month in the year.

Darling,

It was lovely hearing you on the telephone. I do wish you were here. It is a perfectly gorgeous place. I'm writing this in the orchard and there are daffodils in the grass and blossom on the trees and all that sort of thing. I'm afraid I'm not much of a hand at describing things, but it really is rather nice. A bird is singing, too. I shouldn't be surprised if it were a blackbird or a thrush or something. Diana is running the hotel. Everybody goes to her in the morning to say how they hate to complain but if something isn't done about something, they'll have to go somewhere else, but, of course, they don't because it is so frightfully nice here. I think Di would be rather glad if they did go because then she would have more time for her writing. Oh, and one of the women here has lost her manuscript and thinks that Di has pinched it to make a denouement to one of her school stories. As I told you she ran over a child yesterday, the woman I mean, not Diana. It was simply too awful, she was just the same as Peter, except for a month and three days, so you can guess what I felt like. I rang up again this morning and she is all right, but it does show how dangerous the roads are and you might just remind Nanny about motorcars coming along when you are not expecting them...

She paused and looked round the orchard. Arthur Smythe was approaching, carrying a deck chair and some writing materials.

"Good morning," said Lupin. "Isn't it a gorgeous day?"

"A day borrowed from heaven," replied Arthur, settling his deck chair near hers, although there was the whole orchard to choose from.

"Absolutely," agreed Lupin.

He looked at her for a moment. "I was repeating what my mother said, as a matter of fact," he replied.

"Good idea!" said Lupin. "It saves a lot of trouble to repeat what other people say. I mean it's such an effort thinking of things to say oneself, isn't it? And it is a good description, though I should never have thought of it for myself."

"I hope I'm not disturbing you," went on Arthur. "I felt I must come here, I, er..." and he shuffled his papers.

"Oh, I expect you are going to write a poem or something," said Lupin. "Would you rather I went away? I mean, I don't want to interfere with the inspiration or anything."

"No, of course not, you were here first. Besides, you are writing yourself."

"Oh," said Lupin, "I was only just writing to my husband."

"I expect you are very happy," said Arthur.

"Yes, I am," replied Lupin. "I am frightfully lucky, as a matter of fact."

"It must be wonderful to be happy," sighed Arthur.

Oh, dear, thought Lupin, he is in love with Grizel and she is in love with Colonel James. How too sickening for him! I must say that I should prefer Colonel James myself. Still, it's frightfully hard on this one and he can't help having no chin. Grizel seems to be a regular Helen of Troy or whoever it was who launched a thousand ships. One would never have guessed it, although I suppose she is quite pretty in a quiet way. Aloud she said hopefully, "I expect you will be happy one day." After all, she told herself, there are far more women than men in the world and he has rather nice eyes.

"I am a feeble ass," he said, throwing down his papers. "But it is awfully difficult standing up against people when you are fond of them. I am not really a funk, at least, I don't think I am, but my father and mother have always been so good to me. They are not very well off and they saved like anything so that I could go to Marlborough and Cambridge. The least I could do was to spend my holidays at home instead of going off with other fellows, but, of course, it meant that I never really made any friends. They wanted me to take orders but they were awfully decent when I told them I couldn't. Now I've slipped into being a schoolmaster, but I simply hate it."

"What about your writing?"

"Damn my writing! Oh, I say, I'm awfully sorry."

"It's all right, but don't you write poetry?"

"It's not poetry. I'm enough of a poet to know that. I used to write a bit as a boy and unfortunately I won a prize in a magazine when I was ten, and Mother is still so proud of it, anyone would think I was Keats. I write a poem for the parish magazine every month, and I've had one or two in other magazines. A guinea or two comes in useful every now and then, but they are awful tripe. If only Mother would leave me alone, I might do something. It's beastly of me to say that, and I am absolutely devoted to her, but I try to write what she would like instead of what I want to write myself. I sort of try to live up to her idea of me instead of making an idea of my own." Lupin nodded. It was a pity he and Grizel could not get together, as they were both mother-ridden. Arthur went on, "I loathe schoolmastering and I'm sick of writing poems to the snowdrop and the hawthorn tree."

"What would you really like to be?"

"An engineer."

"An engineer!"

"Are you surprised?"

"Well, I suppose I'd thought of you more as a bookish sort of person."

"That's the trouble, everyone does. I wanted to read engineering at Cambridge, but poor old Daddy looked so hurt at the idea of anyone choosing engineering when they might do classics that I didn't like to hold out. Then when I let them down over being a clergyman they seemed to think that being a schoolmaster would be the next best thing, so I gave in. But I am a rotten schoolmaster, and I am sure I should be a good engineer. It has always been the dream of my life. I wrote a poem about an airplane once. In fact, it is the only real poem I have ever written. But Mother did not like it. She said it was not up to my usual standard. I didn't say anything about it looking like a great, white bird against the blue sky, but I described its engine. Well, anyway, I burned it in a rage."

So it isn't Grizel he's in love with! It's an airplane or a Brengun carrier or something. How queer! Aloud she said, "If you really are a good engineer, I think you ought to be one. I don't expect your people would really mind so frightfully once they got used to the idea, and after all, you stood out about being a clergyman, so you might as well go the whole hog. Think of all the harm you must be doing to those little boys if you are really such a rotten schoolmaster as you say."

"Of course, I might not get a job. There must be a lot of chaps who know much more about it than I do. I've really taught myself all I know, from books and things, and there is a fellow with a garage at home who lets me go there and mess about in the holidays, but I got mumps, of all childish complaints, this term and Mother brought me here for a change. As a matter of fact, I am frightfully glad she did, and yet I don't know, perhaps it would have been better if I had never come." He lit a cigarette, looking rather embarrassed.

Oh, dear, I am afraid he is in love with Grizel, thought Lupin sadly. Still, if I can persuade him to take up his engineering, I dare say he will forget her. He doesn't stand much chance against Colonel James. "Do you have to pass exams and things to be an engineer?" she asked aloud.

"Yes, but if I could get a job as a mechanic I could work for those in my spare time. As a matter of fact, I have mugged up a good deal of the theoretical part. I've got a little money of my own and I might buy a partnership, only mother would hate it so. She likes to think of me turning out sweet little poems in between influencing the boys for good."

"Instead of which you will turn up late for meals in dirty overalls and smelling of grease. I quite see her point. I expect I shall be just the same with my boy when he grows up and will worry him to do something different from what he wants to do, but I hope he will defy me and choose for himself. I shall respect him much more and I expect your parents will too, when they have got over the shock."

"It's awful good of you to be so decent," said Arthur. "I expect people confide things to you a lot, don't they?"

"Yes, most of the time. Which reminds me—Miss Dyson-Drake asked me to find out whether you had stolen her manuscript."

"Why ever should I?"

"She thought you might have interpolated her plot into the middle of one of your poems. It was about someone being in love with someone and marrying someone else and getting murdered. I shouldn't think it would fit frightfully well into a poem about snowdrops nor into one about cylinders and ball-bearings, but, of course, I don't know much about these things."

"It wouldn't fit in frightfully well," agreed Arthur.

"Good, then I'll tell her it wasn't you," and Lupin returned to her letter as Arthur rather hesitatingly picked up a book on engineering. He wants to tell me about his love for Grizel, thought Lupin. I hope he won't as I can't give him any encouragement and, in any case, she will probably be in prison soon for stealing that manuscript. I think it must have been her.

CHAPTER 7

LUPIN heard voices behind her. "Well, I'll do my best, but you know what he is."

"My dear, you are not a slave."

"No, but I hate rows and—" Here Lupin coughed loudly.

Paul Ramsden and Ruth Rennie appeared. Paul looked perfectly unconcerned. "Good morning, Lady Lupin. I hope you had a good night."

Ruth looked a little self-conscious. "Oh, good morning," she said. "I was just taking a breath of air and ran into Mr. Ramsden."

"I've run into nearly everyone, or they've run into me," remarked Lupin. "I suppose it's because it's such a nice day. Here's Miss Dyson-Drake."

"That woman!" muttered Ruth with venom, and walked away.

Paul looked rather amused and turned to greet his friend. "My dear," he said, "I can see you have no news. If only there were anything I could do. I do so feel for you. I lay awake last night thinking of you."

"Thanks, Paul," said Miss Dyson-Drake, as she took his arm. "I know you understand. People say 'but you can write it again,' but one cannot write the same thing twice. Even if you remembered it word for word the original fire would be lacking."

"How true, Lavinia! Something of the artist goes into all creative work and if it is cut off it leaves a wound."

"I don't know what I should do without you, Paul. Our thoughts run together. It is as if our minds were twins."

Lupin thought it was time to remind them that she was among those present. "Good morning," she said to Miss Dyson-Drake.

Miss Dyson-Drake looked at Lupin as if wondering who and why she was. "Good morning. I hope we have not interrupted your meditations."

"Oh, no, not a bit. As a matter of fact I'm not much of a hand at meditation. I was only writing to my husband."

"Ah, you are very happy," exclaimed Miss Dyson-Drake.

Lupin wondered why everyone made that remark when she told them she was writing to her husband. Was it a very rare thing for a wife to be on speaking, or rather, writing terms with her husband? Surely Mrs. Smythe sometimes wrote to Mr. Smythe!

"Happy? Oh, yes, rather! By the way, I asked Miss Turner if she had taken your manuscript, and I asked Mr. Rennie, too, and it wasn't either of them. I don't think it would fit into either of their books frightfully well. I mean hers is a school story, and his is a scientific work."

"So they say, but thank you, anyhow, for trying to help me in my great trouble. Yours is a very sympathetic nature, I knew it at once. I am a wonderful reader of character and I summed up yours directly. Not deep, the mind undeveloped, floating on the shallows of life, yet good-hearted and ready to help others according to your limitations."

Sounds like one of my old reports from school, thought Lupin, 'she does her best but it is poor.' To Miss Dyson-Drake she said, "Oh, and I asked Mr. Smythe, too. He writes poetry about snowdrops, so it can't be him. I can't think of anyone else. Of course, Colonel James is a publisher, but he is so nice, I am sure he wouldn't do a thing like that."

"I don't like publishers. They make money out of other people's brains. Don't you agree with me, Paul?"

"I hate the commercialism of art."

"I must write, I must write, my head is bursting."

"Oh, if you only could, it would do you all the good in the world."

"Not my novel! Not my poem in prose, my maimed stillborn child! But an article, a mere article. However, it is forming, I think I see it, I must go."

"Oh, talking of children," said Lupin, "I rang up the hospital this morning. She is much the same."

"Who is much the same?"

"Rosie, the little girl."

"What little girl?'

"The one you ran over yesterday."

"I remember a child ran in front of the car, but luckily I avoided it. Thank heavens I always keep my head in a crisis. What would have been my feelings if I had had a child's death on my hands? An imagination like mine is a curse. You are lucky, my child, you live in the present, you skate lightly on the surface of things, so sorrow can never really come near you. Not what I mean by sorrow."

"Hurray," said Lupin. "That is good news," and she went on with her letter to Andrew.

That woman writer I told you about who knocked down Rosie has just been talking to me. She says I shall never know sorrow, isn't that splendid? She and Diana's cousin, who is an artist, have just been talking to me and I feel quite giddy. If they marry each other their children will be quite mad, but I dare say they won't, as she is old enough to be his mother, and I think he is rather keen on that other man's wife. It all sounds as if I had landed into a very fast place, but it isn't really. There is a vicar's wife, and a widow, and a young man with an Adam's-apple, so it is quite all right really. Bother, Di's cousin is coming back...

Paul threw himself on to a grassy bank near to Lupin. "What she needs," he said, "is to relieve herself."

Lupin looked a little surprised for a moment, then she had an inspiration. "You mean, do a spot of writing? Jolly good idea. I expect it will relieve her, as you say."

"Yes, we artists must fulfill ourselves. The urge comes and if we suppress it our whole being is thrown out of gear. For ten years I've struggled in my father's engineering firm. It was purgatory. I was never well, my head ached, and I had acute indigestion all the time."

"Like Mr. Gower," murmured Lupin.

Luckily Paul did not hear nor at any rate notice her. "Then an aunt died and left me a small income. I broke away from my home, from my family and from the works and took up the life I was meant for. Now I never have an ache or pain."

"It must be beastly doing something you don't like."

"To me it is the greatest crime to force anybody out of their mold. Take yourself, for instance. Your role is just to be decorative. To set you to work or to make you think would destroy you. You fulfill yourself by simply being. To sit under the cherry blossom, nicely dressed, is your function in life."

"But I am just having a holiday. When I am at home I do a lot. I am a vicar's wife and have to do all sorts of things—mothers' unions, Sunday-school teachers, girls' clubs, missionaries to tea, and I've got a child, too."

"That is all wrong. You should not do it. You will make yourself ill. In fact, I'm sure someone told me you had been ill."

"It was only influenza."

"Whatever it was, it was brought on by your unnatural way of living. You will have illness after illness if you do not break away before it is too late. You are disturbing your whole equilibrium if you try to force yourself out of your mold."

"Oh, dear, how awkward!"

"It is everyone's business to develop their own personality in their own way. Only so shall we have a perfectly balanced world."

"I should find it frightfully tiring. Besides, I should not know where to start."

Paul ignored the interruption. "People talk about being good or bad, but there is no such thing. All that matters is to express your ego. If you are naturally good, be good, and if you are naturally bad, be bad. Among the great people of the earth there have been sinners and saints."

"Would you have people be criminals just because they feel like stealing and murdering?"

"I would rather be a successful criminal than an unsuccessful saint."

"I wonder if I should be a greater person if I smacked people's faces whenever I felt like it."

Paul laughed. "I'd rather you didn't, as I believe you are feeling like that now. But you shouldn't, for smacking faces isn't your métier. As I have said, you should never do anything except look lovely."

"Sounds dull to me! Still, I suppose if I started smacking faces I might get my own smacked back one day, which would be a pity. But I mustn't keep you from your painting. I can't imagine anything lovelier than being able to paint this orchard. I mean, all this blossom and the blue sky and the daffodils underneath."

He shrugged his shoulders. "I don't paint that sort of picture."

"Oh, don't you? What a pity! But I am sure yours are awfully good."

"I don't know if they are good or bad. I just try to paint life as I see it, and it is not all apple blossom and daffodils, you know," and he looked round him with a hostile air.

"No, but some of it is. I mean, why not enjoy it while we've got it? One doesn't often have oysters, but there is no point in thinking about prunes while one is eating oysters, if you know what I mean."

"You are a realist, in spite of looking as if you lived on rose petals and dew. Perhaps it is as well. There is always an awakening for the dreamers of the earth."

Lupin was not quick, but somehow she had an inspiration at this moment. He has had a sorrow, she told herself. I wonder if it was a sad love affair. I wonder if it is a woman, or a tank, like Arthur Smythe. I shall probably soon know all about it.

"I suppose you know this place well," she said. "I mean, before it was a hotel, it belonged to your aunt, didn't it?"

Was it her imagination, or did an angry expression pass over his pleasant, well-featured face? It passed in a moment, and he replied casually, "Oh, yes, I spent most of my holidays here when I was a little chap. My people were in India."

"Did you like it?"

He lit a cigarette, and she could not see his face. "I quite liked it as a child," he said. "But a child is happy anywhere so long as he gets enough to eat. It is a long time since the 'splendor in the grass, the glory in the flower departed'."

"Oh, is it?" asked Lupin. Oh, dear, I am afraid the scene of his sorrow must have been here. What a pity I mentioned it. "I should love to see some of your pictures sometime," she said aloud. Not that this was strictly true, but she hoped it might take his mind off his sorrow.

"I have only just a few sketches here that I hope to make pictures from later. I am by way of having a one-man show presently." His portfolio was lying beside him and he picked it up. "Just a few ideas," he said as he laid out his sketches on a smooth piece of grass.

"How nice!"

"These are just ideas, you know, nothing finished."

Lupin gazed at the first sketch. There was a very realistic fishmonger's slab. A codfish eyed her with just the same malignant eye that so often greeted her when she did her morning shopping at Glanville. In the background some sailors seemed to be being very sick in a boat. But suddenly the sight of a fishing net gave her the idea that they were deep sea fishermen. "How clever!" she said. "Fishermen catching fish! That cod might almost be speaking."

"And there," he said, pointing to the other side, "I've only just roughed it in."

A fat man in evening dress was rolling his eyes over what Lupin thought at first must be a dish of oysters, because one would hardly roll one's eyes over a bit of cod. Still, it must be the cod or there would be no point. "Marvelous," she said, "you get the whole history of the fish, don't you?"

"Its just an impression I got when passing a fishmonger's shop."

"Well, I do think it's clever. I can't think how you get such impressions. I am afraid I never get any at all except that salmon costs more than I ought to give, but that I'd better have it as most fish is so frightful and my husband will have it on Fridays."

"Now this will interest you, I think."

Lupin gazed at what at first sight she took to be the Massacre of the Holy Innocents. But on seeing a large locomotive ploughing through the center, she rejected her first idea, for surely they hadn't had trains in those days. "Oh, er, a railway accident," she hazarded.

"No," said Paul, "that is the train deluxe, in which you and I travel, and all around are the victims who made it possible for us to do so."

"Oh, dear! What a horrible thought! But what are all those dead children?"

"They are the ones who died working in the mines. Think of the men who dug the railways! And of the men who smelted the iron! Of men, of women, and worst of all, of children, who produced the fuel! Blood and sweat went to the making of the railways."

"Thank goodness I came down by car. I should expect to see the line strewed with dead bodies if I went by train."

"And look at those dead trunks of trees, once a sturdy forest, but now cut down to make room for the line, and the mangled buttercups and daisies in the meadows."

Just then Colonel James approached. "Good morning, Lady Lupin. Ramsden showing you his pictures?"

"Yes, they are so interesting."

"May I have a look, Ramsden?"

"Yes, of course, but I must be getting along. I have work to do."

Colonel James looked cautiously at the sketches Lupin had already seen and expressed the hope of seeing the others at some other time. Paul Ramsden departed ,and Lupin and Colonel James sat trying to avoid each other's eye. "The funny thing is, they are really rather clever in their way," he said.

"I suppose they are, but think of having them on your walls!"

"It wouldn't be restful, would it? I see you are writing letters. Don't let me interrupt you."

"Well, I've been trying to write to my husband since teatime yesterday, but first Miss Dyson-Drake took me for that frantic drive and then this morning as soon as I had got started people kept coming along to tell me the story of their lives, and I have promised Miss Dyson-Drake that I'll ask everyone if they've stolen her manuscript, but no one seems to have done so. Diana is writing a girl's school story, and Mr. Rennie a book on natural science, and Mr. Smythe a poem on snowdrops, and from what Miss Dyson-Drake told me about her book I don't see how it would fit into any of theirs."

"No, from the one manuscript of hers I was privileged to see, I shouldn't think it would."

"Oh, have you seen one of hers? I suppose you didn't take this one, did you? I mean, you are a publisher, aren't you? I am not sure she doesn't suspect you. At least, she said she didn't like publishers because they made fortunes out of other people's brains or something."

"To be perfectly frank with you, I don't think any publisher will make a fortune out of hers. As a matter of fact, if I had a passion for Miss Dyson-Drake's writings, I don't think I should need to steal them. I think I could obtain them in a perfectly normal way and at no very great expense. However—this is in confidence—I am only telling you so that you can wipe me off your list of suspects."

"Well, that seems to be about the lot, unless, of course, Mrs. Mydleton and her daughter are secret writers."

"No, I think I can vouch for them. I have known them a good many years."

"Still, you can't always tell. I am sure I should never have known that you were a publisher unless Diana had told me."

"Well, as a matter of fact, I don't think I should have guessed that you were a vicar's wife."

"No, I suppose not," said Lupin, regretfully. "And talking of vicars' wives, we are forgetting Mrs. Smythe. She might be a writer. It is true she told me that she did not like Miss Dyson-Drake's books, but she may have said that to put me off the scent while she is working it up to put into one of her own."

"Will she publish it in the parish magazine?"

"I should hardly think so, from what Miss Dyson-Drake told me about it, if I got it correctly, that is, which I easily might not have done, as I am never very bright and am less so than usual when I am simply terrified. I mean, I do think driving at sixty miles an hour without any hands on the wheel is a bit dangerous, don't you?"

"Yes, I should have been very alarmed. Do you think Mrs. Smythe writes her books under a *nom de plume*, Godfrey Marjorybanks or Rupert Dalrymple? After all, clergymen's wives have been known to live double lives, you know."

"I can't think how they find the time," sighed Lupin.

"Personally, my private opinion is that the manuscript may have blown out of the window, or else she may have made her laundry list on the back of it. Writers are supposed to be very absentminded, although I can't say that I have ever noticed it much, not over royalties, anyway."

"Do you like being a publisher?"

"Yes, it is very interesting. I haven't been one long, but I had an accident and had to leave the army. I've always been fond of books in spite of being a soldier. I had a chance of a partnership with my brother, so I took it. I have a little place in Somerset, but I didn't feel like settling down there yet awhile. It's near the Mydletons' old home, so I know them quite well. Grizel has a pretty thin time, for though Mrs. Mydleton is very charming, she is as selfish as they make them. Her husband was a delightful person and she has had a very happy life, so I don't see why she should grudge Grizel hers. In fact, it makes me boil to see the poor girl's life absolutely ruined."

"I quite agree," said Lupin eagerly. "I do hope she will get married soon."

Colonel James smiled. "So do I," he said. "She was engaged to quite a nice chap a few years ago. The wedding was fixed, then her father died and they had to postpone it. His regiment was ordered to India not long after, so they arranged to get married just before he sailed, but at the last moment Mrs. Mydleton said she could not be left, and Grizel's fiancé lost his temper. I can't say that I blame him. I tried to make arrangements for her to follow him out with a woman I know, but it was no good. Mrs. Mydleton had hysterics whenever it was mentioned and the young people had a violent quarrel."

"I think he sounds rather selfish," said Lupin. "I dare say she's well out of it. There is not much point in leaving a selfish mother for a selfish husband. She wants someone kind and considerate who will cosset her up a bit."

"Yes, she does," he agreed. "And I hope she gets it," he added earnestly.

"I think she will," said Lupin, in what she meant to be an encouraging manner. Colonel James gave her a grateful smile as he walked away. I shouldn't be surprised if he had gone straight off to propose, thought Lupin, as she turned back to her letter.

I've just been doing a spot of matchmaking, or at any rate, egging it on, if you know what I mean. He is a publisher and a bit lame but really awfully nice. He's got a place in Somerset, which I always think sounds a romantic sort of county. Didn't someone write a sort of poem or something about it once? She is quite pretty, but inclined to wring her hands a bit, which would pall on me, but he is one of those strong,, silent ones, who would like to have someone leaning on them. At least, he's not exactly silent, now I come to think of it, as he has just been telling me the story of his life and hers, too. But people always seem to do that the minute they see me, however rugged and reserved they are supposed to be. Is it because I am a vicar's wife and the next best thing to the confessional? Or is it because I have a sympathetic nature? I do wish you...

"Oh, hallo," said Ruth Rennie. "Have you seen Paul Ramsden anywhere?"

Lupin looked up from her letter. "Oh, yes," she replied. "He was here not long ago. He was showing me his pictures."

"Was he?" Ruth sounded rather surprised. "He doesn't show them to everyone."

"Doesn't he?"

"What did you think about them?"

"I thought they were very clever."

Ruth looked at her rather intensely. Lupin felt uncomfortable and wondered if she had a smudge on her nose. "Paul feels things very deeply," explained Ruth. "And unless he paints them they turn sour inside him."

"How uncomfortable," murmured Lupin.

"He has a wonderful mind. It is a privilege to talk to him. He is like me. He hates the obvious. Take this orchard, for instance. It is very pretty, but what is it but sugar on the cake?"

"Sugar on the cake is rather nice," said Lupin.

"Life is not all sugar," said Ruth profoundly.

"No, I suppose not," agreed Lupin, feeling rather lost. "Oh," she added in a relieved voice, "there is Mr. Ramsden with Miss Dyson-Drake."

"That hag!" exclaimed Ruth.

"I can't say I like her much," said Lupin. "She doesn't seem to be a bit interested in that child she knocked over yesterday."

"I'm sure she bores Paul to tears. She must be fifty if she's a day, and I bet her books are tripe. Hallo, Paul, are you coming?"

Paul strolled towards them with Miss Drake in his wake. "Oh, there you are," he said. "Have you eluded your keeper?"

"I haven't got a keeper," said Ruth indignantly.

"No?" said Paul. "Then let us away."

Miss Dyson-Drake looked at Ruth through her eyeglass as if she were something not very nice. "Goodbye, Paul," she said. "I'll take your advice."

"Do, my dear, it will do you good," and he followed Ruth across the grass.

"Shoddy stuff!" said Miss Dyson-Drake. "What fools men are! To think that a man with Paul's gifts should run about with that."

"Oh, I don't think there is anything in it," said Lupin. "After all, if her husband is writing books all the time, it is a bit dull for her."

"My dear child, I am no moralist. Life is beautiful, one must live, and how can one live without love? It is like the rain, flowers cannot bloom without it. No, what I deplore is men's taste, the way they seem to be enslaved by the second-rate."

"Paul Ramsden didn't strike me as the sort of person who would be easily enslaved."

"My dear, what do you know of men?" Lupin couldn't help feeling that she probably knew more than Miss Dyson-Drake, but did not like to say so. "They are unfathomable creatures. Now, as a matter of fact, Paul is just the sort of man who might easily succumb to a grand passion."

"Is he? Well, I hope he doesn't get one for Mrs. Rennie. I mean, her husband might not like it."

"I care nothing for that. All I fear is that Mrs. Rennie is not worthy of Paul."

Lupin was thankful to see Colonel James walking towards her. She did not care for talking to Miss Dyson-Drake; it gave her a feeling of utter inadequacy. "Hallo," he said, "have you seen Mrs. Rennie anywhere?"

Lupin was taken aback. She had hoped that Colonel James might have been about to announce his engagement with Grizel. It is true he had not had very long in which to fix things up, and it would have been rather funny to break away so soon to tell the news to someone whom he had only known for two days. But what did he want with Mrs. Rennie? He had been driving with her yesterday and here he was clamoring for her again. Perhaps Miss Dyson-Drake was right and men were rather unfathomable. "She has gone for a walk with Paul Ramsden," she said.

"Oh, has she?" Lupin noted with disappointment that Colonel James looked very much taken aback and rather cross. Happily married herself, she was always anxious to couple as many others as she could, and Grizel Mydleton and Colonel James had seemed a very promising pair. Bother Ruth Rennie!

"I suppose nothing has turned up?" said Miss Dyson-Drake.

"About your manuscript? I fear not."

To Lupin's great relief they strolled together towards the house, leaving her to finish her letter.

Oh, dear, the whole thing has blown a fuse, and he has just come back not having proposed at all but in search of rather a tiresome little thing with a cross husband who flirts with the artist cousin of Diana—the wife, not the husband, I mean, and he is sort of the property of that lunatic woman I told you about. I don't know if this a very clear, but the whole place seems to abound with love interest. Was it Tennyson or Wordsworth who said, "Comfort me with apples, for I am sick of love?" That is how I feel. I think I will go and have a chat with Diana. It will be rather the same as the apples, if you know what 1 mean. Anyway, I love you a lot.

Lupin

CHAPTER 8

LUPIN drove over to the hospital that afternoon to see how Rosie Gower was getting on. Diana had to stay at home as she was expecting people to come to look over the hotel with the idea of taking rooms. Lupin was rather nervous that she would be waylaid before she could get off, and would somehow find herself joined up with one of the temperamental guests and be compelled to listen to the history of their love life. But luck favored her and at half-past three she was walking into the hospital, carrying grapes, daffodils, and a large teddy bear.

The hospital was rather depressing. There were long corridors smelling of floor-polish and disinfectant. Purposeful-looking people kept walking briskly by, obviously regarding Lupin as one of nature's worst mistakes but not having time at the moment to do anything about it. At length she found a porter who told her that Rosie Gower was allowed no visitors, and she was about to leave her gifts and depart in shame when a kind-faced doctor came up. "Have you come to see Rosie Gower?" he asked. "She mustn't see anyone but her mother today, but her father is in the reception room and he will like to see you, I expect. Take the young lady along, Brown."

Brown looked at Lupin with dislike, but grudgingly pointed along a corridor and told her that it was the third door on the right. With a sinking heart, feeling sure that she would make a mistake and step into the operating theater just as someone was having some of the more intimate and unpleasant organs removed, she set off. The teddy bear slipped from under her arm and in recovering him she dropped the flowers, but at what seemed long last she found herself in what she supposed must be the reception room. Two women were sitting on a slippery sofa, having a highly technical conversation, but to Lupin's great relief she spied Mr. Gower sitting on a chair near a popping gas stove.

"Oh, how do you do, Mr. Gower?" she said. "I do hope Rosie is going on all right."

"Couldn't keep down a thing!" exclaimed one of the ghouls on the sofa.

"Why, it's the young lady," said Mr. Gower. "I'm sure I'm very pleased to see you, miss. They say Rosie is going on all right but has got to be kept quiet. What I say is, either she's all right or else she isn't, and if she is all right, why can't we take her home?"

"Well, she had rather a shock, you know."

"Shock! I'd say she did, miss. If I had my way that woman would be locked up. Not that I want to say anything against a friend of yours, miss, but I was never one to mince my words."

"And her legs, my dear!" came from the sofa. "Proper bolsters they were. I knew we wouldn't have her long."

"Miss Dyson-Drake isn't a friend of mine. I only met her the day before yesterday. For some reason or other she asked me to go for a drive with her to help her look for her manuscript, and like a fool I went."

"What manuscript?"

"She's written a manuscript and it has been stolen from her room. She woke me up the first night I was there to tell me all about it, only I was half asleep at the time and I thought she said she'd lost her child, so, of course, I was frightfully upset. I got up and tried to organize a search party, and just when everyone was dragging ponds and climbing about the roof ,it turned out that it wasn't a child she had lost after all, so, of course, everyone was a bit sick."

"Well, I never should have thought she was a mother! I am sorry for her child, that I am."

"No, she isn't. That is what I am trying to tell you. I misunderstood her. She said her manuscript was her child."

"She must be barmy, isn't she?"

"Yes, I rather think she is, but don't say I said so, she might have me up for libel."

"She ought to be shut up, driving about the place like that running over kids, and she's never been to ask how our Rosie is, either. Might be dead for all she cares! But she'd better look out for herself or she'll find herself in Queer Street one of these days. I am a socialist, I am, and I don't believe in one law for the rich and another for the poor."

"Oh, I didn't know you were a socialist," said Lupin with interest.

"I am that, and the times are coming sooner than you think, when the roads will be safe for the children of the poor."

"What about the children of the rich?"

"There won't be any."

"Oh, dear, no, I suppose there won't really. But won't there be any motorcars or buses or anything?"

"Yes, there will be motorcars, but they will be driven by the workers."

"Well, so long as they don't run over anyone's children, that will be something. I quite agree that Miss Dyson-Drake shouldn't be allowed to drive."

"You're fond of kids, aren't you, miss?"

"Yes, I suppose I am. You see, I've got one of my own."

"You married?"

"Oh, yes, absolutely." And Lupin took off her glove and displayed her wedding ring. "And he's a clergyman, too," she added proudly.

"You, a parson's wife! You sure you're not kidding me?"

"No, why should I?"

"Well, you don't look like one. No offense meant, but you look like a toff—not that you weren't good to the wife, a fair comfort you were to her, and I say, speak as you find, and I hope as how you and your husband and kid will flourish. There's parsons and parsons and some are straight chaps enough. They'll have nothing to fear from the workers."

"Thanks awfully. I'm sure you'd like my husband and you'd love Peter. He is two and just beginning to talk and stagger about as if he were drunk, just the same age as your Rosie."

"Thanks, miss, or madam, I suppose I should say. They are a treat at that age. Thanks, too, very kindly for these here, which I take in the spirit in which they are meant."

"Oh, good! I do hope the next time I come they'll let me see Rosie." And she shook hands with her socialistic friend. Oh, bother! she thought as she got into the car, I never told him about poor old Daddy being an earl. I wonder if it was deceitful of me, but I had forgotten about it for the moment and it is an awkward thing to bring into the conversation, anyway.

Lupin garaged her car and went in search of tea. The drawing room was empty, as she was rather late, and she thankfully sat down on a chair in the window and began to spread honey on a homemade scone. But she was not left long in peace. Mrs. Rennie burst in through the French window and, throwing herself in a chair opposite Lupin, exclaimed: "Thank God it is you. The end has come."

"What end?" asked Lupin placidly.

"The end of everything."

Lupin looked anxiously at the scones and finding that, at least, they had not come to an end yet, took another so as to be on the safe side.

"I was afraid I should find one of the old cats here," went on Mrs. Rennie. "I know they all think the worst of Charles and me."

"Why?"

"Oh, I don't know. I feel they always suspect us of not being married."

"Do they?" asked Lupin, surprised. "Whatever makes them think that? After all, you share the same room and everything."

"Well, I suppose I am rather a weird, unconventional sort of person," went on Mrs. Rennie, absentmindedly taking a cake off the plate and starting to eat it. "And now they'll know it's true."

"Why? Aren't you married?" asked Lupin, genuinely astonished.

"Well, I suppose I am at the moment, but I shan't be much longer. I am leaving Charles tonight."

"Oh, are you? I thought you'd made it up."

"Made it up! I suppose we've made it up a hundred times since we got married, but I am through. After all, other men like me, it's no use pretending. I know I am attractive to men."

"How nice!" said Lupin.

Mrs. Rennie took another scone and spread it with honey. "Don't you sometimes wonder what it's all about?" she asked.

Lupin sat up with a jerk, feeling that she had lost the thread of the conversation. "What's about what?" she asked.

"Everything," said Mrs. Rennie.

Lupin gaped at her; she was feeling very sleepy and would have liked to have gone and lain down for a bit before dinner.

"I mean," went on Mrs. Rennie, "why am I here?"

That was what Lupin was wondering, too, and wishing that she were not, as Mrs. Rennie quoted:

"Into this universe and why not knowing,
I came like water willy-nilly flowing
And out of it like wind along the waste
I know not whither, willy-nilly blowing,"

"Oh, absolutely," agreed Lupin, feeling that her companion expected an answer.

Mrs. Rennie folded her arms round her knees. "There must be an answer to the riddle," she said.

Lupin felt that if they were going to start asking each other riddles it was time she went upstairs. After all, one associated riddles with puns and great uncles, not with somebody like Mrs. Rennie who must be younger than she was herself, and fairly rapid if all she said about herself were true. "I am not much of a hand at riddles," she said, getting up to go.

"But don't you ever wonder about things?" persisted Mrs. Rennie.

"Sometimes," replied Lupin, who at the moment was wondering what on earth they were talking about.

"Look at all this," and Mrs. Rennie pointed out of the window at the orchard. "Spring and beauty," she said. "Doesn't it look as if one were meant to be happy?"

"I should think so."

"Then why isn't one?"

"Aren't you happy?"

"No, I'm in hell."

"Oh, dear," sighed Lupin, and rather unwillingly sat down again.

"I feel this more deeply than other people. Some people can be satisfied with the second-best, but I can't."

"Can't you?"

"No, I thought I loved Charles, but I find I don't. Am I to spend the rest of my life at his side, starved of all that makes life worth living?"

Lupin did not know the answer to this one, but luckily it was only a rhetorical question, and her companion went straight on. "Think what life might be," she said. "Think of the blossom on the trees, of the sunshine and even of the beauty that can be found by the initiated in chimney stacks and factory buildings! Think of dew on the grass and moonlight on the sea! Think of the stars singing together as you stand hand-in-hand with your lover on the threshold of a new heaven and a new earth! Think!"

Lupin tried to think, but it wasn't a success. She thought of Andrew and hoped Cook would remember his favorite puddings. She thought of Peter and hoped Nanny wouldn't let him stray about the roads. She also thought that it must be nearly time for a drink. She pulled herself together and tried to take in what Ruth was saying, but it made her feel very giddy, flitting about from trees to chimney stacks, from dew on the grass to moonlight on the sea. Her own thoughts never came out consecutively and she always had a great difficulty in expressing herself, but just now a vague picture did form in her mind—a picture of a wet winter afternoon, and Andrew coming in at teatime and sitting there talking about Peter or the parish or anything for the matter of that, and how utterly happy they had been, but even if she had been able to explain it, it would have sounded very prosaic to Mrs. Rennie, who seemed to need sun, moon, and stars, not to mention a few chimney stacks and factory buildings thrown in, to celebrate her romance.

"I don't want to butt in," she said truthfully, for she would have much referred to hear nothing about it. "But why are you so unhappy?

Don't tell me if you would rather not," she added, without much hope.

"I fell in love with Charles at the beginning. He was staying with some people who brought him to the tennis club. We played together and as soon as he handed me the balls I knew that I loved him and I thought that he loved me. We met every day and went for long walks together. It was June. I shall never see wild roses in the hedges again without thinking of those days. We danced together and we seemed made for each other. It was absolute bliss. Then we got married and everything changed. I was prepared to be happy in a little house, so long as we loved each other. I gave up my parents, my friends, the tennis club, and all my old life so as to devote myself to him. But he did not want my devotion. From the beginning his work came first. For one thing, he would start off at the same time every morning."

Lupin felt that it would have been much more trying if he had started off at a different time each morning, but did not like to say so, for fear of seeming unsympathetic.

"Sometimes at the beginning he would come home to lunch, but he was always in a hurry and wanting to get back to his work. He was furious one day because lunch was late. Then he took to having his lunch out and I had to have mine all alone. In the evening he would talk about his work all the time, and afterwards he would write his book and be angry if I made a remark, and at last I realized that his love was dead."

"I don't see why. I mean, men are always interested in their work."

"Then they shouldn't get married. By the end of the winter he had killed my love by his cruelty and neglect."

"You know I think you are making a sort of mistake in a sort of a way, if you know what I mean. After all, one can't make love all the time, it would be like never eating anything but caviar and oysters, and I don't think one would really like a man very much if he never did any work. I've heard you and your husband laughing together. Don't you think that perhaps you do still really like each other, and have just got a bit fed up? Of course, people do seem a bit more glamorous at the beginning, but they get nicer and nicer, I think," and Lupin subsided, rather exhausted after her real effort at explanation.

"You don't know what love is," announced Mrs. Rennie.

Lupin felt that if it were the series of emotions described by Mrs. Rennie, she was glad she didn't.

"Love to you is just ordering your husband's dinner."

Lupin turned a giggle into a sneeze. For one thing she never did order her husband's dinner. Cook had been with him before his marriage and she knew his tastes much better than Lupin did, so the daily interview was chiefly an account by Cook of her aunt's last illness, her sister's matrimonial troubles and her nephew's brilliance at school. It was all very friendly and interesting, but hardly to be described in the terms of a great love story.

"I suppose no one with potentialities like mine is ever happy," pondered Ruth. "I could be a great saint or a great sinner. You are one of the lucky ones who play about on the fringe of life, you paddle in shallow water while I plunge out into the depths."

Lupin had not the heart to try to cheer her up any more as she seemed determined to be miserable. "Oh, well," she said comfortably, "it must be very dreadful for you."

"Sometimes I think I shall end it all. Perhaps that would be the best way out. Oh, hallo, Paul."

"Hallo, care for a drive?"

"Yes, I should like a drive, I want to get right away from everything, out into the air. I feel stifled." She threw her arms wide.

"You won't be stifled in the car—you had better get a coat:"

Ruth left the room and Paul grinned at Lupin. "Don't be disapproving, it doesn't suit you. All you should ever do is to sit still and look lovely."

Lupin had never been accused of being disapproving before. She was all for people being happy, and a motor drive was probably Just what Ruth Rennie needed. All that talk about leaving her husband and doing away with herself was so much hot air, like the Sunday-school-teacher who had threatened to go on the streets when she quarreled with the superintendent. All the same, Lupin wished that Paul would not flirt with Ruth, because she was obviously in a discontented mood and ready to do anything silly. Well, it wasn't her business. Being a clergyman's wife was giving her quite a sense of responsibility. If she weren't careful her teeth would start sticking out. She laughed and said to Paul, "I should get awfully bored sitting quite still all day, and I should soon stop looking lovely if I didn't get any exercise!"

"Now you are being argumentative and that doesn't suit you, either. I should like you to sit forever under the cherry blossom, with the sun shining on your hair."

"I thought you despised cherry blossom."

He looked at her sharply, then turned away to light a cigarette. "Sometimes," he said, "one is in the mood for cherry blossom and sometimes one is not."

He looked as if he might have said more, but at this moment George, the porter, came up. He was the old-fashioned type, with charming manners and always ready to do anything for anybody. Lupin had made friends with him already. "Please, my lady," he said, "Miss Turner was inquiring after you:"

"Oh, I'll go and find her," said Lupin, getting up.

"Might I ask how you found the little girl, my lady?"

"Getting on very well, I am thankful to say."

"I am very glad to hear that, my lady."

"Get my car round for me, will you, George?" asked Paul. "I am going for a run before dinner."

"Certainly, sir," replied George.

Lupin went up to Diana's office. "Hallo, my dear. George said you were wondering what had happened to me. Did you think there had been another accident? George is rather a lamb, isn't he?"

"Yes, he is a great help. Paul found him for me and I must say I am much more grateful for him than I am for the guests he found. He gives a good look to the hotel when people arrive, definitely an asset."

CHAPTER 9

THE dining room was very empty that evening. Miss Dyson-Drake was already at her table, always the first to come and the last to go, as Diana remarked. Lupin stopped at her table on her way in. "Rosie is going on all right," she said.

"Who on earth is Rosie?" asked Miss Dyson-Drake, scraping her soup plate for the last drop.

"The little girl, the one you knocked down."

"Oh, is she? I suppose you haven't found out anything?"

"Nothing new, it's a concussion, you know. I wasn't allowed to see her."

Miss Dyson-Drake gave a last despairing look at her soup plate and tried to catch the waiter's eye, then she looked again at Lupin. "It's got to be found," she said.

Lupin looked at her vaguely. "Have you lost anything?" she asked.

Miss Dyson-Drake gave her the look that Lupin had known from her youth up, starting with her aunts, going on to schoolmistresses and leading up to the Sunday-school superintendent at her husband's parish in Glanville. The look seemed to say, "Can any human being be quite so lacking in any glimmer of intelligence as this?" Lupin knew the answer was "yes," and she had always been sorry about it, but she was afraid there was nothing to be done. Luckily the waiter came up at this moment, and while Miss Dyson-Drake transferred her attention to him and entered into a long and animated discussion about the boiled turbot which she would have preferred to have been fried sole, Lupin escaped to her own table.

Diana talked well and amusingly about the prospective visitors who had arrived that afternoon and who had told Diana that they had never stayed in a boardinghouse before. Lupin suddenly interrupted her. "I know what she was talking about;" she said. "Her manuscript."

"Who was talking about whose manuscript?"

"Miss Dyson-Drake about hers."

"Probably—she seldom talks about anything else except food. The other night she asked me why we never had pheasant, and though I pointed out that it was April, I don't think it conveyed anything to her. She has a mind above such mundane matters."

"She doesn't seem very interested in Rosie," said Lupin, knitting her brows. "I should not be able to think of anything else if I were she. Rosie's father is a dear little man. You can see he is absolutely devoted to her. We had an awfully nice talk. I told him about the time Peter had croup and he was frightfully sympathetic. Rosie had the most awful diarrhea last summer and they were simply terrified, but it was only plums."

Charles Rennie was sitting alone at his table, looking furious. It was a pity, he had been quite nice yesterday. Perhaps his inside was upset, men had such awkward insides. She wondered whether he had ever tried prunes. Or was it because Ruth was so late coming in from her drive with Paul Ramsden? She was a silly idiot. Lupin was sure she really did like her husband, but she seemed to expect him to spend his time making love to her, which husbands didn't.

At this moment Barker, Mrs. Mydleton's maid, came in. "Excuse me, miss," she said to Diana, "but could you come to Mrs. Mydleton? Miss Grizel has not come in yet, and my mistress is very upset."

Diana left the room as Mrs. Rennie came in; she was looking rather pleased with herself. "Oh, sorry I'm late," she said, sitting down opposite her husband.

"Are you late? I never noticed."

"Well, I suppose I can go for a drive if I like, or would you like me to sit at home and hold your hand while you write about the fauna of South Africa?"

"It is Central Africa, as it happens."

"Well, it is all the same to me."

"It would be."

Lupin wondered why she found herself thinking of the house study at school. It was a long time since she had thought about it. Then she realized that the Rennies' conversation, which she could not help overhearing, closely resembled that of herself and her friends when in the fourth form. It seemed a pity, but there it was. Perhaps it was rather restful after being with Paul Ramsden.

Mrs. Smythe came in looking worried. "Where is Miss Turner?" she asked.

"She has gone to Mrs. Mydleton," replied Lupin. "Her daughter's not back yet and she is a bit upset."

"Arthur isn't back yet, either."

"Were they together?"

"No, Arthur had gone for a walk, to meditate upon a poem. He needs solitude. Miss Mydleton has gone for a drive with Colonel James, I believe," she added coldly.

"Oh," said Lupin, rather pleased. She did hope Colonel James would get on with it.

Just then Paul Ramsden lounged in and sat down at his table. "Where on earth have you been, Paul?" shouted Miss Dyson-Drake.

Lupin wondered why they did not sit at the same table as they never stopped talking to each other and were bound to take the whole room into their confidence.

"Ruth and I went over to see the new council houses at Brayside."

"Why on earth? I'd have come with you if you'd told me, it might have taken my mind off. I tried to work but it was no good."

"My dear, you have so often told me that ugliness jars on you. I knew it would only hurt you."

"In some moods beauty only mocks one. Waiter, some more cream! When one's soul is in torment," she went on, adding sugar and cream in large quantities to her chocolate souffle, "the burgeoning of spring is but an additional ache. The stark ugliness of council houses might have braced me." The cream having come, she fell on her souffle avidly.

"To me they were beautiful," said Paul.

"Nonsense," said Miss Dyson-Drake, with her mouth full. "I defy even you to find beauty in council houses."

"I will try to show you their beauty in my next picture," he replied.

"That will be interesting," said Miss Dyson-Drake, "very interesting. Waiter, I will have some more of that souffle."

"You seem to have a rival," remarked Charles Rennie to his wife in a low voice which Lupin could not help hearing.

Ruth laughed contemptuously. "As a matter of fact," she said, "we brought Grizel Mydleton back with us. Colonel James's car had broken down and she asked us to bring her along. She was worrying about her mother. The people here all make me sick. They've been dead a hundred years and want burying."

Lupin, who was trying to persuade Mrs. Smythe to have some dinner, hoped they did not realize how audible their conversation was. "You will feel much better when you have had something to eat," she said. "I remember my husband was away at a meeting one evening and he was frightfully late home and I was simply terrified. I rang up the Bishop and he said that Andrew had started for home and that if I'd take his advice I'd start my dinner and before I'd finished he'd be with me. And so I did and so he was. It just shows that bishops do know some things, doesn't it? Bring Mrs. Smythe's dinner here, John."

Mrs. Smythe sat down reluctantly and had just taken a halfhearted spoonful of soup when Arthur came into the room. He walked rather jauntily and there was a slightly defiant expression on his face that Lupin liked to see.

"There, I was right, just like the Bishop," said Lupin.

"I am sorry I'm late, Mother, but it was such a splendid day I thought I'd make the most of it. I shouldn't be here now if Colonel James hadn't picked me up in his car."

"Naturally, dear, I am only too glad that you did, but if you had rung up to say that you were going to be late it would have saved me much anxiety. As you see, Lady Lupin has kindly asked me to sit at her table and now we shall have to have everything moved back again."

"Why?" asked Lupin. "Won't Mr. Smythe sit here, too?"

"Thanks, I'd love to. I hope you won't mind my not having changed.

But as I was so late I thought I'd better just come in as I was."

"I hope you washed, dear," said his mother.

Arthur flushed angrily. "Oh, yes, I washed," he said shortly. "And I'm sorry I didn't telephone. I didn't see a callbox."

"I suppose he was wandering about in the open country composing a poem," said his mother indulgently.

"Must have been nice," agreed Lupin.

"Oh, rather," said Arthur, "It was great." And he grinned rather fatuously.

Mrs. Mydleton, Grizel, and Colonel James all came into the room together, and to Lupin's intense surprise Mrs. Mydleton was beaming. Colonel James was sitting with them and Lupin felt sure that he and Grizel had just become engaged. Did Arthur know? She did hope he wouldn't be disappointed, but after all, Grizel was much older than he was. "Well, I am thankful everyone is back safely," she remarked. "I've been feeling awfully nervous ever since we ran over Rosie. I mean, such frightful things might happen in a car, mightn't they?"

In the meanwhile, Diana had returned and greeted Mrs. Smythe and Arthur. "I hope you don't mind our having joined you, Miss Turner," said Mrs. Smythe. "Lady Lupin kindly asked me to sit here while I was waiting for Arthur."

"That was a very good idea. Where had I got to, Lupin? I think I had had soup, but am not sure."

"I should start from the beginning if I were you," said Lupin.

"It is funny that everyone should be so late tonight," said Mrs. Smythe. "Arthur, Grizel Mydleton, Mrs. Rennie, Mr. Ramsden, and Colonel James."

"Well, the evenings are rather nice. I think I must see if we can't have dinner a bit later, though it is rather difficult with the staff. What did you say, John?"

"The police are here, miss," said John in an awed voice, "and wish to see you."

"Oh, dear, it seems just like old times, doesn't it?" exclaimed Lupin.

Mrs. Smythe gazed at her in astonishment.

"It does, indeed," sighed Diana, getting up. "I wish they had waited until I had finished my fish."

"Whatever can they want?" asked Mrs. Smythe.

"I wonder," murmured Lupin. "Oh, John is fetching Miss Dyson-

Drake! I know—" and she had one of her occasional brainwaves, if they could be called that. "She has called them in about her manuscript, the one that was lost, you know."

"Well, if the police question me," said Mrs. Smythe, "I shall have to say what I think about it."

"Yes, you will. It's always best to be quite frank with them. I found that out last time. Oh, there goes Colonel James. What, John? You don't mean to say they want me? Well, all right, but mind you keep me some chocolate soufflé. I do hope they don't think I took it, it will look so bad in the papers, 'Vicar's wife steals manuscript of improper book.' They'll think I wanted to read it in private, or else that Andrew did," and she walked off.

"What did she mean?" Mrs. Smythe asked her son. "Has she been mixed up with the police before?"

"I don't know, I'm sure, Mother."

"I wonder if she really is the wife of the vicar of Glanville."

"I wonder," replied her son, with his thoughts elsewhere.

A solid-looking policeman sat at Diana's desk, while she sat in her armchair with Colonel James standing beside her. Upon Lupin's entrance he drew up a chair for her.

Miss Dyson-Drake stood facing the police. "The manuscript was in my room when I dressed for dinner."

"Will you please give me particulars of the accident?"

"Accident! I don t believe for a moment that it was an accident."

"How do you mean, madam, that it was not an accident?"

"I think someone took it on purpose."

"Took what on purpose?"

"My manuscript."

"What manuscript?"

"The manuscript that I have been working at with my heart's blood for the last six months."

"What has that to do with the accident?"

"You will keep on talking about an accident. I tell you that it has been stolen."

The policeman looked helplessly at his notes. "You reported that at seven P.M. approximately you were proceeding along the main road from Barton to Exford, when you saw a child standing in the middle of the road."

"I never reported anything of the kind."

Colonel James interposed. "I reported the accident on behalf of Miss Dyson-Drake, as she was naturally feeling very much upset at the time."

"You had no right to do so," snapped Miss Dyson-Drake. "It was no business of yours."

"It was lucky for you that he did, madam, or you would have found yourself in an awkward position. Failing to report an accident is a serious offense."

"I really don't see that any of this has any bearing on the theft of my manuscript."

"It hasn't, madam. I know nothing about any manuscript."

"Well, I am trying to tell you, but you won't listen."

"I wish for particulars about this accident. Mr. Gower, the father of the child, tells me that there was a Mrs. Hastings in the car at the time. Is she here?"

"Yes, I expect he means me."

"This is Lady Lupin Hastings," explained Colonel James.

"Lady Lupin Hastings," said the policeman doubtfully.

"Yes, but don't say anything to Mr. Gower about it because he's by way of being a communist or something and it might put him right off and that would be a pity as we are such friends."

"Your husband is Lord Hastings?"

"No, rather not, just plain Mr., at least, Reverend, to be exact. He's a clergyman, you know. It's my father who's Lord Lanchester. Mr. Gower would like him if he knew him, everybody does. He is a perfect darling and after all, he didn't do it on purpose."

"Who didn't do what on purpose, madam? I mean your ladyship."

"Daddy being an earl, I mean, he couldn't help it."

"Was he there at the time of the accident?"

"Oh, no, rather not. I haven't seen him since Christmas."

"Who was in the car at the time of the accident?" asked the policeman patiently.

"Just Miss Dyson-Drake and me. We were dashing along, I mean, driving along, and suddenly we saw Rosie standing in the middle of the road."

"Who is Rosie?"

"The child, the one we had the accident with."

The policeman referred to his notes again. "Oh, yes, the child, Rose Gower. Please go on, miss."

"Well, it was too frightful, I didn't really see what happened because I shut my eyes and began to pray. I am a clergyman's wife, you know."

"Very natural, I'm sure, your ladyship. But could you tell me about what rate you were going?"

"I am afraid I am awfully bad at anything like that. But we were going a little bit fast, it's true, but that was really my fault because I said I wanted to get home, quickly. You see, I wanted to write to my husband before dinner."

"Would you say that Miss…er…Drake was driving with all possible care?"

Lupin looked uncomfortable. "That is an awkward sort of question," she said. "I mean, after all we all have our own ways of driving and one so often feels the other person's driving badly if they don't drive quite like you do yourself. I mean, I often think that my husband drives too slowly."

"And you thought that Miss Drake drove too quickly?"

"I didn't say so, I only meant that neither she nor my husband drive quite the same as I do."

"That will do, Lady Hastings, I quite understand," and he gave her a very nice smile.

"I understand, madam," he went on to Miss Dyson-Drake, "that the child is not in any immediate danger and there is no actual evidence that you were driving to the danger of the public, but you may think yourself lucky that there have been no further consequences. Of course, Mr. Gower may decide to take the matter to court, but I don't think he will. I should like to see your driving license, please."

"Oh, dear," said Lupin to Diana, when at last they were alone. "I wonder if I ought to have told that nice policeman that Miss D.-D. is a menace on the roads. She really oughtn't to be allowed to drive at all, and if she runs over anyone else it will all be owing to me for not speaking up, but the habits of the old school die hard and I couldn't bring myself to say that she drove at sixty miles an hour, with her hands off the wheel, and her head turned round the other way, which no one could call first-class driving."

"I shouldn't bother, I think the policeman gathered exactly what you thought about Miss Dyson-Drake's driving. He is not a fool."

CHAPTER 10

LUPIN was just walking out of the dining room, having finished her breakfast, when Grizel Mydleton came hurrying up to her. “Oh, Lady Lupin, the most frightful thing has happened.”

“‘Is anything the matter?” asked Lupin.

“Yes,” and Grizel gave a great gulp. “Mother’s pearls!”

“Your mother’s pearls?”

“Yes.”

“What about them?”

“They have gone.”

“Where have they gone?”

“I don’t know.”

“You mean she has lost them?”

“She thinks they were stolen.”

“Oh, does she? Like Miss Dyson-Drake’s manuscript! I wonder if there is someone in this place who pinches things.”

“I can’t find Miss Turner.”

“Why, you don’t think she has got them, do you? I can assure you she would never do a thing like that. She has never even been accused of stealing.”

“No, no, of course I didn’t mean that, but mother wanted to tell her all about it.”

“Oh, does she? Well, I suppose I had better come along,” she said, in a resigned voice, though she could not help feeling that Mrs. Smythe, as the senior vicar’s wife in the establishment, might have been given the first refusal of the job. I wonder what made the thief choose Mrs. Mydleton’s pearls, she pondered, or Miss Dyson-Drake’s manuscript, for the matter of that.

“Aren’t they insured?” she asked aloud.

“I don’t know, but anyhow, Daddy gave them to her. She is in a terrible state about them. Do come and see what you can do.”

Mrs. Mydleton lay back in her chair and her maid was hovering over her with smelling salts. “I couldn’t find Miss Turner, Mummy, explained Grizel apologetically, “so I brought Lady Lupin.”

Lupin felt rather like the time she had had to substitute in a school match owing to half the school being down with measles. “Perhaps I’d better go and look for Diana," she said. "Have you any brandy? It sometimes makes one feel a little better."

"Thank you, dear," said Mrs. Mydleton. "You are always so thoughtful. I think a little brandy would make me feel better."

Lupin felt a little less like an unsatisfactory understudy called on at the last moment. "I was so terribly sorry to hear of your loss," she said.

"If my pearls have gone, my heart will be broken," announced Mrs. Mydleton sadly. "They were the last gift my dear husband ever gave me. I always think about him whenever I put them on." Lupin felt that she would sometimes spare a thought for Andrew even without a gift to remind her.

"When did you last think, I mean, where did you last see them?"

"I wore them last night with my black velvet," replied Mrs. Mydleton, after a pause.

"Oh, yes, I remember. I thought how nice you looked," said Lupin.

Mrs. Mydleton gave her a wan smile. "There is no one to care what I look like now," she said.

Grizel stood wringing her hands. No wonder she exasperates her mother, thought Lupin. And the silly idiot has forgotten her cue.

"I think it is kind of you to look so nice," she said out loud. "It is such a relief to look at you, after looking at Miss Dyson-Drake and Mrs. Smythe." Belatedly she remembered that Mrs. Smythe was a friend of Mrs. Mydleton's. "Though, of course, Mrs. Smythe is very nice," she added hurriedly.

Mrs. Mydleton began to cheer up a little. "So sweet of you, dear, and you always look charming yourself. But my pearls...yes, I wore them last night and kept them on in bed. They say it is always a good thing to sleep in one's pearls, and then this morning I went to the bathroom. Unfortunately, there is no private bathroom to this bedroom, but Barker always goes to the one at the end of the passage and keeps it until I am ready. I would have left the pearls as I always do, on the dressing table. It appears that Grizel called to Barker to go to put a stitch in her frock and she did not come back to my room until after I had returned from my bath. I suppose she took it for granted that I had the pearls with me."

"I ought to have noticed, madam, but I was feeling a little rushed," Barker apologized. " I shall never forgive myself, but Miss Grizel wanted a fresh collar sewn into her dress. Of course, if I had known yesterday—"

"It is all my fault," said Grizel miserably.

"Well, my child, if you had only thought about your collar yesterday evening, Barker would have come straight back to my room and seen the pearls." Lupin could not help thinking that if Mrs. Mydleton had put away her own pearls before going to the bath, or else had taken them with her instead of leaving them lying about on the dressing table, it would also have prevented the tragedy.

"Looks as if they were taken while you were in your bath, doesn't it?" remarked Lupin brilliantly.

Diana arrived at this moment, and Lupin thankfully made her escape. Later in the morning they sat together in Diana's sitting room. "I can't think whatever made me start this guest house," she said.

"It all seemed to be going so well," replied Lupin. "But I must say I have noticed whenever you get several people together, something seems to go wrong."

There was a knock at the door and Colonel James came in.

"Can I help?" he asked.

"I don't know," replied Diana. "I should be glad if you could."

"Let's write down all the alternatives," he suggested.

"Yes, let's," agreed Lupin. "Things always look better written down, except when they look worse."

"Number one," said Colonel James. "It is just possible that Mrs. Mydleton may have put them somewhere and forgotten where she put them."

"Yes, that's quite possible, of course," agreed Diana.

"Number two, someone came into her room while she was in her bath and took them. A, a servant; B, a guest; C, an outsider."

"Well, then," said Diana, "we had better go through the servants. One: Nanny, head housemaid. She has been with me for thirty years, and I should suspect either of you or the Archbishop of Canterbury of stealing something before I suspected her.

"Number two: Kate, a good worker with excellent references, but rather grumpy. She has been with me for two years, but I don't feel I know much about her. I can't imagine her stealing a pearl necklace. She was in her last place ten years and she is too disagreeable to be dishonest.

"Number three: Shirley Walker. I gave her notice last week. She is very dressy and probably spends all her money on clothes. She skips her work and is thoroughly unsatisfactory, but, of course, that doesn't mean she is a thief."

"And anyway, I don't see why she should have stolen Miss Dyson-Drake's manuscript," put in Lupin. "I mean, she couldn't wear that."

"You think the two things hang together?" queried Colonel James.

"Well, I should hope so," said Lupin. "Otherwise there are two thieves in the house, one stealing manuscripts and one stealing pearls."

"Well," said Colonel James, "I think we shall have to put Shirley Walker on the list of possible suspects."

"Number four: Daisy Bray," went on Diana, "a young girl from a good home. She works well and teaches in the Sunday school."

"Ah," said Lupin darkly. As a vicar's wife, her opinion of church workers was slightly suspicious.

"Then there are the waiters, John and Ferguson. John I've known most of my life. He was my aunt's butler and stayed on with me in spite of me turning the house into a hotel—decent of him, wasn't it? He is absolutely reliable. But Ferguson I don't know much about. Nanny saw him kissing Shirley Walker, but there is no harm in that, and his references were all right. I have never cared for him much, but I have nothing against him."

"It would be rather a difficult thing for the waiters to get into the visitors' rooms before breakfast, I should think," pointed out Colonel James. "They would not have any excuse if they were seen."

"That's true," agreed Diana. "Besides, I was having my breakfast at the time and I should have noticed if Ferguson had not been in the room, at least, I hope I should. Let me see, you were at breakfast, weren't you? And Mrs. Smythe and Arthur, and Charles Rennie, I think. Of course, we do not know the exact time that the pearls disappeared. Mrs. Mydleton was so vague, but I should think it was roughly between nine and nine-thirty."

"Have you gone through all the staff?"

"Well, there is Cook, and there are two kitchen-maids, but I don't see how they could very well pop up to the guests' bedrooms just at breakfast time. They are too busy, for one thing, and the same applies to them as to the waiters. They would look silly if they were seen coming out of one of the bedrooms. A chambermaid would be the only one who could get away with it."

"What about George?"

"Oh, I forgot about George. I suppose it would be pretty casy for him. He could be carrying up shoes, or mending a sash-cord, or putting in a new electric bulb. Yes, there are a thousand excuses George could make. Of course, I don't know much about him except that he is a treasure. Paul produced him for me. Oh, I do hope it isn't George."

"I hope not," agreed Colonel James, but he looked a little thoughtful.

"Bother it all," said Diana. "It is just the sort of thing that would happen when I want to get on with my book. If only they hadn't been Mrs. Mydleton's pearls it wouldn't have been so bad. After all, Lupin's are much more valuable, and she usually leaves them lying about in the soap dish, so why on earth couldn't the thief have taken them?"

"I am glad he didn't," replied Lupin. She was a kindhearted girl, but could not help feeling that if a necklace had to be stolen, she would prefer it not to be hers.

"What I meant was that you wouldn't be making such a fuss as Mrs. Mydleton is making," explained Diana.

"Well," said Lupin, "if it comes to that, it is a pity they did not take *your* manuscript. I am sure it is better than Miss Dyson-Drake's, and you didn't write it with your heart's blood. Or did you?"

"No, just Quink."

"What about the guests?" broke in Colonel James.

"Well, I can't say I know much about any of them except Lupin and Paul. I don't think either of them would have taken Mrs. Mydleton's pearls."

"No," agreed Lupin, "I don't think I should, and I certainly shouldn't have taken Miss Dyson-Drake's manuscript."

"I don't know about the Rennies. I suppose they might be professional thieves. It doesn't seem likely, but then no one seems likely and it must be someone. I must ask Paul about them, he introduced them here, but I don't think he knows them well."

"As you say, it must be someone, unless, as I rather hope, Mrs. Mydleton has just mislaid them. All the same, I should be surprised if it turned out to be the Rennies," said the colonel.

Oh, dear, thought Lupin. I do hope he isn't in love with Ruth. He does seem rather keen, taking her for a drive and not liking the idea of her being a thief. Still, I think it's Grizel he's really in love with. It's not as if he could marry Ruth, and it will be too sickening if Grizel has another disappointment.

"I wonder if it's Mrs. Smythe," she said aloud. "It's always the most unlikely person, and it would be a very clever disguise. No one would like to suspect her. She is the very living spit of a clergyman's wife. In fact, now I come to think of it, no real one could ever be quite so typical. At least, I've never met one."

"Well, you ought to know;" said Diana. "Set a thief to catch a thief."

"Thief!" replied Lupin, rather taken aback.

"Clergyman's wife, I mean, of course, silly. No, you couldn't do it off your own bat, but you could ask Andrew to set you a list of questions about church schools, and ecclesiastical commissions, and the date of Quinquagesima, etcetera, and then try them on her at unexpected moments."

Well, I suppose I might try," replied Lupin doubtfully.

"It's a long shot," said Colonel James. "And, as a matter of fact, I am pretty sure that she is a clergyman's wife. I don't fancy either her and Arthur, or the Rennies. If the pearls really have gone, I should be inclined to guess it was your Shirley Walker, although I have no earthly right to say so, but from what you tell us, she is unsatisfactory, and then, of course, there is George; you don't know much about him. Still, I hope it's not. I like George."

"I'd much rather it were Ferguson than George," said Diana. "I've never liked him, though, as you say, it would be difficult for him to get into the bedroom."

"I have got to go to London today," went on Colonel James. "And I've promise to call in at Mrs. Mydleton's insurance office and they may insist on an investigation."

"Oh, dear, we seem to be in for it now."

"If they do, I know a chap who is awfully good at that sort of thing."

"Do you mean a detective?"

"Yes, but you would never guess he was one. He could just come along and stay as a guest and gave a look round."

"Everyone will know that he is a detective if he comes in a bowler hat," pointed out Lupin.

"He won't."

"I suppose," said Lupin thoughtfully, after Colonel James had left them, "that Grizel didn't take them."

"Why ever should she?"

"I don't know, but she looked a bit guilty, I thought. As a matter of fact, I rather wondered yesterday whether she hadn't taken the manuscript. I am sure she has something on her mind. I mean, it would be rather ironical if Colonel James got detectives down here and they traced the crime to her. On the other hand, I don't quite see what I can do about it. I mean, it is a bit difficult to tell a man that you think the girl he is in love with is given to stealing manuscripts and her own mother's pearls."

"I shouldn't try if I were you," replied Diana, dryly.

CHAPTER 11

LUPIN went to see Rosie that afternoon and drove Mr. Gower back to his garage afterwards. "Well," he remarked, as they drove out of the hospital gates, "so your father is an earl, is he?"

"Well, yes, I suppose he is in a way, but I did ask the policeman not to tell you, because I had an idea that you didn't like earls, and after all, its not altogether Daddy's fault, is it? He's got the sweetest nature and, anyway, my husband is only a plain mister, not that he's exactly plain. In fact, he's very good-looking, but you know what I mean."

"You ran away with a humble suitor, did you?"

Lupin pondered. She remembered the surprised and incredulous delight her family had displayed on learning that she was engaged to Andrew. So many girls nowadays were prone to marry film stars, crooners, and broadcast announcers who, though no doubt excellent husbands and fathers, were something of an unknown quantity to people like the Lanchesters. They had always felt that Lupin was just the kind of girl who might do something eccentric, and that her eccentricity should take the form of marrying a clergyman instead of running away with a member of the Left Book Club was a great relief to them.

Clergymen were a race with which the Lanchesters had always been familiar, and this particular one had the advantage of being related to families they had known all their lives. Then he was old enough and sensible enough to keep Lupin in order, which was a distinct advantage. Not that there was any harm in her, but she had an impulsive nature which often led to trouble. At twelve she had adopted six sick dogs from a neighboring dogs' home, at fifteen she had become engaged to the gardener's boy, to his intense embarrassment, and at eighteen she had absentmindedly gone to a neighboring hunt ball in fancy dress. Three more years had passed while her parents felt themselves treading on the edge of a precipice, and then she had become engaged to this young, or not so young, clergyman, and they had felt themselves on firm ground at last.

Lupin remembered her pretty wedding in Lorrimer Church, packed to overflowing with friends, relations, and tenants. She remembered her father's thankful, "I do," when the vicar asked, "Who giveth this woman to be married to this man?" She remembered her mother's beaming face at the reception and her brother's air of relief as he kissed her good-bye. She remembered the happy crowd standing round the car, waving and calling out good wishes as she and Andrew drove off. She did not really feel it could exactly be called running away, but if Mr. Gower preferred the more romantic story there was no need to disillusion him. He probably pictured Andrew arriving on horseback and snatching her from under her father's nose and them both riding off together on one horse.

Humble suitor, too! Well, if Mr. Gower liked to fancy Andrew as humble, well and good! Humility had never struck her as one of his most outstanding characteristics, but as it was one of the Christian virtues, no doubt he possessed it. "My marriage was rather romantic," she said out loud. And that was true enough, anyway.

"I bet it was, and I think the better of you for it. I dare say it wasn't easy to brave your father's wrath. But why don't you drop that flummery and call yourself Mrs. Hastings?"

"Well, you see, other people would go on calling me Lady Lupin and it would look as if my husband had two wives. That sort of thing doesn't do a clergyman any good, you know."

"No, I suppose not," admitted Mr. Gower. "Well, I'm one of those as speaks as they find and you've been very kind to my Rosie. But, I tell you what, that Miss Dying-Duck of yours, she simply won't do."

"I agree with you there," replied Lupin fervently. "But, of course, she is mad."

"Then she shouldn't be allowed on the roads. If a poor person goes mad, they are shut up in an asylum, but if a rich person goes mad they are just called eccentric and encouraged to drive motorcars about the roads, murdering the children of the poor, and not once has she as much as called at the hospital to inquire."

"I know. I don't believe she even took in what she had done," replied Lupin. "I was sorry for her at the beginning, as I thought she must feel so awful, but not a bit of it ! She has lost a manuscript and she can think about nothing else."

"What sort of manuscript?" asked Mr. Gower.

"The manuscript of a novel," explained Lupin. "But I can't tell you any more about it," she added primly.

"One of them improper ones, eh? Well, that just shows, and it's a good thing you broke away from all that sort of thing when you did. Decadent aristocracy! What do they ever do but write improper novels and get into the divorce courts?"

Lupin thought of her father and mother and felt bound to make a protest. "But they are not all like that," she assured him. "And Miss Dyson-Drake isn't particularly aristocratic, if it comes to that. As for Daddy and Mummy, I'm sure they've never read a rude book in their lives, much less written one."

"That's as it may be, but the world has got to be changed by the time my Rosie grows up. It will be an individual's own merit that counts then, not his grandfathers'."

Lupin felt bewildered. She could only just remember her grandfather, but she imagined dozens of them, hemming her round on every side and counting loudly. She was relieved when Mr. Gower remarked, "Well, thanks very much for the ride, miss, this is my little place," and he waved his hand towards a garage flanked with petrol pumps. "Not that it really is mine—belongs to a capitalist chap who doesn't know a car from a piece of cheese. If only I could get enough together to buy it from him, I could make something of it, but I suppose one of those rud—, I beg your pardon, one of those combines will buy it up and put in their own manager, as likely as not, and then where do I get off? Oh, well, mustn't grumble, and I'm very grateful to you, miss, for bringing me back. I'm shorthanded today, one of my chaps is ill. I can't really afford any time off, but I had to see my Rosie."

"Naturally," said Lupin. Then a sudden idea flashed into her head. "Are you really very short-handed?" she asked, "Because I believe I know someone who might come and lend a hand."

"What sort of chap?" asked Mr. Gower suspiciously.

"Well, he's only an amateur, but he does spend all the time he can with machines. You will be doing him a kindness if you let him come and mess about, do a few simple things, you know."

"I don't want anyone messing about my garage." He paused. "Not but that one good turn deserves another, and I don't know what the missus would have done without you. What does this friend of yours call himself? A mechanic or a laborer?"

"Oh, neither. He is a schoolmaster and his mother makes him write poems about snowdrops, but he wants to be an engineer. To him the inside of a car is what going to the pictures is to other people, if you know what I mean. He would be so happy here, if you didn't mind."

Mr. Gower did not know what she meant at all, but he grunted that any friend of Lupin's would be welcome. She was a nice girl, all right, he told himself, but obviously a bit batty. Whatever was this chap she wanted to palm off on him? Wrote poems about snowdrops! And thought he was at the pictures when he was in a garage! Had he got to pay him a union wage while he was playing about thinking he was at the pictures? He scratched his head gloomily. He supposed it was all right and her husband knew about the boyfriend. She didn't seem the sort that would be up to any games. Straight girl, or he'd eat his hat!

Lupin waved and drove off, and leaving her car in front of the hotel hurried off into the garden in search of Arthur.

"Oh, there you are," cried Miss Dyson-Drake. "I've been looking for you everywhere."

"I'll be back in a minute," replied Lupin, hurrying on to the orchard.

"Lady Lupin," said Grizel Mydleton, appearing from between two trees, "I must speak to you."

"Yes, rather, back in two ticks," responded Lupin, avoiding a deck chair in which sat Mrs. Rennie, gazing soulfully into the distance, as well as the bench on which Mrs. Smythe sat correcting the proofs of the parish magazine. She hurried on to the garage where, sure enough, she found Arthur gazing at the inside of Diana's car with a yearning expression. "Look here," she said, "a friend of mine, a Mr. Gower, is short-handed at his garage, and I wondered if you would like to go and lend him a hand."

Arthur stared at Lupin as Stout Cortez had stared at the Pacific. "I say, are you sure?" he asked.

"Yes, if you are quick. He wasn't too keen on having you, because he naturally thought any friend of mine would be bats, not to mention decadent—whatever that is, I'm never sure. But he is very decent, so I expect it will be all right. Come as you are, you look quite workmanlike."

"If you don't mind," stammered Arthur, pulling down his sleeves as he hurried after Lupin. They were lucky and got to her car unobserved by dint of going the other way round, and were soon at Mr. Gower's garage.

"Here he is," cried Lupin, decanting her passenger.

"I say, it's awfully good of you, are you sure?" stammered Arthur.

"You can clean the plugs on that Vauxhall," said Mr. Gower, shortly. Arthur, his face alight as if he were being vouchsafed a glimpse of paradise, sprang to the Vauxhall, and Lupin, feeling that she had done her good deed for the day, hurried home and sneaked up to Diana's sitting room unseen.

Diana was typing. She finished the sheet she was at, numbered it and tidied up her work. "I hope you have had a quiet afternoon," she remarked, ringing for drinks. "Andrew will be cross if you spend your whole holiday looking for other people's manuscripts and pearls."

"Well, I went to see Rosie and then I drove Mr. Gower back to his garage. We had a nice talk and he quite sees that Daddy is more sinned against than sinning. He thinks I ran away with Andrew, young Lochinvar sort of stuff. I used to think that was a lovely poem—it is one of the few I ever knew by heart. 'He rode all unarmed and he rode all alone.' Can you see Andrew and me riding off together on one horse, staying not for break or stone? Well, what I mean to say is that it's all right and he has taken Arthur into his garage."

"Arthur Smythe! Why?"

"Because I asked him to, and he says one good turn deserves another. He is a perfect lamb, that man. If I weren't married to Andrew I might marry him."

"But did Arthur want to work in his garage?"

"Rather. He went quite red and flustered, as if he had seen the only girl he ever loved. He is simply mad about machinery."

"But I thought he was a schoolmaster."

"He is, but he simply hates it. He hates snowdrops, too—funny, isn't it? I used to think he was in love, the way he mooned about, but it was really a craving for machinery, so now he will, at any rate, get a few happy hours before he has to go back to his schoolmastering."

"He did do something to my car yesterday, now I come to think of it. I was quite surprised when he offered, as I had always thought of him as a poetical sort of young man who would not like to get his hands dirty."

"Diana, promise me something."

"What?"

"If I start trying to plan things for Peter and decide what sort of a man he's going to be, wring my neck."

"Right you are!"

"Have you heard any news of Mrs. Mydleton's pearls?"

"I have heard of little else, of the pearls, I mean, not news. But if any of the visitors had stolen them you would have heard about it by now—you seem to be in everyone's confidence."

Lupin took a sip from her glass. "They say that kind hearts are more than coronets, though I don't quite see how you can compare them. I mean to say, you might as well say that hot baths are more than niblicks. It depends on what you are doing at the moment, but a kind face is a perfect curse at all times. No one can look at me without telling me the whole history of their past life."

"I wish whoever has stolen those pearls of Mrs. Mydleton's would tell you about it."

"Yes, I wish they would in a way, for your sake, I mean. It is not Mrs. Rennie. She would have been frightfully proud of being a thief and blurted it all out at once. I am afraid it is Grizel. I am sorry for Colonel James's sake, but I dare say they will bring it in as justifiable kleptomania."

"I don't see why she should have taken them."

"She could pawn them and get away from her mother with the money."

"I don't think it is money she needs. I think it is more moral courage. I rather fancy that she has her own money and could go away quite easily if she weren't afraid of her mother."

"There is something a bit steely under all that sweetness, isn't there? I rather liked her at first, but I don't much now. I wish Colonel James would hurry up and propose to Grizel and get her away."

Diana smoked in silence for a moment or two, looking out of the window. "Oh, talking of Colonel James," she said casually at length, "he rang up at teatime. He is having to stay in town for the night but hopes to bring that detective friend with him when he comes. The insurance company will probably send down one, too, so they will be company for each other."

"In the meanwhile both Miss Dyson-Drake and Mrs. Mydleton will call in the police, so there will be plenty going on."

"I am glad you're not finding your visit dull. Come in," she added on hearing a knock at the door. Mrs. Smythe came violently into the room.

"Oh, Miss Turner, my brooch, my garnet brooch has gone!"

CHAPTER 12

LUPIN was dawdling over her breakfast the next morning and reading Andrew's letter, when she found Charles Rennie standing before her, his face quite ashy and his eyes hurt and bewildered. He handed her a note appealingly. "She has gone, Lady Lupin, what am I to do?"

Lupin read the note, as that seemed to be what he wanted her to do.

Dear Charles,

It is no good going on now that our love is dead. I need love as the flowers need water and I go to find it.

Good luck,

Ruth

"What am I to do? What am I to do?"

"You must go after her and bring her back."

"But I don't know where she's gone."

"There is that, of course."

"Besides, she doesn't love me any more. I shall set her free," and he drew himself up. "I shan't play the heavy husband. If she prefers someone else, blast him, she shall have him. All I want is her happiness."

"I don't think she loves anyone else. I think she is very fond of you really, but she thought marriage was going to be all one long honeymoon and didn't understand about your having your work. Of course, it is much easier for a clergyman's wife. She can help him in his work, at least. Personally, I rather hinder mine but, at least, one can join in. But with yours there was nothing Ruth could do, so naturally she got a bit bored and sort of felt cut out of things, and if you don't mind my saying so, you are frightfully cross sometimes, aren't you?"

"You think I am a brute, don't you?"

"No, just a bit peevish. I think you and Ruth ought to have gone on the stage. You are both rather fond of acting, and you could have done it together. Lots of husbands and wives do and everyone thinks it's so beautiful."

Charles began to laugh in spite of himself. "You mean that we both pose?"

"Yes, but why shouldn't you, if it gives you any pleasure? You like to seem superior and she likes to seem misunderstood. I expect its great fun. All the same, I think I should go after her pretty quick and stage a grand reconciliation scene. She will enjoy that and when you get her back I'd make a bit more fuss of her. It needn't interfere with your work, but just tell her once or twice a day how pretty she is. After all, women like to be told that, and if their husbands stop doing it they find someone else who will."

"But she knows I think she's pretty. Why on earth should I keep on telling her?"

"Because women are like that. At least, I suppose the sensible ones aren't, but you wouldn't like to be married to a sensible woman, would you? Their teeth are so inclined to stick out."

"What a fool I've been!"

"Yes, haven't you? But it will be all right. She has probably gone to her mother's or to a girlfriend. Don't let's waste time. Get your car out and go after her."

They walked to the garage. "Hell, she's taken the car!"

"Are you sure? I suppose you will have to take mine. Anyway, it shows she's gone alone. I mean, if she'd gone with someone else she'd have gone in his car."

"Where's Ramsden's car?"

"I don't know, he may be having something done to it, or it may have been stolen or—"

"It isn't here."

"I am sure they can't have gone together, if that's what you mean. They would have gone in the same car. It would be very funny to elope in two cars, wouldn't it? Such a waste of petrol, too! Besides, Paul never would. He may make pretty remarks and hold hands, or perhaps give a chaste salute, but he would never seduce someone's wife, and I don't think he would steal a car."

"If I thought that he had I would break every bone in his body."

"Oh, well, I am sure he hasn't and in any case she wouldn't. If you don't mind my saying so, I think at heart she is very respectable."

He laughed shortly. "Her mother is and all her family. She was always scoffing at them. She has a friend, though, with rather advanced views. She may have gone there. I say, do you really mean that I can take your car?"

"Yes, I suppose you'll have to, but just tell me one thing first. I've always wanted to know."

"What is that?"

"When you break every bone in someone's body, do you start from the top downwards, or from the bottom upwards?"

"Do you never take anything seriously?" asked Charles Rennie, backing angrily out of the garage.

"Yes," replied Lupin, "my car!" She walked thoughtfully back to the house. She did not really think that Paul Ramsden would be very likely to elope with anyone, and probably Ruth Rennie had just gone off like that to be dramatic. As a matter of fact, it would very likely be the best thing in the end, because Charles would make more fuss of her in future. But one nasty thought kept jabbing her mind. Colonel James! She did hope here was nothing between him and Ruth, but he had seemed rather keen. Of course, she was prettier than Grizel and she didn't wring her hands. On the other land, she would always be working up scenes and she was the most frightful bore. No, she was sure Colonel James would not do anything caddish. He really was nice and she pushed the idea away from her.

The first person she saw on going into Diana's sitting room was Paul Ramsden, sitting on the edge of Diana's desk.

"Oh, I am glad to see you," she blurted out before she could stop herself.

He looked slightly surprised. "That is very nice of you," he said.

"Well," said Lupin, "your car wasn't in the garage and, er, well, I just wondered what had happened."

"That fellow Smythe has got it at his garage. Wonderful fellow with a car, and he likes it, too. I told him he should never do anything else, and I don't think he will."

"Paul's notecase has gone now," said Diana.

"I shouldn't have mentioned it," said Paul, "knowing how worried Diana is, but I thought under the circumstances we all ought to pool what information we have."

"Quite," said Diana. "How much was there in it, if you don't mind my asking?"

"Well, I shouldn't like to be too positive, but I cashed a check for ten pounds on Saturday and except for a few cigarettes and two and sixpence worth of stamps, I don't think I've spent any of it."

"Probably nine pounds," said Diana, making a note."

"Yes, unless, of course, there was a pound or two there before I cashed the check. I don't care two hoots about the money, as you know, but nearly everyone has had something pinched during the week and it seems to me you'll have to do something about it."

"Yes, I feel that, but what?"

"Well, I suppose it is the sort of job the police are paid to tackle."

"Yes, but do you think Mrs. Mydleton and Mrs. Smythe will dream of staying on here if I have the place filled with policemen, turning out their drawers and asking them embarrassing questions?"

"Why should they ask embarrassing questions?"

"Most questions are embarrassing."

"Of course there is the danger of them not liking it, but will they stay anyway, knowing that there is a thief at large in the place? They will expect to be murdered next."

"I don't know. I am living from hand to mouth at the moment, but I don't want to bring in the police if I can possibly help it. I rather think Mrs. Mydleton will stay here in hopes of finding her pearls. Mrs. Smythe goes next week, anyway. Miss Dyson-Drake is certain her manuscript is on the premises so she will stick on, and the Rennies—"

"I am afraid they have gone," said Lupin.

"Gone?"

"But they will come back. At least, I hope they will, because he's got my car."

"Got your car?"

"Yes, she took theirs, so I had to let him have mine to go after her. That's why I was so glad to see Mr. Ramsden, because Charles was going to break every bone in his body if he found them together."

"Did Rennie honor me with suspecting me of eloping with his wife?"

"Yes, if you like to put it that way. I said ten to one she'd gone to her mother and he had better hurry after her and bring her back, and the sooner they come the better so far as I'm concerned, as I want my car."

"Oh, Lady Lupin, Lady Lupin,' sighed Paul, "what did I tell you? Your role is to sit still looking beautiful, not to meddle in other people's affairs."

"Meddle? I like that!" said Lupin. "All I wanted to do was to sit still, eating my breakfast, but when someone comes up to you while you are taking your last mouthful of roll and marmalade and waves a letter in your face, saying that their wife has run away, what can you do?"

"I am afraid it was a put-up job," said Paul. "I feel dreadfully guilty, Di, because I recommended them to you in the first place. I ought to have found out more about them, but he seemed quite a decent chap, and he has or had quite a decent position at London University. I had only met her once or twice."

"You have been meeting her quite a bit lately," threw in Lupin.

"Yes, well, for one thing I was rather sorry for the little thing. Her husband is such a surly beast and I thought it might help things if I kept her amused. But I suppose all that quarreling was put on and they had the whole thing planned out."

"I wonder," mused Diana.

"I don't think so," said Lupin. "I think they are a couple of silly idiots, but quite decent, and I bet they will be back before long with my car."

"Do you think they have taken the missing things?" Diana asked Paul.

"It looks rather like it," he replied.

CHAPTER 13

RUTH drove along the long white road towards London. She had done it at last—she had escaped from marriage and conventions and the old-fashioned ideas of right and wrong. Was she being pursued? There was a car close behind her. Her heart beat quickly. No, it had passed her. There was nothing to be frightened of. What a fool she had been. She should never have married Charles. He wanted to shut her up in a little house, to be there when he wanted her, to have his meals ready for him, to listen to him when he felt like talking and to be silent when he wished to work. It was Paul Ramsden who had shown her what an unnatural life she was leading. She had been feeling vaguely discontented for some time, but it was he who had pointed out that she was being treated like a canary in a cage. When Charles felt like it he gave her a lump of sugar or a piece of groundsel, and when he felt like it he covered her with a dark cloth.

Paul! How clever he was! Ruth had never met anyone quite like him before. There had been men at the art school where she had studied who had been interesting to talk to and who shared her own unconventional views on life, but their hair had been too long, they were often badly shaved and their fingernails had needed attention. Paul, in spite of being so brilliant an artist, had well-brushed hair and beautifully kept nails. He really was very attractive and she wondered if he were in love with her. He had never actually said so, and yet he was always seeking her out and talking to her. Obviously he found her an intelligent listener. Then he had a flattering way of looking at her when he was talking, as if he were really noticing her. She did hope that he thought her pretty. She went over their various conversations together. He had said she was wasted on Charles. How true that was! But Charles had thought her pretty once. She remembered one special walk beside the river beneath the lime trees last June. Was it only last June? But it was no good thinking about that, sentiment took you nowhere. Her mistake had been in marrying Charles. She should have had an affair with him and worked it out of her system that way.

Ruth remembered the time that one of the art students had suggested a love affair. He had kissed her, and he had smelled of paint and stale tobacco. She had been terrified and run home the next day to her mother. But she was much younger then and easily shocked. Now nothing could shock her any more. She had crossed the boundary line between those who were shocked and those who shocked others. In the future she would live lightly, taking what she wanted as she wanted it. She would write to Paul, a friendly, careless, lighthearted letter which would show him that she would like to see him again and yet that she was not taking things seriously.

She was going back to her friend Anne, with whom she had lived before when she was at art school. It would be great fun living that bohemian life once more. She hoped Paul would come to see her. She would enjoy showing him off to Anne who had so many men friends, but all rather grubby. She had been very proud of Charles when they were first engaged. Well, she must not think about him any more. Suppose Paul wanted her to live with him! Well, why not? Charles, of course, would divorce her and then she and Paul would be able to get married and settle down comfortably together. She pulled herself up sharply—whatever was she thinking about? She did not want to get married again. The whole point was that she wanted to be free, to live with anyone she chose and to leave them when she grew tired of them, but something within her shied away from the idea.

What she really wanted was a profession. All women ought to have professions nowadays and then they could meet men on equal terms instead of being regarded either as playthings or housekeepers. What should she take up? She knew she would never make an artist; six months at art school had taught her that much, and she shuddered to think of what Paul would say if he were ever to come across any of her efforts. What about writing? She had tried to write when she was a girl, before she married. She remembered the novel she was writing when she first met Charles. She had put it away, thinking to herself: "Now I am going to live romance, not write about it." How wrong she had been! The romance was so soon over. She would start another novel. After all, she knew something of life now; she was very different from the ignorant little schoolgirl whose idea of romance had been marriage bells and an old shoe tied on to the car.

She would write something stark and realistic. Suddenly, against her will, a vision of Miss Dyson-Drake flashed into her mind. Would she grow like her? She hoped not. She remembered the day that Lady Lupin had asked Charles if he had incorporated Miss Dyson-Drake's plot into one of his scientific works. How they had all laughed. Would she ever laugh with anyone again as she had laughed with Charles? How attractive he was when he screwed up his eyes and threw back his head and burst into shrieks of laughter. How she loved the little lines round his eyes and mouth. At least, she had once, but that was over now. All the same she would miss his laughter. Now that she came to think of it, Anne and all her friends took life rather seriously and Paul did not seem to find it very amusing, although occasionally he would give a dry little laugh, usually at something Ruth did not understand.

Lady Lupin Hastings was amusing,. She seemed to enjoy life and to find it funny. Of course, she was terribly stupid and had probably always lived a very narrow kind of life. Ruth did not know much about people like Lupin except from what she had read in books, but she was sure that Lupin thought people who did not hunt and play cricket were outside the pale. All the same, she was very friendly. Would she still be if she knew that Ruth had never been on a horse in her life and would be terrified if she were to find herself on one? Still, she had got a brain, she could think things out for herself, and she had the courage of her opinions. Lupin seemed quite contented with her clergyman husband

and her child and home. She probably spent her time carrying soup to the poor and opening bazaars and never even wished for a fuller life. How shocked she would be when she knew what Ruth had done. No, she would not change places with her, although it would be rather fun to be called Lady Ruth, and to wear clothes like Lupin's just for a little while. Not for long, of course, because she did not really approve of that sort of thing—her politics were definitely left, as were those of all thinking people.

Suppose Charles were to fall in love with Lady Lupin! He liked her, Ruth knew. He made her laugh and he loved laughing although he was often so cross. Ruth supposed there could be no doubt that she was very pretty; even Paul had often remarked on it. That had made her rather jealous in a way. It was so dull listening to a man praising another woman's looks. Was Lupin really prettier than she was, or was it just that she was better dressed? Surely she had a much more intelligent expression! And then Lupin was older, she told herself hopefully, she must be at least twenty-four, so her looks would soon start to fade. But Charles left all alone might turn to her for comfort. There was something comforting about Lupin, Ruth had to admit. When you were talking to her you forgot that her father was an earl and even that her husband was a clergyman and that she herself was outstandingly pretty and well-dressed. You just felt you were talking to someone frightfully kind and understanding who was really interested in all you had to say and who would do all she could to help you.

She would have no one but herself to blame if Charles fell in love with Lupin. Suppose he started to talk to her as he had talked to Ruth beneath the lime trees, suppose they laughed together at little secret jokes, and suppose they went back together to the little house near University College. She had forgotten the clergyman husband; he had always been something of a myth, anyway. She blinked back her tears. Never mind, she would have Paul. Paul, who was so clever and so modern. Paul, who saw her as she really was, a woman with great potential for good or evil. She had given way to the evil, but according to Paul that was right. One's duty was to follow one's own star wherever it might lead one and to fulfill one's own destiny. She was meant to be a bad woman, so it would be wrong for her to try to be good.

What would Charles do when he found the car was gone? He would miss the car, even if he didn't miss her. Would he come after her? Would she be caught? She felt rather mean having taken Charles's car.

She wished that she had taken Miss Dyson-Drake's. She hated that woman. It would serve her right to lose her car as well as her manuscript. Why ever was Paul so attached to her? She was old and far from beautiful and Ruth did not really believe she was so frightfully clever. "Paul admires her," she told herself, "because she is always herself. She never bothers about conventions or other people's opinions, but just goes her own way. Well, that is what I am doing now, so he will admire me, even if he doesn't already."

She stopped at a nasty little tea-shop, in a nasty little town, and had a nasty egg and some nasty beans and a cup of tea. Somehow she had not been able to bring herself to go alone into a hotel. She was not used to going into hotels alone. She thought of Lady Lupin. She would go into a hotel and have a drink and order lunch without thinking about it. She and Miss Dyson-Drake were alike in that, different as they were in every other way. Neither would care two hoots what anyone was thinking about them. It would not enter into their heads to wonder about such a thing. Ruth envied them, in spite of what she had done, she had not reached that state of detachment yet. Even now she was wondering what Anne would think about her. Would she admire her for what she had done or not? Dear old Anne. What fun they had had together. How exciting life had been, cooking their own meals on the gas ring in the little kitchen, coming in at all hours and lying in bed till they felt like getting up.

At least, it had been fun for a bit, but it had soon begun to pall on her. Anne was always coming into her room to borrow something, and spilling powder and cigarette ash over everything. She would go off with her lipstick or a pair of stockings and forget to return them. Then the kitchen was so horrid, the sink got stopped up and everything was stick and nasty. Ruth was naturally tidy and her mother had always had things so nice at home. Everything there was clean and cozy, meals were regular and well cooked, friends came when they were asked but did not keep dropping in and sprawling about the place and clamoring for gin. She hated to admit it, but she did not really like cocktails, nor did she like the cheap little restaurants where she and Anne had their luncheons nor the scratch suppers they cooked for themselves. Of course, at home it was very dull and suburban and she had done with all that. All the same, as she drove drowsily along, she could not help thinking rather wistfully of her father and mother and of their nice little house in Magnolia Avenue.

Paul had told her she was meant to live splendidly, and she was determined to do so, but how did one start? It was no use pretending that life with Anne was very splendid. She had always felt herself that she was meant for pearls and fur coats and orchids, for first-class hotels, ocean liners, and first nights. She had been the prettiest girl at the tennis club and at the art school, and boys had always wanted to take her to dances and to the pictures, but none of them had ever given her a pearl necklace.

Ruth remembered walking down the corridor and seeing Mrs. Mydleton's door open. She had peeped in. Even dreary old Mrs. Mydleton and poor, drab Grizel belonged to that life of country houses and ladies' maids after which she hankered in spite of her left-wing views. The room was fresh and tidy and there was a slight scent of eau-de-cologne hanging over it. Everything was in order on the dressing table, the beautifully kept silver and the numerous cut-glass jars and bottles. There was no loose powder or untidy odds and ends, except...what was that? Yes, there, lying in the middle, carelessly thrown down, was the pearl necklace. Ruth was certain they were real pearls, it would never have occurred to Mrs. Mydleton to wear artificial ones, and she had just left them there for anyone to pick up. It would serve the old woman right if someone did take them. Then she had heard footsteps in the corridor and she had hurried away. Had anybody seen her?

She trod on the accelerator and hurried on. Only thirty miles more and she would be with Anne. She wished she could put the clock back. No, that was ridiculous, what she had done, she had done, there were to be no regrets. She would feel better when she had had a drink. She must get over her dislike of spirits—it was ridiculous in a woman of the world. She would like to stop for a cup of tea, but she had better push on if she wanted to reach London before the shops shut. She had not much money with her. She would have to visit a pawnbroker. The idea horrified her, but Anne would know how to do it. It was quite an ordinary occurrence in her set, Ruth believed.

Mother would be getting tea now, and Father would be coming back from the office. How she wished that she were with them. She remembered how thrilled she had been during the first few weeks of her marriage, when she had made the tea herself while she waited to hear Charles's key in the lock. It was no good thinking about that now. She had chosen the wider life, she must get on to London and to Anne and get the visit to the pawnbroker over. She blinked back her tears once more and sent the needle of the speedometer up to forty.

CHAPTER 14

CHARLES drove fast and furiously. What a fool he had been! He had fallen in love with a pretty face and a pretty figure and an enchanting manner. He remembered the first time he had seen Ruth on the tennis court at Clement's Green, in her white shirt and shorts, her lovely legs bare, and a blue ribbon in her curly hair. He had written a poem to her that night. Hardheaded scientist that he was, he had a streak of romance running through him, and that night he allowed it to have full sway as he likened Ruth to a wood nymph playing in the woods of Arcady. Two nights later he met her at a dance, dressed in pale green and he likened her to a water sprite. Then came a picnic, with Ruth in a blue frock and she became the Goddess of Spring. After that they met almost daily and every time he saw her she seemed lovelier than the time before. Yet, with it all, there was something pathetic about her. Her people were dears but they did not understand her. The art school, of which she had hoped great things, had failed her. She had many friends and everyone was very kind, but somehow she had never met anyone with whom she could really be herself. Poor little darling. Charles longed to stroke away the little line between her brows, to kiss the droop from the charming mouth, to take her, away and make her happy as she had never been happy before.

He remembered one evening in June when they had strolled together beneath the lime trees and he had told her that he loved her. He had quoted:

> "How many loved your moments of glad grace,
> And loved your beauty with love false or true;
> But one man loved the pilgrim soul in you,
> And loved the sorrows of your changing face."

And then, wonder of wonders! It had turned out that she loved him, too, and they had become engaged.

It had been an enchanted summer. He had just been appointed a lecturer of natural science at University College and was to take up his post in October. They had found a little house not very far from the college, and what fun they had had choosing furniture and arranging where it was to go. They had had one or two little quarrels over this, but the making up afterwards had been so pleasant that it was well worth it. It had been delightful to give in to her in the end, to see the pleasure in her eyes, to receive her tremulous thanks. "You spoil me, darling," she had said one day as he dried away her tears.

They were married in September on a glorious, golden day. Ruth had looked so ethereal and mysterious as she came up the aisle on her father's arm that it hardly seemed right for her to be marrying a mortal man. Charles was not a religious man, but he had felt religious at that moment and he had vowed to God that he would make her happy. How had he kept his vow? He trod angrily on the accelerator and the car bounded forward while he tried to keep his thoughts under control.

It had been a beautiful autumn and on Sundays they had gone for long walks in the country. They would take the car to East Grinstead and walk for miles in Ashdown Forest with the golden leaves overhead and golden bracken beneath their feet. Ruth would pretend she really was a wood nymph, and she would run away from him down the forest glades and would hide behind trees when he tried to catch her. Then they would arrive home tired and happy, to find themselves alone in the house, for the maid went out on Sunday evening. He would help Ruth cook the supper and wash up, for Ruth would never leave the dirty things till the morning. She insisted on leaving everything neat and tidy before she went to bed, and though he had laughed at her, he had been proud of her dainty ways.

Sometimes he would dash home for luncheon, although it was not easy, just for the sake of seeing her in the middle of the day. But he had gradually given that up for it was one of the few chances of meeting his colleagues and talking thing over with them. And then it was not always easy to get back punctually for his afternoon lecture. Ruth was rather hurt if he appeared in a hurry. She was easily hurt, but she was easily made happy, too, at least, in those early days. She was like a little kitten, wanting to be stroked and caressed, and upset if her hair was rubbed the wrong way. She was happy in her new home, she laughed and she sang and she kept everything as clean as a new pin.

In the evenings when Charles came home from work, Ruth would meet him at the door and throw her arms round his neck and he would pick her up and carry her into the sitting room. Then she would make the tea and toast the crumpets, and afterwards she would sit on his knee and tell him everything she had done while he had been away, and she would ask him what he had been doing, and they would build plans for the future when he had made a great name for himself in the scientific world, and they were rich and famous and traveled all round the world in a luxury liner and went to dinner at Buckingham Palace.

Charles had no particular wish to be rich or famous. He enjoyed his work for its own sake. He liked his house and his friends. He enjoyed the little bridge parties he and Ruth gave and the ones they went to among their neighbors. He suggested that in the summer they should both join the tennis club at Clement's Green again. He could easily get down there after his day's work, during the long evenings. To his surprise, Ruth had burst into tears and said she hated Clement's Green, that the people there were stuffy and suburban and that she would like to belong to Ranelagh.

Charles was nonplussed. Where had she got her ideas from? She had seemed happy enough since her marriage, but now it transpired that all his friends were bores, and their wives frumps; and that she had always hated the people at Clement's Green and even the people at the art school were second-rate and she wanted to meet really nice people. They had had their first really serious quarrel. He had called her a snob, and she had made herself quite ill with crying. Then he had relented. After all, she was his precious little wood nymph and no one was really good enough for her. He wished that he were rich and famous and could give her everything that she ought to have. He took to bringing her home something every evening, flowers or chocolates, or even once a jar of *paté de foie gras*, which he could ill afford.

Then he had started his book and become interested in it to the exclusion of everything else. It was not that he loved her any less, but his mind was so occupied that he forgot to tell her that he loved her and that she was the prettiest girl in the world. He tried talking to her a bit about his book, but she was not very interested, so he stopped. He became so absorbed that he did not notice when she was looking tired or sad. And then she began to get on his nerves by talking about unimportant things, when he wanted to think about his book.

Gradually their quarrels became more and more frequent. They still made them up—still, from time to time, they laughed together as in the old days, but the glamor had gone. He was glad to escape for walks with other men who were interested in natural science. And Ruth would spend Sunday afternoons with Anne and her friends in spite of their being second-rate. Sometimes she talked bitterly of the dreary life she led, of how she longed for a house in the country, to meet congenial people, to wear pearls and…

Pearls? Had she really had a hankering for pearls? A terrible thought flashed into his brain. She had always said that she was a socialist, as he was himself, but she had never been a socialist at heart. She loved looking at the pictures in the *Tatler* and the *Sketch,* pictures of house-parties and cups at race meetings and nonsense of that kind, as he deemed it. But, then, he had known she was silly when he married her. He wouldn't have called it silliness then, he would have called it her sweet, childlike mind, but it was all the same thing and, anyway, as Lady Lupin had said, he would not have cared for a sensible wife. He had known plenty of sensible and intellectual women when he was up at Cambridge, but he had never wanted to marry any of them. He loved his silly, pretty little Ruth, although he had been such a pigheaded fool lately that he had forgotten that he loved her. He had taken her for granted, and now perhaps he had lost her. Had she gone to her mother as Lady Lupin had guessed or had she gone to Anne? Charles did not like Anne. Ruth had been quite right about her being second-rate.

But those pearls! She was such a child, and that bounder, Paul Ramsden, had been putting a whole lot of ridiculous notions into her head, about how she should always have what she wanted, and that it was bad for her to deny herself anything. But if he had not been such a thrice-accursed fool himself, she would never have become mixed up with Paul Ramsden. He had neglected her and he had sneered at her when she talked nonsense, his poor little kitten! It was small wonder that she encouraged anyone who would listen to her and make a fuss of her. And now she had run away and perhaps she had got herself into an awful mess. Would he be in time to get her out of it?

He did not stop for anything to eat, he did not even know he was hungry. He tore savagely ahead, thinking of nothing but of how soon he would find his wife and of whether he would be able to extricate her from the difficulties into which he had driven her by his selfishness. The whole question was where had she gone? To her mother, he hoped. He liked her nice, homely, plump mother who was still very good-looking in a comfortable sort of way. He liked her father, too, and he liked the pleasant, well-run house in Magnolia Avenue. He did not like

Anne nor her untidy, dirty flat, or studio, as she called it, and he did not like her friends. He and Ruth would have a much better chance of reaching an understanding if they met in her mother's house.

The car went well; it was a lovely piece of work and Charles would have thoroughly enjoyed driving it on an ordinary occasion. But now it was merely a means of getting to London and he pushed it along ungratefully. He did just spare a thought to Lady Lupin, she was a decent sort and seemed to understand Ruth. She would be a nice friend for her if he ever got her back again, much better than Anne. She was the sort of person Ruth wanted to know, too. It had been luck meeting her because they would not have been likely to run across her in the ordinary way. He wanted Ruth to have everything she wanted. After all, she had every right to be fastidious, his little wood nymph. He would spend the rest of his life trying to make her happy, if only he got her back again. But he did hope she had not helped herself to what she wanted in her simple, childlike way; other people might not see it in the same light as he did.

He decided to try her mother's house first. He might even confide his fears to her father. He was an understanding sort of person and might prove helpful. Charles turned left as he reached the outskirts of London and drove straight to Clement's Green. The place was full of memories for him. How often he had driven through these quiet roads with their well-kept gardens while his heart beat fast at the thought of seeing Ruth! The trees were covered with powdery-green leaves, the gardens were gay with daffodils, tulips, and wallflowers. Spring was everywhere around him. Would it ever be spring again for him, or was autumn closing in on him? Without Ruth his life would be a perpetual winter.

Magnolia Avenue. What memories it held for him. A car was approaching from the other end of the avenue, an elderly Morris, rather like his own. It was drawing up outside number thirty-six! Could it be? He drew into the side of the road, jumped out of the Vauxhall, and ran. Ruth was getting out of the Morris, her hand was on the gate. "Darling!" cried Charles.

Ruth turned, let go of the gate and ran. "Darling!" she cried. They were in each other's arms. A delivery van, two boys on bicycles, and a couple of middle-aged men returning from the city, passed by. But Charles and Ruth were oblivious to everyone but each other.

"Oh, Charles, I've been so silly!"

"Not so silly as I've been. Promise you'll never leave me again. I'll throw my old book on the fire."

"No, you won't. You know how proud I am of it. I don't know why I've been such an idiot lately."

"You haven't. It's been all my fault."

"No, it wasn't."

"Never mind, we'll spend tonight with your mother and tomorrow we'll go back to Orchard House to finish our holiday and then…"

"Oh, no, Charles I—I couldn't go back to Orchard House, you see, they'll all know by now."

"Darling, you haven't…you didn't… as a sort of joke, of course, I mean, Mrs. Mydleton's pearls?"

Ruth lifted her head from his shoulder and began to laugh. "Oh, darling, you didn't really think I'd taken the pearls, did you? I meant they would all know about my running away; not that that wasn't much worse than taking the pearls. You poor boy, what a state you must have been in. I know what made you think of it—you've stolen Miss Dyson-Drake's manuscript."

Eventually Ruth's father and mother found them, standing in the middle of the road, hugging each other and laughing at the tops of their voices, while an interested group of spectators gathered round.

CHAPTER 15

"BUT why Great-aunt Jemima's brooch?"

"I couldn't say, my lady."

"No, but just imagine for a moment that you were a thief, Staines."

"Well, my lady, I couldn't really imagine such a thing."

"Just have a try. After all, I could never have imagined myself a clergyman's wife, but I am. It just shows what unexpected things do happen."

"I suppose it would have been more natural to have taken the pearl necklace or the diamond ring, my lady."

"That's what I mean. Miss Dyson-Drake's manuscript and Aunt Jemima's brooch don't make sense."

"No, my lady, it seems more like the work of a kleptomaniac."

"Klepto what? Oh, I know what you mean, someone who takes things."

"Yes, because they can't help taking things, my lady, not because they want them."

"Um, there's something in that; no one can have wanted Miss Dyson-Drake's manuscript, nor Mrs. Smythe's garnet brooch; of course, Mrs. Mydleton's pearls were quite nice, but they were nothing to write home about, were they?"

"They were certainly not so good as yours, my lady."

"And Aunt Jemima's brooch. No one could have had a yearning for that, unless they were quite potty, could they? How did you find out that it had gone, by the way?"

"I found the key of your jewel case lying on the writing table."

"Did you? Oh, I must have left it there, I suppose. I meant to give it back to you, but Miss Mydleton came in before breakfast to say she had had toothache all night and must go up to London to see the dentist. Why she has adopted me as her governess or elder sister or something, I can't imagine. She must be years older than I am. However, somehow she inveigled me into being a daughter to Mrs. Mydleton and I had to spend the whole morning walking about the grounds talking about who was related to whom, a thing I never know, and I can't see that it matters, anyway. But I did very well and I rather think that my Uncle George's second wife's first husband's son married Mrs. Mydleton's third cousin's daughter-in-law's aunt, but I couldn't be quite sure. I shall lie down for a bit, my head is in a whirl. I don't think I'll say anything to Miss Turner about the brooch. She has enough to brood on without that, and I don't mind about it, though I shouldn't like to hurt the old lady's feelings. Still, I dare say as she is dead she won't notice." There was a knock at the door. "Say I am dead, Staines," begged Lupin.

Staines went to the door to find Diana on the threshold. "It's all right, Staines," she said. "I am not going to bother Lady Lupin for more than two minutes. Time me, and if I haven't gone by then you can turn me out."

"I was afraid it was Mrs. Mydleton having woken up," said Lupin.

"No, it's only that Colonel James is getting back by the five o'clock train and bringing his friend with him."

"I hope he'll bring Grizel with him. I say, I wonder if she really went up to meet him, and not the dentist at all."

"I wonder. What I wanted to say was, don't say a word to anyone about the friend, not even to Staines."

"Not to Staines?"

"No, not even to Staines," Diane repeated. "I haven't told Paul. I feel rather mean, but he does talk a bit and he might let it out to Miss Dyson-Drake, and if she knows he may as well come in a bowler hat straightaway as you suggested."

"I am afraid I do rather run on a bit sometimes myself, though there is no likelihood of me letting it out to the guests because they never let me get a word in edgeways, but Staines doesn't talk much. However, I'll try to think about something else."

"Right you are. I think I hear her coming to turn me out. Have a nice rest."

Lupin stretched herself comfortably in her bed and prepared to go to sleep. It had been very tiring entertaining Mrs. Mydleton all the morning. She wondered if Grizel really had gone to the dentist. She had seemed very agitated, but then she usually did, and the toothache must be horrid. Could she have gone up to London to pawn her mother's pearls, Mrs. Smythe's garnet brooch, Great-aunt Jemima's ditto, and Miss Dyson-Drake's manuscript. No, surely she couldn't pawn that! Had she taken that to Colonel James? No, Lupin was pretty sure he had nothing to do with it. After all, he had suggested bringing this detective man down, or wasn't he really a detective at all, but in the plot with Colonel James and the Mydletons? Perhaps Mrs. Mydleton had put on all that fuss this morning about Grizel going to London, while really making her go with the manuscript. One could invent a good story about it, but somehow Colonel James did not seem to be the sort of person to be mixed up in anything shady. Lupin remembered his solid-looking Jaeger dressing gown. But he might have persuaded Grizel to marry him secretly, knowing how frightened she was of her mother. Perhaps that was what she had gone to London for, to get married! Bother! Lupin could not sleep. Anyway it was rather stuffy, lying down in the afternoon, and she went out into the garden.

It was very pleasant wandering about alone. It was a thing one so seldom did. People leaped up from behind trees to tell one that their husbands did not love them, or that their lives had been frustrated by their parents. Today, however, everyone seemed to be otherwise occupied. Bother! It was beginning to rain and she had on only a thin jumper and skirt. It had been such a lovely, sunny day when she was eating her luncheon. It was April, of course. What was that poem she had learned at school about April? "April and her something laughter and her something tears." By Browning, she believed. Well, it was no use staying here and getting soaked through while she recited poetry, she would have to run back to the house. But what was that roof between the trees: a cottage? A shed? Something, anyway. She ducked under the overhanging branches and made her way towards it. It was a little summerhouse with a veranda and French windows. She tried the door but it was locked; then she tried the windows. One gave way; she opened it thankfully and escaped from the rain.

Inside it was clean and tidy. There were chairs and a table and in one corner an easel. Lupin wondered if Paul Ramsden used it as a studio. There were books on a shelf, and she looked at them with interest: *The Cock House at Felsgarth, The Speckled Band,* and *Robinson Crusoe.* They did not seem like Paul, somehow. He would read rather advanced things, she would imagine, about philosophy or something, or poems which didn't mean anything, but these books had been favorites of hers and her brother's, and she would rather like to read them again. There was a cupboard in another corner, and in it there were some cups and saucers and a tin of biscuits; evidently someone had been here quite lately as the biscuits were fresh. She helped herself to one. It would make quite a good studio, as on one side there was a clearing with no trees, so that the light would be good, whether it was north or not she couldn't say. She believed artists liked north lights, though she couldn't think why. There would never be any sun, which she would have considered a pity, but then, she wasn't an artist. There were some canvases stacked against the wall and she went up to them eagerly, rather hoping they might turn out to be Paul's. If those were really his books, he must be much more human than he seemed.

No, they weren't Paul's. One look at the first canvas told her that. It was a picture of Orchard House on a winter afternoon. It looked quite different and yet just as lovely as it looked in the spring, although in another and more somber way. The trees were bare, but how beautiful the branches looked against the opal sky. There were lights in several of the windows and also shining through the half-open front door, making a golden pool on the patch of drive, and welcoming all who came. The gracious, mellow, red brick was softened by the rays of the setting sun. It is a beautiful house, thought Lupin. It is almost more beautiful in the winter than in the summer. It looks the sort of house one ought to be happy in. I wonder if it hates being a guest house. How whimsical I am getting. Paul would be horrified if he knew that I suspected him of painting here. He would sneer at that picture. I wonder whose it is. There must be a secret artist about the place. Oh, there's the sun again, good. "Laugh your girlish laughter," is that right, I wonder? I should never have thought of the sun as girlish. Oh, no, it's April who is girlish, of course.

Well, I had better get back before it starts weeping its girlish tears again. But I do wonder who painted that picture. Someone who liked the place awfully, I'd think. She remembered that Grizel had taken up painting at one time, but could poor, ineffectual Grizel, paint a picture like that? Lupin did not know much about painting, but even she realized that there was a certainty and mastery about it that would be hard to associate with Grizel. But, then, she might have two sides, one reads about people like that in books, Dr. Jekyll and Mr. Hyde, for instance. One side of her was an accomplished artist and the other a shrinking woman, who was frightened of her mother. But even then, even if she were an accomplished artist, when could she ever have had time to paint that picture? She was seldom out of her mother's sight for more than five minutes. Or did she get up and do it in the middle of the night? What about the other night when she had come to Lupin's room for the brandy? She had been out then and her mother had been upset. She said she had been strolling in the garden with Arthur Smythe, but perhaps she had really been here snatching a few hectic minutes painting. Was that her secret?

Then another thought struck Lupin. How could she have painted the house as it looked in the winter? She had never been here in the winter. This was her first visit. Whoever had painted that picture had seen what they painted, of that she felt sure. There was something so real about it. Unless...could it be possible that Colonel James had described it to her? He had been here several times. Could the power of love be so strong that she had seen it through his eyes? I had better ask Miss Dyson-Drake, she told herself, this is getting beyond me. Or Ruth Rennie perhaps, she seems to be an authority on love. I wonder if Charles has found her yet? I hope they will soon come back, having made it up and bring my car with them. She picked her way back through the wet grass to be met by Staines, who made remarks about wet stockings to which Lupin submitted grudgingly.

In the middle of the process of changing, Lupin heard a telephone bell ring, and she thought how nice it was to hear it and to know that it could not possibly be the Sunday-school superintendent, the Girl Guide captain or the secretary of the parochial church council.

Staines was called from the room and came back looking upset. Lupin's mind at once darted to Andrew and Peter. "What is it, Staines?" she demanded. "Tell me quickly."

"Please, my lady, there has been an accident and both Miss Turner and Miss Dyson-Drake are in the hospital."

CHAPTER 16

"MISS TURNER? Is she bad?"

"I hope not, my lady."

"Oh, dear, my car. Mr. Rennie has taken it. Ring up Mr. Gower and tell him to send a car for me quickly."

"Very good, my lady."

Nanny was standing in the corridor, white and shaking. "You had better come with me, Nanny," said Lupin. "Miss Diana will want you. Put on your hat and coat. The car will be here in a minute."

One of Mr. Gower's assistants arrived shortly in a car. Lupin was rather disappointed it wasn't Arthur Smythe, but learned that he had gone up to town for the day. They were soon at the hospital and Lupin found herself once again in the familiar entrance hall.

She walked down the corridor thinking hard. She was very fond of Diana. Nanny followed her with a wooden expression, while the smell of disinfectant rose up all around them.

"Hallo, Lupin, hallo, Nanny, I'm glad you've come. That confounded nurse has no more idea of how to arrange a pillow than of how to keep the peace in Europe. Don't both gape at me as though I were a corpse. I've only broken my arm. Thanks, Nanny, that's better. Lupin, my child, do cheer up, you look just like the vicar's wife visiting the repentant sinner's deathbed. Do you want me to say something edifying? I will if you like, but as I keep telling you it is only a broken arm."

"Well, you gave me an awful fright," said Lupin. "And I hate hospitals at the best of times. You must admit things are getting more sinister every day. First of all there was Rosie getting knocked down and all those things being pinched, and Mrs. Rennie running away and Charles going after her in my car, and now Miss Dyson-Drake goes and tips you out of hers—of course, she's at the bottom of the whole thing."

"She didn't tip me out. I was driving," said Diana.

"Are you sure?" asked Lupin, surprised.

"Yes, I am sure I was, but…" Diana frowned.

"I shouldn't bother about that now, Miss Diana," said Nanny primly. "I should just have a nice rest and tomorrow you will be back home again."

"Yes, of course," agreed Lupin. "And do you want me to help Nanny run the hotel for you while you are away?"

"Please. I wish I could be there to see you—"

There was a knock at the door and Colonel James hurried in. He looked very much upset. "Di," he cried.

"It's all right, sir," said Nanny. "Miss Diana has only broken her arm and sustained a slight shock."

"Thank God!"

Lupin got up and walked through the door, which Nanny held open for her. "I had no idea," she remarked.

"No, my lady?"

"Well, we may as well get back home. We don't seem needed here. Oh, ought we to do something about Miss Dyson-Drake?"

"Perhaps we might inquire, my lady."

"Oh, there's Sister." Lupin saw a sister whom she recognized, and who was really quite human, and went up to her. "I say," she said, "do you know anything about a Miss Dyson-Drake?"

"Yes, she is suffering from shock, following an accident, and is in one of the private wards. Do you want to see her?"

"Not a bit, but I know her slightly and thought I ought to ask if there was anything I could do."

"I'll fetch her nurse."

The nurse arrived. "Miss Dyson-Drake is a little overexcited. The doctor does not want her to have any visitors today, I am afraid."

"Thank goodness for that," said Lupin. "Give her my love."

"Excuse me," said the nurse, "but Miss Dyson-Drake seems to be worrying about a manuscript. Could you throw any light on that?"

"It's a manuscript she thinks she's lost. She came into my room to tell me about it three nights ago. I expect you will be hearing a good deal about it. Well, if there is really nothing I can do, I must be getting back. Good evening, nurse."

Lupin and Nanny drove home. Her head was in a whirl. How dense she had been! Naturally Colonel James was in love with Diana. Anyone would prefer her to Grizel Mydleton or to Ruth Rennie. Why had she never thought of it? Somehow she had never thought of Diana as being likely to get married. Not that she was really very old, and in any case Colonel James wasn't young himself; and now she had gone and offered to run the hotel and she had not the vaguest idea how one started to do such a thing. "I say, Nanny," she said, as they drew up at Orchard House, "you will have to tell me what to do about the hotel."

"Yes, my lady," agreed Nanny.

A pleasant-faced young man was standing in the hall. "How do you do?" said Lupin. "Are you staying here? I am the manageress," she added proudly.

"Lady Lupin Hastings?" he asked. "My name's Borden."

"How on earth did you know that? My name, I mean, not yours. But, of course, you are the detec— I mean, you are Colonel James's friend. He is at the hospital—there has been an accident. I say, let's go up to the office. I am sure to say something wrong. Oh, yes," as Mrs. Smythe passed by, "the country is very nice, isn't it? So much to look at. Do you play golf?"

Meanwhile she led the way to Diana's office and rang for sherry. "Well," she said when they were alone, "I expect Colonel James has told you everything. As a matter of fact we know who it is, because she is quite loony and sees things. And now she has smashed up poor Diana."

"Do you mean Miss Dyson-Drake?"

"Yes, how clever of you. Let me think now. First of all, she stole her own manuscript, and then she ran over a little girl, then she took one pearl necklace, two brooches, and a notecase, and now she has broken my friend's arm and is in the hospital suffering from shock."

"I should think that is the best place for her."

"Yes, if they will only keep her there. Oh, here is Colonel James. I was just telling Mr. Borden who it was who has been taking the things. By the way, a lot has happened since you went away. Paul's notecase has gone now, and Mrs. Rennie has run away, but that's all right if you are engaged to Diana, as Charles won't have to break every bone to your body."

"I wish I knew what you were talking about," said Colonel James rather wearily.

"Aren't you engaged to Diana?"

"I hope I am, now you speak of it. I don't believe I ever asked her."

"How like a man. Andrew went on for ages about how old he was, and how he wouldn't dream of asking me to marry him. I nearly got engaged to someone else just to spite him. So you had better look out. I saw a very nice-looking doctor in the corridor at the hospital, and I dare say a clergyman will get in while she's there, they usually do, and they are often very fascinating."

"Thanks very much for your kind advice. I will get things put on a business footing as soon as possible. Now about the other business, did you say you thought you knew who it was?"

"Miss Dyson-Drake, of course."

"Why?

"Well, it must be a lunatic, and she is the only lunatic here. And now she has gone and tipped out Diana from her car."

"But Diana was driving herself. It wasn't Miss Dyson-Drake's fault."

"So she said, I remember now," exclaimed Lupin. "I was taking for granted that Miss Dyson-Drake was driving because she is the world's worst driver and Diana drives very well."

"But it was Miss Dyson-Drake's car," added Colonel James.

"Oh, well, that accounts for it," said Lupin.

"I can't quite see why."

George came in. "Please, my lady, Mr. Smythe wants to see you very special."

"All right, I'll come, George. I wonder what's happened now. His mother has been murdered, I expect."

Arthur was in the library, which was deserted at the moment. He looked rather worried, but for once Lupin did not notice his Adam's-apple. It struck her for the second time what nice eyes he had got. "I say, Lady Lupin," he said, "that car of Miss Dyson-Drake's has been tampered with."

"Tampered with?"

"Yes, someone has been monkeying about with the steering. The nut was quite loose. I had to go up to London on business today, but I went straight to the garage when I got back and Mr. Gower sent me to salvage Miss Dyson-Drakes' car, and I noticed it at once."

"Are you sure?"

"Yes, quite. We had it in to oil and grease two days ago. I did it myself and it was quite all right when we sent it home last night."

'Did you bring it?"

"No, Mr. Gower did."

"Yes, so he did, I met him," she replied. Then she stopped quite still where she stood, as a frightful suspicion came over her. Mr. Gower! She remembered the story at the beginning of A *Tale of Two Cities,* about the man whose child had been run over and who had murdered the aristocrat who did it and was in his turn hung. Lupin's sympathies had always been with the father of the child. "Arthur," she said, "do you think you need say anything for an hour or two?"

"I shouldn't think so. The only thing is that I don't think I ought to do anything to the car till the police have seen it."

"No, I see that. Couldn't you just leave it and get on with something else? I mean, I've Just got a sort of an idea. I won't be long and I will come straight back to the garage."

"You know that I would do anything in the world for you, Lady Lupin."

"Yes, I know you would, Arthur. You are a brick," and she hurried up to the garage. Bother, of course, her car wasn't there. Oh, there was Diana's. Why on earth had she gone out this afternoon in Miss Dyson-Drake's? She might have known she would be bound to have an accident. Still, it was lucky hers was here now. Lupin jumped into it, and within ten minutes was knocking at the door of the Gowers' house.

"Come in, your ladyship, and welcome," said Mrs. Gower.

"Good evening, Mrs. Hastings, come in and have a cup of tea," said Mr. Gower.

"For shame, Bert," said his wife.

"Good evening, Comrade Gower," returned Lupin.

"Lady, lady!" cried Rosie ecstatically, embracing Lupin's knees.

Lupin picked her up. "You are a great lump," she said. "You are heavier than my baby, I do believe. No one would ever guess you had been ill."

"She is fine now, miss, isn't she?" said the proud mother.

"I hope she's all right," said Mr. Gower gloomily. "But a fall on the head is a nasty thing. You never know what it may lead to."

"Oh, do be quiet, Bert."

"She seems to me bright enough," said Lupin. "After all, people often ask if I had a fall when I was a child, but no one can remember it. So it just shows one can grow up silly without one and vice versa, if that is what I mean. What lovely jam!"

"Well, and how is Miss Dying-Duck?" asked Mr. Gower.

"She is no lady," said Mrs. Gower. "Never so much as inquired once."

"I know," said Lupin. "But she is still alive. It was Miss Turner who broke her arm. Miss Dyson-Drake is in the hospital, suffering from shock, but I don't think there is much wrong with her."

"So I heard," said Mr. Gower. "Young Smythe went to salvage the car. A smart young chap, that! I thought he'd be some la-di-da young fellow, but he understands cars as if they were his own mother."

"That's just the trouble, he knows too much. He's found something wrong with Miss Dyson-Drake's car."

"Oh, he has, has he?"

"Yes, I'm afraid so, but he has promised not to do anything for an hour or two."

"Why not?"

"Well—er—it is no use beating about the bush, is it? I mean—er—have you ever read *A Tale of Two Cities?"*

"Have I ever read *A Tale of Two Cities?"* and Mr. Gower stared at her.

"It's a book, Bert," said his wife helpfully.

"You don't say," said Bert sarcastically. "I thought perhaps it was a kipper. No, I haven't read it. By Charles Dickens, isn't it?"

"Oh, he wrote that lovely picture, *Oliver Twist,"* broke in his wife. "How I cried!"

"You'd cry over this, too," said Lupin. "I think *Pickwick Papers* is the best, myself. But then I really like laughing better than crying."

"I must say I like a good cry," said Mrs. Gower.

Lupin felt that was perhaps a good thing, as she would have ample opportunity for it when Mr. Gower was arrested for attempted murder. "There really isn't any time to be wasted," she said aloud.

"I mean I told Arthur I would go back and tell him when he could report about the car."

Mr. Gower laughed good-humoredly. "Well, I like that," he said. "Boss of my garage, are you? Never mind, you can do what you like," and he looked affectionately at Lupin, who was giving Rosie's doll a drink out of her own cup to Rosie's great joy.

"It's only that, in *A Tale of Two Cities,* a man ran over a man's child and the other man went and killed him," she explained lucidly.

"Quite right, too," said Mrs. Gower. "Sit down, Rosie, and let Lady Hastings have some tea."

Mr. Gower looked at Lupin with a puzzled expression for a few minutes, then he burst out laughing. "I've got there," he said. "You thought I might have tampered with Miss Drake's car so as to cause her death, and you were going to give me time to put on a false beard and make my getaway before your young friend blew up."

"I'm sure Lady Lupin never thought anything of the kind," protested Mrs. Gower.

"Never you mind, Betty;" he said, giving her an affectionate smack. "If anything had happened to our Rose I might have done it. Anyway, Lady Lupin is a trump. We'd better go along to the garage and put that young fellow out of his misery."

CHAPTER 17

AFTER dinner, Lupin, Colonel James, and Mr. Borden retired to Diana's office. "You say that Miss Dyson-Drake's manuscript was the first thing to disappear?" asked Mr. Borden, looking at his notes.

"Yes, but, of course, that was just to put us off the scent. Then she took Mrs. Mydleton's pearls, Mrs. Smythe's brooch, Paul Ramsden's notecase, and Aunt Jemima's brooch."

"Who is Aunt Jemima?"

"Well, she's a great-aunt, really. Mummy's aunt you know. She refused twelve men before she was twenty-one and died an old maid at ninety-seven, or was it twenty-one before she was twelve? Anyhow, they always told me the tale as a hideous warning But I don't believe anyone ever asked her. Her teeth were always falling out and she was always in the foulest rage because she couldn't hear what anyone said. I believe she thought they were proposing when they were asking her to pass the salt. She always used to yell at one, 'What's that? What's that? Why can't you speak out?' I was simply petrified of her."

"Was she in the hotel last night?"

"What a ghastly thought! But I don't see why she should haunt this house, it's not as if she'd ever stayed here."

"I thought you said her brooch was stolen?"

"Yes, it was taken out of my jewel case. I had left the key on the writing table and the thief walked in, opened the case, chose Aunt Jemima's brooch and shut it all up again. No one but Miss Dyson-Drake could have done a thing like that. And then there is this accident."

"We can hardly blame Miss Dyson-Drake for that," pointed out Colonel James, "as she wasn't driving."

"But it was her car," said Lupin, "and Arthur Smythe said it had been tampered with."

"She would hardly have tampered with her own car," said Mr. Borden, "if she were going in it herself."

"You don't know Miss Dyson-Drake," said Lupin. "The first night I was here she woke me up to tell me that her child had disappeared and then it turned out to be a manuscript, so you see, she might do anything. But whatever made Diana go in her car?"

"I think Diana was in a hurry to go to the town and found Miss Dyson-Drake just starting, so she asked her to give her a lift," said Colonel James, "to save getting out her own car. But she seems to have persuaded Miss Dyson-Drake to let her drive."

"I don't blame her, not that it was much use if Miss Dyson-Drake had loosened the screws before she started."

"No, I don't think she did that," said Colonel James. "Someone else must have tampered with the car."

Mr. Borden was writing. "You say the manuscript went first and then the pearls?"

"Yes, not the next day, but the day after, I should say. Mrs. Mydleton left them on her dressing table while she had her bath and then when she came back again they had gone."

"What was lost next and when?"

"I should say it was the next evening just before dinner. I was having a drink in here with Diana when Mrs. Smythe came in. And, you know, it does seem funny to think of anyone stealing that. It was just the sort of brooch that a clergyman's wife would wear, but I can't see it on anyone else and as I am the only other clergyman's wife here it could only have been me, and I am sure it wasn't. At least, as sure as I can be of anything."

"Then when did your brooch go?"

"This morning. It's a frightful-looking thing, rather like a pancake with currants in it. That is what makes the whole thing so queer. I left my engagement ring in the cloakroom the whole of one morning and there it was at lunch time, so why didn't they take that?" And she handed it across to the detective. "And my pearls, of course. My maid runs around all the time picking them up and putting them away when I'm not wearing them. I am a bit careless, I'm afraid, and she is always finding them in strange places."

The detective examined Lupin's pearls and her engagement ring through a glass and handed them back to her. "You have been lucky," he said, "and the thief seems to have been lacking in discrimination."

"Oh, I only meant that I couldn't think why they had hit on Aunt Jemima's brooch."

"Then you mentioned a notecase. I don't think James told me about that."

"Yes, that was Mr. Ramsden's. It had nine or ten pounds in it. It's the only sensible thing that's been stolen. Oh, that was before Aunt Jemima. Yes, this morning, quite soon after breakfast, just after the Rennies had run away. What a long day it has been."

"Who are the Rennies?"

"They are a young married couple who are always quarreling, and this morning she ran away, leaving a note on the pincushion, and he went after her in my car, but I don't think they'd have taken anything. Unless, of course, she wanted to draw attention to herself."

"Is she that sort of person?"

"Yes, but she was brought up in a London suburb, so she is really very respectable underneath. I don't think she would really like to be mixed up with stealing. Running away from your husband is different, isn't it?"

"I should imagine there is a certain difference."

"Especially when you have gone to your mother's, which I expect she has. Well, I think that's everything. I must go to bed. I shall need my good eight hours if I am to be in good shape for running this hotel tomorrow. Good night."

CHAPTER 18

"PLEASE, my lady. Shirley has gone."

Lupin had just settled herself in Diana's office the next morning when Nanny brought in this piece of news.

"Gone? Shirley? What a place this is! No one ever stays put for a moment. Let me see, wasn't she the one that Miss Turner gave the notice to?"

"Yes, my lady, she was due to go next Tuesday."

"Oh, is there anyone else coming?"

"I think that there was a young person coming to be interviewed today."

"Well, I'll have to see her, I suppose. Show her in here when she comes, Nanny."

"Very good, my lady."

Lupin looked round the office with a self-satisfied air. Certainly she was running this hotel very well. She had been down to breakfast at eight-thirty and seen that everything was as it should be. She had seen the cook and heard about the meals. Then she had been round the bedrooms and had even made a note that two electric light bulbs were broken and that one chair needed re-seating. Yes, she really would have made a good businesswoman. Now about Shirley Walker! She had gone off without a word a week before she was due to go and without asking for her wages. It looked suspicious, but surely if she had taken the things she would have waited one more week so that suspicion would not have fallen on her. Going off like this was tantamount to hanging up a notice saying : "I, Shirley Walker, have taken one manuscript, one pearl necklace, one garnet brooch, one peridot ditto, and one notecase, and have sabotaged one motorcar.' The manuscript and the motorcar seemed most incomprehensible. From what Lupin had seen of Shirley she doubted if she could even read, much less tamper with a car. Of course, she may have had a grudge against Miss Dyson-Drake and taken her manuscript and loosened a screw, if she knew how to, out of spite, but that didn't account for the other things. Her thoughts were interrupted by a knock. "Oh, come in."

Kate opened the door. "Miss Graham, my lady."

"Ah, yes," said Lupin. "Sit down. Let me see now." As a matter of fact she had not had much experience in engaging servants. When she married, her husband had the house and staff all ready for her, except for Staines, who had come with her from her own home. "Where was it that you were before?" she asked.

"I have come from London."

"Oh, have you, what part?"

"West Kensington, but I feel I need a thorough change."

"Yes, of course, I can quite understand that. Are you—er—pretty strong?"

"No, as a matter of fact, I am very delicate, and I have been very ill this winter. People are surprised at the way I am able to carry on, but it is pure willpower. I will not give in."

"Oh, well, do you like work?"

"Yes, I have always been a worker. I can never sit idle, so long as there is anything I can do to help others, I must be up and doing. I am made like that."

"That's splendid. Now how soon can you come?"

"I haven't settled whether to come at all yet. I must find out more about the place."

"Well, if you do come, what about money?"

"Well, I had thought of four guineas a week, not more."

"No, not more, but I am afraid it will be a good deal less. I mean, four guineas a week would be," and Lupin wrinkled her forehead, "why, it would be more than two hundred pounds a year."

"What would you suggest?"

Lupin searched feverishly among Diana's papers. "Thirty shillings a week," she hazarded. "After all, there are always tips."

"Thirty shillings a week. Do you mean that you would like me to come here for thirty shillings a week?"

"If the references are all right, of course."

"You would want a reference?"

"Well, it's usual, isn't it?"

"I have never been asked for such a thing before."

"I am sure Miss Turner would not take anyone without a reference."

"Aren't you Miss Turner?"

"No." Lupin felt herself on firm ground here; she knew that she was not Miss Turner. "No, I am not Miss Turner."

"Then I should like to see Miss Turner."

"I am afraid that is impossible as she is in hospital."

"Well, will you kindly show me the room?"

"What room?"

"The room that I shall sleep in."

"Well, I suppose you can see it if we arrange anything."

"I shall want it to face south or southwest, not east. I do not wish to be woken up early in the morning and I find an east window very trying."

Lupin had always thought Diana very clever to write books, but now she realized that she had underrated her cleverness. Engaging servants was much more difficult than writing books, she was sure, not that she had ever tried the latter. She really must pull herself together. "Are you an early riser?" she asked.

"No, I am not."

Well, it was a pity because they probably wouldn't get anybody else, but she did not think that it would be good policy to engage somebody without a reference, especially if they weren't an early riser, which she was sure was expected of housemaids and, in any case, she had no idea in which direction Shirley's window faced. "I'd better talk it over with Miss Turner and let you know," she said. "I am sure she will want a reference."

"You needn't trouble. I am sure the hotel wouldn't suit me at all. If the rest of the staff are as impertinent as you are I shouldn't think you get many guests. Anyone would think that I was a servant come to apply for a post."

"Aren't… I mean, I see what you mean. Come in. Oh, Nanny, will you show this lady downstairs?" Oh dear, she said to herself when the door was shut, I don't seem frightfully good at running a hotel after all, but how was I to know?

"Come in. Did you get rid of her, Nanny?"

"Yes, my lady."

"I thought she'd come after Shirley's place and really she wanted to come as a guest."

"So I gathered, my lady."

"Well, now I've lost her and done Miss Turner out of the weekly envelope."

"There is a young person downstairs."

"But how do you know she's a young person? She's probably a prospective guest.

"No, she mentioned that she was after the place. She seems a respectable girl and she has been in private service," said Nanny triumphantly, as if that were the highest target at which to aim.

"Well, if you have given her the onceover, I suppose it is all right, but I hope she has got a reference."

"Of course, it all depends on that, my lady:"

"That's what I thought," said Lupin triumphantly. "But the last one said she had never heard of such a thing."

"But then she was not applying for a post, my lady."

"No more she was, Nanny. I suppose that accounts for it. Well, send this one in."

The girl was a well-behaved young woman of about nineteen, and Lupin felt quite at home with her. After all, she had not been a vicar's wife for three years without getting to feel at home with all manner of people. And although the interview might have varied slightly from the usual interview between employer and employee, it was quite pleasant. They had an interesting talk about Rangers, films, and dogs, and they parted pleasantly on the understanding that Ruby, as the young woman was called, should take up her duties on Friday if the reference should prove satisfactory.

"Are you busy, my dear?" asked Mrs. Mydleton, walking in. "I have just come to have a little chat. How good it is of you to take on Miss Turner's work. You must find it very hard. Poor Miss Turner! I do hope she is as well as can be expected. Such a nice woman! But there does seem to be something very funny about this hotel. Such strange people! Miss Dyson-Drake, I mean, and Mr. and Mrs. Rennie. Of course, Mrs. Smythe is quite a nice woman in her way, but that son of hers is impossible. Think of working in a garage as a common mechanic."

"Some people like machinery," said Lupin. "As a matter of fact, my husband rather likes tinkering about with the car, especially when it is going quite all right. He says he hears a tapping or some such thing, and I always tell him that it is noises in his head and he had better have his ears syringed, or go to a brain specialist, or something. It is just the same with the wireless. I can never listen comfortably to a single concert without his turning the knobs about and getting on to the fat-stock prices, but, after all, life would be very dull if there weren't any men, wouldn't it?"

"I heard from my insurance people this morning, and they are sending a man down to investigate the loss of my pearls."

"Your pearls? Oh, yes, well, I think we shall have to tell the police."

"The police!"

"Yes, you see, one of the chambermaids went off today without any warning, so I think we ought to sort of mention it, if you know what I mean, because, of course, she may have taken all the things with her. On the other hand, one has to be very careful because if one accuses people wrongfully one is liable to get put in prison oneself and I am always so frightened of being put in prison. One has to be so careful when one is a clergyman's wife. It would be too sickening if they thought of making Andrew a bishop and then looked up his record and found his wife had been in prison. Just the very sort of thing that would be likely to put them off! I forget exactly what it was that St. Paul said about a bishop's wife, something about her worth being beyond rubies, I think, and getting up and finding her family meat while it is yet dark. I believe on second thoughts I should not like to be a bishop's wife. I hate getting up early, so perhaps I'd better go to prison. Anyway, I'll see what Colonel James says."

"Colonel James?"

"I mean about the police. He is always so helpful and after all, this is…" She was going to say "nearly his hotel," but stopped herself. Perhaps Mrs. Mydleton did not know yet. It would be a nasty shock for her. "I expect he will know what we ought to do," she added rather lamely.

"I think you are quite right, my dear. I have known him for a long time and look on him as one of the family. You could not do better than consult him."

"No, I couldn't, could I? Come in."

"I beg your pardon, my lady, but when you are disengaged Kate would like to speak to you."

"Thank you, Nanny. That always sounds so ominous, I think, don't you?" Lupin said to Mrs. Mydleton, as Nanny shut the door. "They never want to see one to tell one how happy they are, nor how much they enjoy their work, nor how well they get on with the other servants."

"Well, I mustn't keep you, Lady Lupin. I expect the man from the insurance office will be here some time this afternoon."

"Will he?" said Lupin sadly, as she rang the bell for Kate.

CHAPTER 19

"I AM sorry to say I shall not be able to stay, my lady. I would do anything for Miss Turner and I am never one to mind how hard I work. But how I am to be expected to carry on as usual without any help I don't know. Miss Nunn is old—"

"Who is old?"

"Miss Nunn, 'Nanny' as Miss Turner calls her, and I am sure I always do all I can to save her. But these nannies think they run the whole place and, after all, they are no better than the rest of us and I don't see why I should take my orders from her. Daisy is a good girl but quite untrained and the whole thing falls on me. I really don't feel that I can go on any longer and I had better hand in my notice."

"I know just how you feel," exclaimed Lupin. "As Miss Turner always says, 'The whole thing depends on Kate,' and she does not know what she would do without you. As a matter of fact, I could not answer for what might happen if I were to tell her just now that you were thinking of leaving. She is going on very well, but any agitation would throw her back. You see, she has had a terrible shock, concussion, you know."

"I wouldn't do anything to hurt Miss Turner for anything. She is a good mistress and I have always done my best for her. But I don't see how I am to do two people's work. Hotel work isn't easy. (Lupin agreed with her here.) And it is not what I have been used to. I should never have undertaken it if it had not been for Miss Turner."

"That's just it, Kate. That is what makes this place so nice, I mean, you not being like an ordinary hotel chambermaid. It is just like being at home, that is why people like it here. I have engaged another housemaid and she is coming on Friday if her reference is satisfactory."

"That makes a difference, but how I am to get through the next three days, I don't know. If you had seen my feet last night…"

Lupin was glad she had been spared this treat. She did not care for feet. "I should think you must be nearly dead," she said. "I'll see if I can get you some help until Ruby comes. I can't promise anything but I will do my best. In the meanwhile just think of poor Miss Turner, and how you are helping her to get well just as much as the doctors and nurses."

"Well, my lady, if you put it like that I am sure I shall only be too pleased to do what I can."

Lupin sent for Staines. "Oh, Staines," she said, "do you remember when we all had influenza?"

"Yes, my lady."

"I mean, do you remember how you bathed Peter, and did most of the housework and cooked the dinner one day and took a Sunday-school class?"

"You wish me to lend a hand to the chambermaids, my lady?"

"It would be most frightfully decent of you, Staines. You see, one of them has run away. Whether she has taken those things or not, I don't know, but it makes such a lot of extra work for Kate. Not that she minds, but she suffers with her feet. And she is talking of going and it will be so awkward for Miss Turner if she comes back to find all the staff gone as well as the jewelry."

"I shall be very glad to do what I can, my lady. It comes very hard on Miss Nunn."

"Nanny? Yes, of course, she is an old friend of yours, isn't she? All being well, this Ruby Graham—no, not Graham, she was the one I made the mistake about, but Ruby something—will be here in a day or two. I must just write for her reference. Will you bring me something to drink, Staines? I feel rather exhausted after running the hotel all the morning."

"And you coming here for a rest cure! I don't know what the master will say."

Lupin took a sheet of writing paper and started her letter:

Dear Madam,
I shall be very grateful if you will give me a refference—

That did not look right. She looked round the room for a dictionary and finding a copy of *What Katy Did* on one of the shelves she began to read it. "Oh, come in," she said, hoping it would be Staines with her drink, but unfortunately it was Mrs. Smythe.

"I just came in to see if there was anything I could do to help you, Lady Lupin. I hear you are trying to take Miss Turner's place, which is very good of you. If there is anything I can do—"

"Well, do you happen to know how many f's there are in reference?"

"Only one, my dear. Are you writing for a reference?"

"Yes. I saw a girl this morning. She seemed very nice and so fond of dogs. If the reference is all right she is coming on Friday. One of the other chambermaids gave notice but she has changed her mind and Staines is going to help until Ruby, that is the new girl, turns up. So we seem to be getting on fairly well."

"Was Miss Turner short-handed then?"

"No, but one of them ran away this morning."

"Ran away!"

"Yes. I don't know if she has got all our things, but I shouldn't be surprised, except I can't think what she would do with them. Come in." Staines brought in her drink and Lupin wished she had waited till Mrs. Smythe had left the room, as it was evidently not the sort of thing they went in for at her vicarage. Not that she said anything, but Lupin had always been rather sensitive to the raised eyebrow.

"Well, I mustn't keep you as you are so busy." Was there a dig in this? Lupin was not sure.

"Would you ask Colonel James to be so kind as to come up here?" Lupin said to Staines.

Colonel James, accompanied by his friend Borden, arrived shortly and were interested to hear about Shirley's disappearance.

"It seems unlikely, as you say," agreed Borden. "What would she do with the manuscript, and why should she tamper with Miss Dyson-Drake's car? Still, I am not satisfied that all the crimes have been committed by the same person. She might have taken the notecase and Mrs. Mydleton's pearls if she found them lying about. But then why go away a week early and draw attention to herself, when she was going anyway in a week's time? All the same, I think perhaps after luncheon I had better stroll down to the police station."

"We do seem to be in for it now, don't we?" agreed Lupin. "But I don't think Mrs. Mydleton will like it. By the way, she has got a detective coming down this afternoon from the insurance company. So you will be able to forgather."

"That will be charming."

John, the head waiter, came into the room, looking slightly rugged. "I am sorry, my lady," he said, "but I cannot find Ferguson anywhere."

CHAPTER 20

LUPIN was sitting in Diana's armchair after luncheon, having a few minutes' rest, when George came in with the information, "The man to see you, my lady."

"Good afternoon. I was expecting you."

"Sorry I couldn't get here this morning, miss. But we are very busy Just now."

"Yes, of course, I quite understand. Do sit down. Now shall I tell you all about it? Of course, you have heard about it from Mrs. Mydleton, I expect. But you might like me just to run through it all again. I am taking Miss Turner's place as she is in the hospital, but we shall come to that later."

"I understood it was in one of the bedrooms, ma'am."

"Yes, you see Mrs. Mydleton always sleeps in her pearls, but she had taken them off to go to her bath and left them on her dressing table, thinking that her maid would lock them up, but just as she was doing so, her daughter called her to put on a fresh set of collars and cuffs."

"Was that when the gas went out?"

"Did the gas go out? I hadn't heard that but, of course, all these details are important, aren't they?"

"I was told that the gas fire in one of the bedrooms had gone out and would not go on again."

"Now, I wonder how that works in; it is sure to have some bearing on the case. You will soon find out. I expect it will just be child's play to you."

"I dare say the pipe has got blocked up, miss."

"Could the pearls be inside?"

"Pearls, ma'am?"

"Yes, Mrs. Mydleton's pearls, you know. Perhaps the thief has hidden them there at the back of the gas fire. I read something about that once though, as a matter of fact it was a snake, not pearls, and I don't think it was a gas fire, but the idea was the same. We may find the other things there, too. Because I don't know if you have heard there have been a lot of things taken lately, a manuscript, a notecase, and two brooches as well as Mrs. Mydleton's pearls, not to mention a motorcar being tampered with."

"Oh, dear," said the man, scratching his head, "how dreadful! Perhaps if you will excuse me, ma'am, I had better be getting along to take a look at that gas fire."

"Yes, of course, that will be very exciting. May I come, too?"

"Just as you wish, ma'am," he replied, without any enthusiasm. They left the room together.

"Let me think, now," said Lupin. "Which is Mrs. Mydleton's room? Was it the third door along on the left?" She knocked. There was silence and she knocked again.

"Herein," replied a deep voice.

Lupin was surprised both at the language and the voice. She did not think it could be Mrs. Mydleton's room after all, but she opened the door.

Miss Dyson-Drake, in an orange dressing gown, was sitting in an easy chair. She gazed at Lupin and Lupin gazed back, while the man stood uneasily in the doorway, shifting from one foot to the other.

"Where am I?" demanded Miss Dyson-Drake.

"At Orchard House," replied Lupin.

"So be it, but I was far away in another country and another era."

"I thought you were still in the hospital," said Lupin.

"No, I came away this morning. I could not stand it, I could not be myself. As I said to the doctor, if I die, I die, but whether I live or die I must be myself."

"Absolutely," agreed Lupin. "I'm glad you are all right again, but I am sorry I woke you up."

"I was not asleep."

"As a matter of fact I was looking for Mrs. Mydleton's room. The detective thinks the things are all hidden behind her gas stove."

"What?" And Miss Dyson-Drake leaped to her feet. "What things are you talking of?"

"Your manuscript, and the pearls and. Great-aunt Jemima's brooch."

"Ha ha, so it is Mrs. Mydleton who is the thief. I might have guessed it. No woman could be as silly as she seems to be. It is all put on."

"But why should she steal her own pearls?"

"That was just a blind, it was the manuscript she wanted. She is hand-in-glove with Colonel James. He wants to get hold of it without paying for it."

"Do you think she tampered with the car?"

"What car?"

"Your car."

"My car was perfectly all right. The accident was just due to Miss Turner's bad driving. She would insist on driving. I can't think why. If I had driven there would have been no accident, but there, I bear no grudge. What is a motorcar to me? Give me back my manuscript and I shall ask for nothing more."

"Is this the gas fire, ma'am?"

"No, not this one, another," relied Lupin. Then she added to Miss Dyson-Drake, "I don't really agree with you about Mrs. Mydleton, but we'll go and look behind her gas stove, if you like." After all, it was always wisest to humor lunatics and perhaps afterwards they could slip back into Miss Dyson-Drake's room and look behind hers, or she might have hidden them herself behind Mrs. Mydleton's. Lunatics were often very cunning and, in any case, they had better obey the detective.

Grizel, looking pale and distraught, was in the corridor outside her mother's bedroom door. "What is the matter?" she asked as Lupin, Miss Dyson-Drake in her orange dressing gown, and a rather embarrassed-looking young man approached her mother's door.

"It's quite all right," exclaimed Lupin, rather inadequately. "We just want to look at your mother's—er—gas stove."

"You can't go in," protested Grizel, looking rather like Horatius keeping the bridge, although Lupin did hope he had not looked quite so frightened as he kept the foe at bay.

"Shall I came back later, ma'am?" asked the man.

"No," said Miss Dyson-Drake. "If it were done it were best done quickly."

Lupin felt uncomfortable. She did like everybody to be happy, but she did not see how she was to make Miss Dyson-Drake and Grizel both happy at the same time. Poor Grizel looked so wretched that she herself felt just like one of the Gestapo.

Barker appeared. "Oh, Barker," cried Grizel, "they all want to go into Mummy's room. What are we to do?"

"Mrs. Mydleton is resting, my lady," said Barker reproachfully to Lupin.

"I could easily come back tomorrow morning," said the man.

"Perhaps that would be best," agreed Lupin.

"Nonsense," said Miss Dyson-Drake. "Tomorrow will be too late."

Barker had taken her stand beside Grizel in the manner of Spurious Lartius or Herminius, whichever were the firmer of the two, and Lupin was at a loss as to what to do next. She had found herself in many uncomfortable positions in her time. Once her horse had bolted with her in the High Street on market day, once she had had to address the local branch of the Mothers' Union, and once she had found herself engaged to someone she did not like, quite by mistake. But never had she felt at such a loss as at this moment. She could not very well force her way past Grizel and Barker into Mrs. Mydleton's bedroom. It would be so rude. On the other hand, if the stolen goods were really behind the gas stove, wasn't it her duty as manageress of the hotel to make some effort to recover them? Surely it was for the detective to take the lead. She looked round at him hopefully, but he was cowering behind

Miss Dyson-Drake, muttering something about never being one to upset the ladies. Lupin was disappointed in him; she had hoped better things of a real detective, and she felt he would cut but a sorry figure beside Hercule Poirot, or Lord Peter Wimsey, or Father Brown.

Paul Ramsden joined them. "Hallo, what's going on?" he asked.

"Oh, Mr. Ramsden," cried Grizel. "They want to force their way into mother's room."

"Why," asked Paul, interested.

"I am convinced that my manuscript is there," said Miss Dyson-Drake, "unless, of course, it has been removed."

"Whatever makes you think so?" asked Paul. "From what you were kind enough to read to me I don't think it would appeal to Mrs. Mydleton at all."

"I have my reasons for thinking that she took it," declared Miss Dyson-Drake.

"Of course, we know nothing for certain," said Lupin, hesitatingly.

"Madam is resting," put in Barker.

"There you are, Lavinia. She would not be resting if she were reading your manuscript. It would keep a dormouse awake."

"How do you know she is resting?" demanded Miss Dyson-Drake

George approached the party and handed Lupin a card on a salver. "J. Elphick, Detective Agency," she read.

"I have shown him into Miss Turner's office, my lady," he informed her.

"Oh, dear," exclaimed Lupin. "There is another detective turned up. That makes three, I mean, it would if there were one more," she added lamely, remembering Mr. Borden's identity was a secret. "We had better have a conference. Will you come?" she said to the man who was now trying to sidle along the passage behind George. "Or would you rather stay here?"

"Shall I take him along to Mrs. Smythe's bedroom?" asked George.

Lupin's head reeled. "But she is a clergyman's wife," she said.

"But it is her gas fire that is out of order, my lady."

"I am sure I don't want to put anyone out, ma'am."

"That will be all right," said George. "Mrs. Smythe is downstairs."

"But what do you mean, George, do you really think it was Mrs. Smythe?"

"Yes, my lady. Mrs. Smythe reported this morning that she could not get her gas fire to give out any heat. I thought Miss Nunn had told you that she had rung up the gas company."

CHAPTER 21

LUPIN found herself alone in the office with a young man who had beautifully waved hair and a small mustache. He stood up when she came in and remarked jauntily, "Good afternoon, Miss Turner."

"I am afraid I am not Miss Turner," said Lupin. "I am her friend and I am taking her place while she is in the hospital. She has broken her arm and had a concussion. Are you the detective the insurance company has sent down about Mrs. Mydleton's pearls?" She was anxious to get everything quite clear this time.

"That's right."

"Well, she is resting at the moment, but she will be glad to see you when she wakes up. In the meantime, I had better tell you what happened. She left her pearls in the bedroom and when she came back from her bath they were gone."

"Or so she says."

Lupin was seldom annoyed, and she had never cared much for Mrs. Mydleton, so why she felt so angry at this reply she could not imagine. "Quite," she replied, unconsciously reproducing Diana's most freezing voice and manner.

The young man took out his cigarette case and offered it to Lupin. She refused a cigarette and watched him light his own resentfully. "I should like a list of everyone in this joint," he said.

"I am afraid I don't follow you," replied Lupin.

"The names of everyone in this hotel, guests, help and so on."

"Certainly," replied Lupin. She went to the writing table, miraculously found the list she wanted, and handed it to him in silence.

"Who is Lady Lupin Hastings?" asked the detective.

"I am," replied Lupin.

"How did you come to get mixed up in all this?"

"I don't quite understand what you mean by being mixed up. I am staying here for a holiday. My friend Miss Turner runs the hotel. She has had an accident, so I am naturally trying to take her place."

"Um, not quite your cup of tea, I should have thought."

Lupin made no reply. He scanned the list. "Can you tell me anything about the staff?" he asked.

"Yes. Miss Nunn, the head housemaid, has been with Miss Turner for forty years, the second housemaid has been here for two years and has very food references, the third housemaid, Shirley Walker, ran away this morning."

"Ran away?"

"Yes, no one seems to have seen her go, but she has taken all her things."

"Well, that sounds pretty clear, doesn't it?"

"I don't know. One of the waiters has gone, too. I have reported the matter to the police. I dare say you would like to have a talk with them."

"I suppose I'll have to, not that they are likely to be of much use. I haven't much of an opinion of the force."

"The police sergeant is here and would like to speak to you, my lady," said Nanny.

"Talk of angels!" said the detective sarcastically.

"Please ask the sergeant to come up, Nanny. Good afternoon, sergeant," said Lupin, pleased to see the familiar face of the policeman who had called after Miss Dyson-Drake's accident with Rosie. "This is Mr. Elphick, the detective from the insurance company. I was telling him that two of the servants have disappeared and that I had let you know."

"Seems a pretty obvious case, doesn't it?" remarked Mr. Elphick..

"Well," said the sergeant guardedly, "I should not like to say that. It may just be a coincidence."

Mr. Elphick gave a contemptuous laugh and the sergeant appeared to be having difficulty in refraining from kicking him, with which difficulty Lupin had great sympathy. "I may as well leave you to have your talk," she remarked, "unless there is anything you want to ask me before I go."

The sergeant gave her an imploring glance but could not think of any reason for detaining her. He opened the door for her and she returned his smile with one of perfect understanding.

"There is something a bit fishy about her, if you ask me," said Mr. Elphick, sitting down negligently on the arm of a chair.

The sergeant looked at him with a look of intense dislike. "We are quite satisfied with regard to Lady Lupin Hastings," he replied stiffly. "As regards the pearls, we only had the matter reported to us this morning, as Miss Turner was naturally anxious to keep the affair as quiet as possible. But when two of the servants disappeared Lady Lupin very rightly felt it her duty to inform us."

"And what are you doing about it?"

The sergeant used rigid self-control. "We are trying to trace Shirley Walker and James Ferguson," he said.

"Oh, you are, are you? I wonder how long that will take! Anyway, there doesn't seem much for me to do until they are found. I think I'll go and see if I can get a cup of tea. Phony sort of place, this, I should say."

Lupin walked downstairs, feeling more annoyed than she had done since someone had gone off with her games shoes just before a match. She walked across the hall and met Mr. Borden coming back from a walk. "Oh, hallo," she said. "Another detective has just turned up, the most frightful bit of work you ever saw. I can't congratulate you on your colleagues. At least, the first one wasn't so bad, just a bit nervous. Besides, now I come to think of it, he wasn't a detective but had come to mend the gas."

"Then you can hardly blame me for him," pointed out Mr. Borden.

"No, I don't, but this last one has been sent down by the insurance company and has a permanent wave. I have left him with the police sergeant and I think he is going to be sick—the sergeant, I mean."

"Well, I don't think I'll join their party, I'm rather easily sick myself. May I stroll round with you for a little, if you are not busy?"

"Yes, do. I am busy, at least, I suppose I ought to be, but I really must relax for a few minutes. I am afraid I am not really most frightfully good at running a hotel. I mistook a guest for a chambermaid this morning and asked her for references and, of course, she went off offended. Then I took the gas man for a detective and nearly threw an inkpot at the real one. And, of course, I have mislaid Shirley Walker and Ferguson. I don't suppose they would have run away if Diana had been here."

"It will do you good to have a breath of air. What a lovely place this is. It makes me wish I were an artist."

Lupin stood stockstill. "That reminds me," she said. "Something rather funny. There is someone here who paints as well as Mr. Ramsden. Either one of the guests paints and keeps it quiet or else someone from outside comes here and paints, someone not on our list and, of course, they might be the one. I meant to tell Diana about it, but just after I'd found out she went and had the accident and since then, what with running the hotel and everything, I had forgotten all about it. But there is a summerhouse all fitted up like a studio. I took shelter there yesterday afternoon—was it really only yesterday? It seems years ago. But it was yesterday because I came in and the telephone rang while I was changing my stockings and I went to the hospital and Colonel James came in and got engaged to Diana, so of course I didn't like to say anything. When I came back you were in the hall, but I am sure it had been used quite lately because there were some biscuits and they were as fresh as anything. I ate one, as a matter of fact."

"How do you know that it is not Mr. Ramsden who used it as a studio?"

"Because they weren't a bit like his pictures. There was one of this place. It must have been painted in the winter, unless it was from memory. I don't want to say anything against Mr. Ramsden's pictures because I don't know anything about art and I'm sure his are awfully clever. But this was the sort of picture that I should like to have hanging in front of me."

"Might we go and have a look?" suggested Mr. Borden.

"Yes, let's, agreed Lupin, and she led him to the summerhouse. "The door was locked the last time I was here, but I got through one of the windows. I suppose in a sort of way I was trespassing, but Diana wouldn't have minded and it was raining when I got here. I am afraid I poked round a bit, but I was rather thrilled about it at the time. It was funny I forgot all about it, but there was Diana's accident, of course, and— Oh, it's open! I didn't open it, I came out of the window I went in by. At least, yes, I am sure I did. The artist must have been in here since." She walked in through the door, followed by Mr. Borden, and the afternoon sunshine fell on the easel, which was standing in the middle of the room with a picture on it. The picture wasn't finished, in fact, it was only just begun, but there was no mistaking the orchard. It had evidently been painted in the early morning. Someone must have been up very early to catch the dew on the daffodils, on the long grass and on the petals of the apple blossom. "I should like to see it like that," Lupin exclaimed. "It is always lovely, but it must be magic in the morning."

"Whoever painted that," said Borden, "had magic in his brush."

"Yes," said Lupin, "and he loved the orchard. It is the same with the other picture I was telling you about. It was by someone who loved Orchard House," and she led him to the stack of canvases in the corner and turned them over feverishly until she found the one she wanted. They had been shifted since yesterday. There it was—there stood the house in the winter twilight, with its warm welcome flowing from the lighted windows and open hall door.

Borden looked at the picture thoughtfully. "You are right," he said. "It is by someone who loves this place."

"That's why I don't think it's Grizel Mydleton," said Lupin.

"Grizel Mydleton? Does she paint?"

"Yes, at least she did. She said she'd given it up but I wondered if she's been going on secretly, like a secret drinker, you know. But I don't see how she could have painted either of those pictures, because she hardly knows the place. She certainly couldn't have painted the winter one, and I don't think she could have done this one, either. I had a sort of mad idea that she had heard Colonel James talk about the place and had seen it through his eyes. That was when I thought she was in love with him, but, of course, now he's engaged to Diana it's different. Oh, dear, I do hope Grizel isn't in love with him because it will come as a dreadful shock to her and she's had one disappointment already. But, anyhow, that idea of the pictures was quite mad. It comes of associating with such strange people and listening to all their talk about love and life, etcetera. All the same, Grizel has got something on her mind, I'm sure. She is always on the verge of confiding it to me."

"Well, I hope she will. It may help us."

"I hope she won't, and if she does it will probably be a secret, so I won't be able to tell you."

"There is that side of it, of course. But as regards these pictures, it ought not to be difficult to discover the artist."

"Diana will know, I suppose. I wonder if it's her, all the time. No, it can't be, because she couldn't have been here this morning. I suppose she lends it to someone. Look, here is a gas ring and a kettle, and here's a cupboard with cups and saucers and everything, and here's the tin of biscuits. They've filled that up since I was here yesterday. It was only half-full then."

The detective took the lid off the teapot and turned it upside down on a little table below the cupboard.

"Good gracious!" exclaimed Lupin as a string of pearls dropped out. For once she was too surprised to speak and stood rooted to the spot. She hoped the unknown artist wasn't the thief. She liked his pictures so much, and there was something so human in his taste in literature. Mr. Borden took a plate and deftly emptied the biscuits on it.

"Great-aunt Jemima's brooch. Aren't detectives wonderful? I do hope that you will find Miss Dyson-Drake's manuscript, if there is one to find, that is. She will never be happy till she gets it."

Borden put the biscuits carefully back into the tin, using a couple of teaspoons for the purpose. Lupin watched him, fascinated. "I should never have thought of that," she said. "I should have put them back with my fingers and covered them with fingerprints, not to mention germs." He moved to the bookshelf and she followed him. "I love *The Cock House at Felsgarth,"* she said, "and *The Speckled Band.* I wonder if, whoever it is, will lend them to me. I haven't read them for ages." Behind the books was a thick packet of paper. "The manuscript," cried Lupin.

"Would you recognize it?" asked the detective.

"I'm not quite sure," replied Lupin.

"Don't touch it," begged Borden. "I'll hold it by the corners."

"Well, don't ask me to read it aloud. Yes, I think it must be the one. I know the heroine was called Rainbow; it struck me as such a funny name at the time. Oh, dear, do take it away. I feel quite hot about the ears. Let us look for Mrs. Smythe's garnet brooch. It is just like 'Hunt the Thimble,' isn't it?"

"And there is a notecase, isn't there?"

"Yes, that seemed the only sensible part of the whole thing. I mean, someone might easily steal a notecase, if they were short of money, I mean, but not a garnet brooch nor a manuscript. Oh, dear," she said after some time had elapsed, "I suppose I ought to be going back to the hotel. What a nuisance! I am enjoying every moment of this game. But something is sure to be happening while I am away. Someone will have stolen Kate's false teeth or tried to murder the cook. That is the sort of thing that would happen to me just before dinner, and I am supposed to wander through the dining room to see that everything is all right. Not that I should notice if it weren't. Anyway, if Staines is helping at dinner she will want to dress me first, not that I couldn't dress myself perfectly well, but she would never believe that." And she hurried off through the grounds, leaving Mr. Borden to his game of "Hunt the Thimble."

The real detective, as Lupin called him in her own mind, was sitting in the hall drinking his tea. "Cheerio," he called to Lupin, not making any effort to get out of his chair.

"Have you seen Mrs. Mydleton?" she asked.

"Not yet. The old bird seems a bit coy. I suppose I had better see her before I go. The whole thing is quite simple—the chambermaid nabbed the things. She and the waiter fellow are in it together, of course. It is just a case of waiting for the police to lay hands on them, and we shall have to wait some time if they are all like that fellow who came up this afternoon. Not much speed there, I should say! Lucky we are not all like that! It doesn't take me long to get to the bottom of things. Considering I only arrived here this afternoon, it's not too bad, is it? Well, I'll see the old lady and then get a move on. I've no wish to spend the night in a country pub. Not quite my line of country, thank you!"

"I'll go and see if Mrs. Mydleton is feeling well enough to come down," said Lupin.

"Tell her to buck her stumps," said the detective.

Lupin ran Mrs. Mydleton to earth in the drawing room. She was looking rather faint, but luckily Colonel James was with her.

"I am so sorry we made such a noise outside your room this afternoon," explained Lupin. "But I thought the gas man was the detective and that you would want to see him. The real one has come now and would be awfully grateful if you would come along to the office. I will send up some tea to you—you must need it."

"I don't think I feel equal to seeing anyone today," said Mrs. Mydleton. "Perhaps tomorrow."

"I think you had better see him now he is here," urged Colonel James. "Then it will be over and done with. If Lady Lupin will send us up some tea, as she suggested, it would make things easier."

"No, I'll have my tea afterward. Please don't think me old-fashioned or snobbish, but I never have had tea with a detective and I am sure he wouldn't feel comfortable, either. Perhaps that nice Mr. Borden will come and have tea with us when it is all over."

"I don't blame you, he really is rather a terrible young man and anyhow, he has had one tea, so it would hardly be fair on Diana to give him another. I don't think, though, that he would feel at all uncomfortable about anything, unless, of course, someone were to kick him," said Lupin wistfully.

"Where is Grizel? One would have thought she would have wished to be with me at a time like this."

"I will go and find her," volunteered Lupin.

Colonel James and Mrs. Mydleton moved slowly down the drawing room. Mrs. Smythe stood up as they passed. She evidently thought they were the chief mourners and that she had somehow, by a stroke of misfortune, missed the coffin. She pressed Mrs. Mydleton's hand and said in meaning tones, "I shall be thinking of you."

Lupin hurried upstairs to find Grizel and ran her to earth in her bedroom, where she stood in the middle of the room with a haunted look on her face.

"Oh, I say," began Lupin, "your mother has just gone to have a word with the detective and she would like you to join her. By the way, I am sorry I made that mistake about the gas man this afternoon, thinking he was a detective, I mean. I hope it didn't upset you."

"Detective? No, no, I couldn't possibly see a detective."

"Oh, couldn't you?"

"No. Oh, dear, what am I to do? Oh, Lady Lupin, do help me."

"Of course I will, my dear old thing. Did you? I mean, if by any chance you accidentally did take some of those things, I should get it off your chest. I am used to people telling me things and, after all, two heads are better than one."

Grizel began to laugh a little hysterically. "No, it's not that," she said, "though I'm not surprised at your thinking it is. It is worse, in a way. I should like to tell you, but I daren't tell anyone, and the detective would get it out of me at once."

"I rather doubt his getting anything out of anybody. He is a terrible young man, and makes one long to tell him just the opposite, quite different from the police sergeant, who is charming. Still, if you like to tell me any time, do. As I say, I'm used to hearing things. Look here, if you really don't want to see the detective—and I don't blame you, because he is rather like a bad dream—I should slip out into the garden. You are sure to be found here."

Grizel hurried off and Lupin followed more slowly. "I wonder if she did take the things," she said to herself. "Of course, she might easily be a secret artist. Temperamental and all that! She has got something on her mind. Still, I am rather glad she didn't tell me. I don't really like hearing things."

She was feeling very tired by this time and was glad to find Staines and fall in with her idea of having tea in her own room. She smoked a cigarette and read a chapter of a novel, then pulling herself together, went downstairs. Mrs. Mydleton was having tea with Colonel James and Mr. Borden and seemed quite cheerful. "Oh, there you are, my dear. You are quite right, he was a terrible young man, but very clever. I suppose one can't have everything. He says that the chambermaid, Shirley somebody, has taken my pearls and run away with one of the waiters. The police are on their track and he thinks it is only a question of days before I get back my pearls. I shall be so glad."

"Oh, hurray," said Lupin, "that is splendid. I am sorry I couldn't find Grizel. I think she must have gone for a walk."

"Very likely, dear child, it will do her good, but I hope she won't miss her tea. Girls are so silly, aren't they?"

"I'll go and have a look for her," said Colonel James.

Mrs. Mydleton looked complacent. "Thank you so much," she said.

Miss Dyson-Drake and Paul Ramsden came into the room. "Well," said Miss Dyson-Drake, "is there any news?"

"Yes, the detective thinks he knows who has got Mrs. Mydleton's pearls," said Lupin. That was true enough. Why Mr. Borden couldn't distribute the missing articles and make everyone happy, she could not imagine, but he evidently had some reason for lying low and it wasn't her place to blurt out everything.

"But what about my manuscript?" asked Miss Dyson-Drake.

"Oh, your manuscript!" said Mrs. Mydleton. "Perhaps the chambermaid has that, too," she replied kindly. She was feeling well-disposed to everyone at that moment, even to Miss Dyson-Drake.

"No, said Miss Dyson-Drake. "What could an ignorant chambermaid know of the value of my work? If she has it, it means she is in the employment of someone else. There is a plot on foot, a well-planned, well-organized plot, and unless I am much mistaken there are many people involved."

"Well, let's hope you are mistaken," said Lupin. "Someone said once that he who never makes a mistake never makes anything and, after all, you have made a manuscript so you might make a mistake, too."

Miss Dyson-Drake looked at her keenly. "I wonder," she said.

CHAPTER 22

LUPIN was awakened by a loud banging on the door. Following Staines's advice, she had slept with her door locked since the first night, and as she had locked the door to prevent anyone coming in, it would be foolish of her to get up and open it. It was probably Miss Dyson-Drake with some new theory about her manuscript or it could be Charles Rennie come back to tell her that Ruth really had eloped with someone or Ruth herself to say that Charles had committed suicide. As these thoughts ran through her head she got up and opened the door, to find the young maid, Daisy, standing there white-faced and trembling.

"Please, my lady, the house is on fire," she said

"On fire!" exclaimed Lupin. "The house? Do you mean the house is on fire?" She looked round her room and wished that it was furnished in the old-fashioned way with a washstand and ewer, but as it wasn't, she took her bottle of drinking water in one hand and her eiderdown in the other and asked, "Whereabouts is it?"

"In Miss Turner's office," replied Daisy.

"Go and ring up the fire brigade. Just say 'fire brigade,' no number," and Lupin dashed down the corridor, banging on everyone's door as she passed and shouting "Fire!" On arriving at the office she was greeted with clouds of smoke and some nasty-looking flames. She recognized Nanny among the fumes, trying single-handedly to smother the flames with a blanket. She joined her with her eiderdown and her bottle of water. It was difficult to see in the smoke what was alight and what wasn't, but after she had been flapping with her eiderdown for some time she realized that at present it was only Diana's armchair that was on fire, although it would probably be the whole house fairly soon. There were some curtains, for instance, unpleasantly near. She renewed her efforts with her eiderdown, but there was not much of it left and as fast as she extinguished one flame, another broke out. "If we had some sand," she remarked chattily, "it would come in handy."

Nanny did not reply; she went on grimly smothering what she could with the remains of her blanket. Staines suddenly appeared with a bucket of water which she poured on to the flames. This had a good effect on them, although the smoke became rather worse.

George then arrived bearing a stirrup-pump, followed by Colonel James, Mr. Borden, and Arthur Smythe. "Thank goodness, here are some men," said Lupin. "Oh, I say, Diana's manuscript." And she dashed to the desk and started seizing all the papers she could find and taking them out on to the landing, tripping over the stirrup-pump as she did so.

"Did you say you had found my manuscript?" asked Miss Dyson-Drake. "So it was Miss Turner who took it, was it?"

"No, not yours. Diana's," explained Lupin, rummaging feverishly.

"And then she or her accomplice had the idea of setting a light to it, so that the world should never behold it!"

"Well, why am I salvaging it?" asked Lupin. "And, in any case, it isn't yours. You can look if you like."

Miss Dyson-Drake knelt down in the passage and began to turn over the sheets eagerly, hoping to find her lost masterpiece.

John, who did not live in the house, had seen the fire through the office window and had arrived by this time with a bucket of sand.

"Hallo, Lavinia, saying your prayers? How nice," said Paul Ramsden, strolling up rather late upon the scene.

"She thinks that Diana has stolen her manuscript and then set fire to the house, and I am sure she is getting it all mixed up and wet, too. Do persuade her that none of it is hers."

"I really don't think my respected cousin stole your manuscript, Lavinia. She has always been a good girl. Besides, you will get rheumatism kneeling in all that water. I came to see the fire, but I must say I am rather disappointed. It is really more like a flood than a fire. Sand, too, to build sand castles. How nice."

"Well, I think that's all right now," remarked Colonel James, ignoring Paul and surveying what had once been rather a nice armchair and was now a mound of ashes and sand with a few shreds of blanket and some feathers sticking out of it, standing in a pool of water.

"Oh, don't say you have put it out," said Lupin, "because I have sent for the fire brigade."

"There is something very powerful about fire," said Miss Dyson-Drake. "The sight of a house in flames is a stirring spectacle and I think it might have stimulated me. I am really rather sorry that it has been arrested."

"I'm not," said Lupin. "Though I don't quite know what I'll say to the fire brigade."

Mrs. Smythe came in. "I have only just heard," she said, obviously rather disappointed at being unable to show her calmness in danger and her powers of organization. "Are you all right, Arthur? Be careful not to step in that puddle. You know how easily you catch cold."

Arthur ignored these remarks and started examining the electric fittings for a possible short circuit. Before anyone could say anything else there was a violent ringing of bells outside as three fire engines arrived in front of the house, then came the tramping of many feet and the shouting of many voices as the whole fire brigade trooped up the stairs.

Lupin hurried out to meet them and was faced with what looked like the Charge of the Light Brigade.

"Where is the fire, madam?" asked the superintendent.

"I'm awfully sorry," said Lupin, apologetically. "I am afraid we have put it out. I was rather afraid it might catch the curtains and spread all over the house, if you know what I mean, so it seemed best to stop it. I do hope you don't mind."

The superintendent smiled and said, "Quite right, but we may as well look and see that everything is shipshape."

"Yes, please do, because it may quite easily break out somewhere else, just when we have got to bed again."

Oh, dear, she suddenly thought to herself, as she conducted the superintendent to the office, I do hope Mrs. Mydleton hasn't been disturbed, and when she had delivered the superintendent to Colonel James she went off post-haste to Mrs. Mydleton's room, to be greeted by a trembling apparition in the doorway.

Mrs. Mydleton, in a becoming dove-gray dressing gown, stood groping at the wall. "What has happened?" she asked in faint accents. "I heard a noise."

"Everything is absolutely all right," said Lupin. "Nothing has happened at all. That was only just the fire brigade coming to put it out."

"Fire brigade! Put it out! Put what out?"

"The fire," explained Lupin, wondering what else a fire brigade would put out. You would hardly send for it to put out the cat.

Mrs. Mydleton tottered and Lupin, taking her arm, led her back into her room.

"It's really quite all right. As a matter of fact, the men had put it out with the stirrup-pump before they arrived, but they are giving it the onceover." Lupin suddenly caught sight of herself in Mrs. Mydleton's mirror and realized that her face was quite black and her eyes red from the smoke. She was enough to frighten Mrs. Mydleton, apart from anything else. She rubbed her face with her handkerchief. "You never know, of course, when it may break out again, but everything is splendid. Oh, good, there's Barker. I say, Barker, there has been a bit of a fire, but it is quite all right now, only naturally Mrs. Mydleton is a bit upset, with all that ringing of bells and stamping of feet, and everyone shouting out 'save the women and children first,' and that sort of thing. Not to mention my face."

"I hope you are not hurt, my lady."

"No, only dirty. I must wash."

"Where is Grizel? Fetch her at once. Why did she not come before?"

"Perhaps she didn't wake up," hazarded Lupin.

"No one could have slept through that noise, not even a young girl. She must be burned. She would not have stayed away if she were safe."

Lupin went to Grizel's room and banged on the door. There was no answer. She shouted "Grizel," with no result. She opened the door; the room was empty and the bed had not been slept in.

"Oh, dear, she has run away now!" But why, had she hidden the things in the summerhouse? Perhaps she had just put them there temporarily, meaning to collect them before she went. Well, now she would not be able to collect them. Mr. Borden had got them. Lupin wondered if he had found Mrs. Smythe's brooch and Paul Ramsden's notecase. She walked thoughtfully back, wondering how she would break the bad news to Mrs. Mydleton.

She was thankful to meet Staines in the doorway, bearing a tray on which was a decanter of whisky, a siphon of soda water, and some glasses. "Good," exclaimed Lupin. "A drink will do us all good." At this moment Mrs. Smythe walked in.

"Well, I don't think there is any further need for alarm," she announced. "The fire was extinguished before the brigade arrived owing to Arthur's prompt action, and Colonel James's, too, of course. No, thank you, I never touch spirits."

"What about a glass of port?" suggested Lupin.

"Well, perhaps this once. I hardly ever touch anything of the kind, but port is really a medicine, isn't it? And this is rather a special occasion. My father was very fond of a good glass of port after a heavy Sunday's preaching."

Lupin guessed where some port might be found and she was quite right, as Staines was entertaining Nanny and Barker in her own room. Another glass was soon found for Mrs. Smythe, which Lupin bore back in triumph, feeling it a great concession on the latter's part to join in a drinking party at midnight.

All was going quite merrily. Mrs. Mydleton had for the moment forgotten her lost daughter as she sipped her whisky and soda and told them what her feelings had been on being rudely awakened by the arrival of the fire brigade.

Mrs. Smythe sipped her port and when she could get in a word told of fires she had put out and of panics she had averted by her good example. "At the sale of work the Christmas before last, the paper chains caught alight and the whole parish room would have been in flames in a minute or two if they had not been put out. Several of the stallholders began to scream and a whole lot of people rushed to the door and nearly got trampled underfoot. 'Stand still, everyone,' I said, 'let no one move.' "

The door opened. "Look," hissed Miss Dyson-Drake. Lupin jumped up and followed the pointing finger with her eyes. There was Grizel, coming out of Arthur Smythe's bedroom.

Mrs. Mydleton and Mrs. Smythe had risen and were standing in the doorway as if frozen to the spot. "Grizel, my darling girl, you are safe," cried her mother.

"What were you doing in my son's room?" demanded Mrs. Smythe.

"Taking him my manuscript," said Miss Dyson-Drake. "I see it all. They started the fire so that we should all be out of the way and then she went to his room with my manuscript, thinking I'd be watching the fire."

"She went to fetch him to put the fire out," said Lupin. "Jolly sound idea."

"He has been out of the room for at least half an hour," said Mrs. Smythe.

"Well, that's all right then, isn't it?" said Lupin.

Grizel stared at them all in rather a vacant kind of way, then in a firmer voice than Lupin had ever heard her use, she said, "Where I have been and what I have been doing is no one's business but my own," and walked straight into her own room.

"Why on earth couldn't you have kept quiet about it?" said Lupin to Miss Dyson-Drake. For once, even her good temper was beginning to feel the strain. "No one need ever have known anything about it if you hadn't come in and drawn attention to it. She could easily have slipped into her own bedroom quietly."

"If she had not got a guilty conscience, she would not have wanted to slip quietly into her bedroom. It is obvious to me that she did not want anyone to know where she had gone."

"Well, as she said, it is no one's business but hers."

"I should have thought my manuscript was my business," retorted Miss Dyson-Drake.

"Bother your manuscript! And now Mrs. Mydleton is upset again, just when I had got her quite jolly. For pity's sake, go for her maid. She is with mine, drinking port."

"I will fetch her, Lady Lupin. I cannot stay here." And Mrs. Smythe, with tight lips, walked from the room.

"My poor, poor child!"cried Mrs. Mydleton. "That scoundrel must have got a hold on her in some way—what have I done that such a thing should have happened to me? I have always been a good mother…I have brought her up so carefully, my little girl, and now she is an abandoned woman. I shall never speak to her again. She is dead to me. I have no daughter …poor, innocent, little lamb, I am sure she is not to blame…her mother will stand by her, whatever she has done."

"Absolutely," agreed Lupin. "I am sure she is not to blame. As you say, I expect she has some very good reason. Personally, I am not at all sure that was Arthur's room. Do have some whisky, or what about some port? Are you sure it wasn't Barker's room? I should go to bed and have a nice rest if I were you. Things will look better in the morning. Oh, Barker, Mrs. Mydleton is feeling rather tired."

"Yes, my lady, and Miss Staines says that the superintendent of the fire brigade wishes to speak to you."

"The superintendent of the fire brigade!" exclaimed Lupin, in an astonished voice. "Oh, of course, I had quite forgotten about the fire. What a long time ago it seems!" and she escaped thankfully from the room.

"No, I have no idea how the fire started," Lupin told the superintendent. "Isn't it funny how if you try to light a fire with plenty of paper and firewood and matches and everything, it is almost impossible to get it to go? Whereas if you drop a cigarette-end on to a bit of glass or steel or asbestos, the house is on fire in no time."

"You think the fire was started by a cigarette-end?"

"Oh, dear, I hope not. Do you think I could have dropped one anywhere? I expect it will all turn out to be my fault. But I don't think I sat in that armchair, though, of course, knowing how things happen, especially to me, it might easily have leaped out of the ashtray on to the chair or something."

"Who else uses this room?"

"No one, except Miss Turner. It is her office, you see. I have only been using it while she is in hospital."

"Hasn't anyone else been in here today, except yourself?"

"Oh, yes, masses of people. Practically everyone, I should say. I mean all the guests and the servants and three detectives—no, one was a gas man, as a matter of fact."

"You have had three detectives here?"

"No, only two. One, as I say, came to look at the gas, but the nice police sergeant knows all about it. Two of the staff have disappeared, I mean."

"You do seem to have been having an unfortunate time."

"Yes, I am beginning to wonder if there isn't a polter-something about the place, you know what I mean, a sort of ghost who does tiresome things like stealing and setting the house on fire."

"You have had a very tiring day, Lady Lupin. I won't keep you up."

"I do seem to be getting a bit light-headed, don't I? Thank you most awfully for all you have done. Good night. Oh, here is Colonel James. He really knows more about everything than I do. I say, they think I probably did it with a cigarette-end. It sounds more than likely, doesn't it? Poor old Di, I can't say that I have run this hotel very well for her, having everything stolen and burning the place down, not to mention everyone running away."

"Oh, I am sorry, Lady Lupin, but there was just one thing. You rang up twice for the fire brigade, didn't you?"

"No, only once. At least, as far as I know. I sent the maid, Daisy, to ring you the minute she told me."

"We got the first message at 11:45 and my men had started when the second message came in a quarter of an hour later."

"How funny," said Lupin. "One of the messages must have been sent by the poltergeist."

CHAPTER 23

LUPIN managed to avoid meeting the other guests the next morning. Arthur Smythe went off early as usual, and Colonel James and Mr. Borden were nowhere to be seen. They were evidently busy detecting. Lupin wished that she could have joined them, but she was very busy. She saw Diana's office put to rights again and she painstakingly sat down and made a list of everything that had been burned, then had all the remains put into the greenhouse ready for inspection, in case the insurance company was of a suspicious nature. She rested after luncheon and then walked down to the drawing room, where Mrs. Mydleton and Mrs. Smythe were sitting at opposite ends, each having an early cup of tea and apparently oblivious of each other's presence.

"Well, there wasn't much damage done after all," remarked Lupin as she passed Mrs. Smythe. "It is a pity about Diana's armchair. I mean, she must want to relax a bit at times. And it's no good saying the carpet looks quite as it did before, but it might have been much worse."

"I am glad to hear that Miss Turner has not lost much of her furniture," responded Mrs. Smythe stiffly.

Lupin walked on to Mrs. Mydleton. "I hope you are feeling rested," she said.

"I could not rest," replied Mrs. Mydleton. "Not that I have anything to worry about. I have absolute trust in my daughter."

"Absolutely," agreed Lupin.

"What was she doing in Arthur Smythe's bedroom?" asked Miss Dyson-Drake, who had just come down the stairs and who never, Lupin considered, had much idea of tact.

"It was not my son's fault," announced Mrs. Smythe firmly, from the other end of the hall.

"He is a very wicked man," said Mrs. Mydleton.

"What about your daughter?"

"I expect there is some quite natural explanation," said Lupin. "I mean, she may have been taking him some aspirin, or lending him her Scripture Union card."

"Or taking him my manuscript," added Miss Dyson-Drake.

"Yes," agreed Lupin, "I shouldn't be a bit surprised, at least—er. Oh, yes, George," she said, glad of an interruption, as she seemed to be floundering rather between the frying pan and the deep sea or whatever it was.

"There are two ladies to see you, my lady, Miss Popham and Miss Witham."

Never was Lupin more thankful to fulfill a duty than she was as she hurried into the hall. Two women were sitting on the edges of their chairs, awaiting her. One had an Eton crop and the expression of one who would stand no nonsense. The other had been pretty once, but now wore a petulant expression and a general air of having worn badly. They both appeared to be between forty and fifty, and Lupin did not feel that they would add much to the gaiety of Orchard House.

"Good afternoon, she said. "I am so glad to see you."

Neither Miss Popham nor Miss Witham seemed to share in her gladness. "Miss Turner?" demanded Miss Popham.

"No, not exactly. I mean, I am not Miss Turner."

"I thought that Miss Turner would be here herself to receive us."

"And so she would be, I am sure, but she has had a bad accident, at least we hope it was an accident, and she is in the hospital. She had a concussion and is having to be kept quiet, but she is going on quite well and may be coming back today with any luck. I believe I hear a car now," and she ran eagerly to the window and saw that it was her own car that she had given up for lost. Forgetting Miss Popham and Miss Witham, she hurried to the front door to greet Charles and Ruth as they came in.

"Is the fatted calf ready?" asked Charles.

"Absolutely," said Lupin. "You can have anything you want. I am glad to see my car again, and you, too, of course."

Ruth threw her arms round Lupin's neck. "You have been a perfect angel," she said.

"And your car is in good condition," added Charles.

"Thank goodness for that! You haven't heard about Miss Dyson-Drake's, I suppose? Someone tampered with it and she took Diana in it, and she was nearly killed."

"Not Miss Turner?"

"Yes, but it's all right and she is coming back this evening, I hope. I have been running the hotel for her. I have lost her one guest, and probably a chambermaid, as well as the one that ran away, and some more things have been stolen and the hotel caught on fire, otherwise I've managed fairly well. Oh, bother, now I am losing her two more. I must fly. I have heaps to tell you later."

She hurried back to Miss Popham and Miss Witham. "I am so sorry. I hope you did not think me rude, but I had to greet those two people. They ran away a few days ago and I never expected to see them again and they had taken my car, so you can imagine how thankful I was to see them back. But you were inquiring about rooms?"

"We shall require one large double room, or two single rooms communicating. My friend is not very strong," explained Miss Popham.

"I am so sorry," reiterated Lupin.

"We have been recommended this hotel as being very quiet," went on Miss Popham.

Lupin was about to reply that it was fairly quiet except for a few burglaries, elopements, fires, and attempted murders, but on second thoughts decided silence would be best.

"My friend is on a diet. She eats no meat."

"Oh, dear, how sickening for you—can you eat fish?" Lupin asked Miss Witham.

"She can eat boiled fish," returned Miss Popham, who always answered for her friend. "But we must be satisfied that your cook understands the boiling of fish."

"Here is Miss Turner," cried Lupin joyously. "I will introduce you later. She has been suffering from a concussion, so she must not have too much excitement at present. Please forgive me if I run over to speak to her for a moment."

Diana, walking between Nanny and a hospital nurse, came slowly through the hall.

"This is indeed a surprise," said Mrs. Smythe, who was lurking in the near distance. "You must go straight upstairs and have a good rest. I have some very bad news for you, but I will not worry you with it now. We will talk about it later."

"That was Miss Turner," explained Lupin, hurrying back to Miss Popham and Miss Witham after embracing Diana and assuring her that everything was quite all right. "She will have to be kept very quiet for a little while, concussion, you know. Oh, I told you, but I shan't tell her about the fire just yet."

"Indeed! About milk, my friend must have unlimited milk. As she eats no meat, I do not consider it should be an extra."

"I don't know," said Lupin. "I mean, what do you call unlimited milk? Oh, there is Colonel James!"

"Unlimited milk is unlimited milk," replied Miss Popham, uncompromisingly.

"Is it?" said Lupin. Visions of milk pouring into the hotel and streaming down the stairs floated before her eyes and made her feel quite giddy.

"Naturally," said Miss Popham.

"Of course," agreed Lupin, wondering if this conversation were going on forever. She succeeded in catching Colonel James's eye, and to her relief he came across to her rescue. "Oh, this is Colonel James," she said. "Miss Popham and Miss Withers."

"Witham," corrected Miss Popham.

"Of course, Miss Witham," agreed Lupin. "Aren't names difficult? We were talking about milk," she explained to Colonel James.

"Unlimited milk," said Miss Popham.

"Instead of meat," explained Lupin.

"My friend does not eat meat," added Miss Popham.

Colonel James and Lupin looked at Miss Witham and thought it was a pity she did not eat meat. There was certainly something lacking in her corpuscles. She looked like one who lived on unlimited milk, with a little boiled fish thrown in, and perhaps an occasional Osborne biscuit.

"Oh, doesn't she?" said Colonel James, rather at a loss for an answer.

"And Miss—er—Wopham, I mean, Miss—er, they were wondering if there would be any extra charge for the milk or if it would cancel out the meat, so to speak."

"Is the meat unlimited?"

"No, no more it is. One could hardly ring up the butcher and say, 'please send an unlimited number of sirloins of beef and saddles of mutton,' could one? There wouldn't be room, either, and I don't see how one can easily ask the milkman to send unlimited milk."

"I hate milk," announced Miss Witham, speaking for the first time.

"When I say unlimited, I mean at least two pints a day," explained Miss Popham.

"Oh, that's all right, of course. Two pints of milk instead of meat. That sounds fair enough, doesn't it?' and Lupin appealed to Colonel James.

"Quite," he replied. "By the way, when you are disengaged, I want a word with you. I hope we shall meet again," he added to Miss Popham and Miss Witham as he walked away.

Now I wonder why he hopes that, wondered Lupin. Of course, if he is marrying Diana, I suppose he is interested in having the place full. I wonder if he knows who it was.

"What about fruit?"

"Yes," said Lupin, her mind elsewhere.

"Not stone fruit."

"Oh, no, of course not." It can't have been the Rennies, she went on to herself, or they would not have come back, and in any case they would have taken the things with them, not left them here.

"We will take a look at the room. This, I suppose, is the lounge?"

"We never call it the lounge. Miss Turner stayed here a lot when she was young, and she said she had always called it the hall and was not going to start calling it the lounge now."

"I thought a hotel always had a lounge," was Miss Popham's disapproving reply.

"This is the drawing room," announced Lupin.

"My friend needs a lot of sunshine."

"Lady Lupin, I must speak to you." Mrs. Mydleton had risen and was looking at her beseechingly. "It is all too terrible for words."

Then it is Grizel, thought Lupin. I felt that she wouldn't be coming out of Arthur's room unless she had a reason, a pure reason, for being there. Poor idiot! Why didn't she tell me yesterday? I could have got back the things before Mr. Borden saw them, or is Mrs. Mydleton brooding about her being in Arthur's room? In a way, of course, it would be worse if she hadn't the excuse of hiding stolen goods there, but then they were in the summerhouse, so she couldn't. I give it up, but she has been very strange lately.

"I'll be back as soon as I can," she said aloud.

"This room is quite pleasant in the evening," allowed Miss Popham, "but there will be no sunshine in the morning. Have you no other sitting room?"

"Yes, there are two more," said Lupin, leading them down the corridor and up two steps. Poor Grizel, she pondered, no wonder she has looked like a frightened rabbit lately, but what was she playing at? Without looking, she threw open a door on her left. "This is the room the guests use more than any other," she said, then realizing it was the W.C. whose door she had opened, closed it hurriedly and led a red-faced Miss Popham and a shrinking Miss Witham into the library.

Arthur and Grizel stood together in one of the windows. Leaving Miss Popham and Miss Witham to find the compass points and decide where the sun would be most likely to come in in the morning, Lupin darted over to them. "Do take my car if it is any good to you," she said. "The Rennies have just brought it back."

"No, we are not going to run away," said Arthur firmly.

Lupin had forgotten for the moment the motor accident, then suddenly she remembered. Suppose Diana had been killed! "Did you mean to hurt Diana?" she demanded.

"Goodness, no," replied Arthur. "Neither of us would ever dream of doing anything to hurt Miss Turner."

Well, if it were Miss Dyson-Drake they had tried to get rid of, she didn't blame them so much. She was an absolute pest. Still, of course, it wouldn't be right to murder her. But perhaps they had had nothing to do with the car, only just stolen the things. What a shock for them when they found they had gone! Grizel must have been down to the summer-house to look, then gone up to tell Arthur they had gone and not liked to come out while all the hue and cry of the fire was going on. After all, Arthur had told her about the car in the first place. No one would have known, otherwise, so that seemed to wipe him out of attempted murder. "I think you are right not to run away," she said, after a minute's thought. "If it's just the things, I'd stay here and make a clean breast of the whole thing, not that I grudge you my car."

"We shall face it out," said Arthur, putting his arm through Grizel's. "We have nothing to be ashamed of."

Lupin did not absolutely agree with him about that, but she did not feel it was her place to judge others. "Good luck," she said and returned to Miss Popham and Miss Witham. "I expect you would like to see the bedrooms," she said.

"Yes, one large double, or two single communicating."

"When would you be wanting them?"

"If we find that we like the rooms we should come almost immediately."

"I shan't be ready to come for a week," protested Miss Witham.

"Yes, you will, dear. The day after tomorrow is Friday. We shall come then if we like the rooms."

"So it is, and the new chambermaid comes that day, too."

"It is most unfortunate that we have been unable to see Miss Turner."

"Isn't it?" agreed Lupin. "About the bedrooms, I always get them a bit mixed up. Whose is whose, I mean, and so on. And so does everybody else, as a matter of fact, and it leads to a bit of awkwardness at times. Oh good, there is Nanny! I say, Nanny, come and help me. Do show these ladies round the bedrooms, otherwise I shall burst into Mrs. Mydleton's while she is resting, or Miss Dyson-Drake's while she is writing, or Mrs. Smythe's while she is praying."

"Certainly, my lady. Perhaps while I am showing the ladies round you would just slip up to the office. The police sergeant wants to speak to you."

"As regards the mattresses," began Miss Popham.

"I am so sorry to have kept you, sergeant," said Lupin, hurrying into the office, "but running a hotel isn't as easy as it sounds. Two women I've just been coping with want unlimited milk, sitting rooms facing north, east, south, and west, and bedrooms communicating with everywhere else. I have handed them over to Nanny for the minute, but I don't expect I've seen the last of them. Now do tell me all. Have you found out who has done everything?"

"I understand that you are responsible for the inmates of this hotel."

"Oh, dear, I hope I am not."

"And I should be glad if you would send everyone up in turn to have their fingerprints taken."

"Well, that means that all the servants will give notice, and one of them has only just ungiven hers. May I send them up first and get it over? I don't mind so much about the guests. But do treat them kindly, if you don't mind," and she rang the bell. "Oh, Nanny, the police want to take all your fingerprints. Do you think that Kate will mind much?"

"I don't see why she should mind more than anyone else, my lady," replied Nanny coldly, "unless, of course, she has a guilty conscience. The two ladies are asking for you."

"Miss Popham and Miss Witham!" exclaimed Lupin. "I must fly. I had forgotten all about them."

"The two ladies I was showing round, my lady. I didn't catch their names."

"Oh, dear, wasn't it awful of me to have forgotten about them?"

"Well, we are quite pleased with the bedroom," said Miss Popham, "provided the terms are reasonable."

"Terms? Oh, yes, of course, they are five guineas a week."

"What does that include?"

"Oh, everything, I think, except coffee and oh, drinks, of course."

"Baths and afternoon tea?"

"Yes, rather."

"And two pints of milk a day?"

"I expect so," agreed Lupin, absentmindedly, and went on thinking to herself. I hope that Kate won't be furious. I think it must have been Shirley and Ferguson, but why did they take such moldy things, and having taken them, why did they leave them in the summerhouse? Or was it Miss Dyson-Drake, or Arthur and Grizel?

"I thought we agreed on two pints a day?"

"Did we?"

"I should be glad to have a confirmation."

Lupin was startled. "What, here?"

"If it is not too much trouble, I should like it before we go."

Lupin gaped round her wildly. Why did things like this always happen to her? As a clergyman's wife she ought, of course, to encourage such wishes, but she did think she might have been done at the proper time like everyone else, not suddenly in a hotel. How was she to get hold of a bishop? For the first time in her life she was pleased to see Mrs. Smythe. "Oh, Mrs. Smythe," she said, accosting her breathlessly, "these two women have suddenly taken it into their heads that they want to be confirmed. What are we to do about it? Very nice, of course, but it is a bit short notice, isn't it? Especially just now with everything else going wrong."

"Really," said Mrs. Smythe. She had been looking rather preoccupied, but this challenge took her mind off her own troubles for the moment. "Would you like me to speak to them?"

"Please do."

Mrs. Smythe advanced towards the two prospective guests. "Can I do anything for you?" she asked.

"We asked the manageress for a confirmation in writing of the terms. One has to be businesslike."

"Yes, of course, but she isn't the manageress. She is Lady Lupin Hastings, a great friend of Miss Turner's. She has been very kindly trying to take her place since the unfortunate accident, but naturally, she has not had experience of anything of the sort before. It is very good of her to do all she does. I, for one, am always ready to help her in any way I can, but what with the fire last night and other things that have happened lately, we have all been in sad trouble. I am sure you understand."

"Will you explain to her that we want a confirmation, in writing, of the terms? Five guineas each a week, including baths, afternoon tea, and two pints of milk a day."

"Yes, certainly. You must forgive us all if we seem a little preoccupied. As I said, we have had great sorrows here during the last few days," and she sighed heavily.

"We shall arrive on Friday," replied Miss Popham, "in time for tea."

Mrs. Smythe moved away from the two ladies, momentarily lost in her own thoughts. It could not be true—not about Arthur! she thought. She did not believe for a moment that he was in any way to blame. He had never given her a moment's anxiety since childhood. This desire to work in a garage was very queer, but he would get over it and they would all be happy again. She wished that they had not come here for their holiday. Ever since they had arrived things had been queer, and Mrs. Smythe was not used to things being queer. First as a clergyman's daughter and then as a clergyman's wife, her life had been useful, busy, and happy. The choirboys sucking sweets and the girls in her club using lipstick had so far been her greatest problems. Of course, there had been the time when the organist had kissed one of the Sunday-school teachers, but he had been so very apologetic afterwards and so anxious that his wife should not hear of it that she had forgiven him, and it had really turned out to be a blessing in disguise as he never after that disputed Mrs. Smythe's choice of chants for the psalms. As she went on her way, reflecting sadly on how queer life had been these last few days, she was stopped by John. "Please, madam, the police sergeant wants to see you as soon as is convenient, in Miss Turner's office."

This was another thing that had never happened to her before, except, once, when her husband had left his car inadvertently in the middle of the High Street. She had the presence of mind to say to John, "You had better give those ladies tea," indicating Miss Popham and Miss Witham, before walking sadly upstairs to the office.

The police sergeant was very polite, but to have her fingerprints taken! Perhaps to be added to the collection of such things at Scotland Yard, among all those who had been mixed up with criminal cases! Arthur's lapse seemed to fade into insignificance beside it. However, a vicar's wife is used to concealing her feelings and she did as she was asked with a good grace.

"The police take the fingerprints of well-known vicars' wives," exclaimed Lupin cheerfully and in what Mrs. Smythe considered bad taste. "I don't expect either of our husbands will be made bishops now. They seem to have chosen us first. I suppose they think we are used to it."

"The two women you asked me to speak to in the hall want a confirmation of the terms."

"Oh, how clever you are! I thought they wanted to be confirmed themselves and I didn't see how we were to arrange it, especially with the police in the house. What shall I put? 'This is to confirm that the terms of this hotel are five guineas a week, including baths and unlimited milk.' "

"Two pints of milk, they said."

"That's a good idea, otherwise they might bathe in it. Anything else? Oh, yes, of course, afternoon tea. I think that is all. How do I sign it? Love from Lupin? Hallo, Mrs. Mydleton, have you come to join the gang of criminals?"

"I feel very ill," announced Mrs. Mydleton.

"No wonder," said Mrs. Smythe. "My heart bleeds for you."

"So it should," said Mrs. Mydleton. "The wickedness of your son."

"My son has not sinned alone," said Mrs. Smythe.

"Here is some brandy," remarked Lupin hopefully.

"Perhaps you would like to blame my daughter," said Mrs. Mydleton.

"I do blame her," said Mrs. Smythe.

"Or would you both prefer some tea?" suggested Lupin.

"My daughter has never had a secret from me in her life."

Mrs. Smythe didn't actually say, "Oh, yeah," but her "Oh, really," obviously meant the same thing.

"I say, what about the jolly old fingerprints?" asked Lupin. "Just the sort of thing to bring us all together, if you know what I mean."

"Never!" cried Mrs. Mydleton. "This is an outrage!"

"Oh, come, Mrs. Mydleton. Things are not as bad as you think," said Colonel James, coming in at this juncture.

"How could they be worse? And you have been betrayed, too. How can I look you in the face?"

Colonel James looked rather embarrassed. "Oh, that's all right, everything is all right. They will explain everything."

"Well, I'll be getting along," said Lupin, "and have a last look at Popham and Witham." She opened the door and fell straight into the arms of Arthur Smythe and Grizel Mydleton.

"How dare you come in here?" demanded Mrs. Mydleton of Arthur.

"I don't see what my son has done," said Mrs. Smythe, goaded beyond all effort at restraint. "Is it his fault if the kind of woman of whom I cannot bring myself to speak insists on going into his room in the middle of the night?"

"Mother, please," said Arthur.

"About these fingerprints," said the sergeant, while Mr. Borden, with great presence of mind, knocked a vase off the mantelpiece.

"If we all keep quite calm," suggested Colonel James.

"I simply must see Miss Popham and Miss Witham," reiterated Lupin, trying to get away, but finding herself somehow entwined with Grizel.

"What we came to say ," said Arthur, stammering a little, "was that Grizel and I were married on Monday. We ought to have told you at once. Colonel James wanted us to, but I have been waiting for the deed of partnership to come through. Mr. Gower and I are going into partnership, and we have bought that garage between us. I have bought it with Aunt Mary's money," and he looked defiantly at his mother.

"My daughter," cried Mrs. Mydleton, "married to a mechanic. And you knew," she said turning on Colonel James. "You knew all the time, and deceived me by pretending that you wanted to marry her yourself."

"I never pretended that, Mrs. Mydleton. I am engaged to Miss Turner, as Grizel and Arthur both know."

"May I congratulate you all?" said Mr. Borden.

"Same here," said the police sergeant. "And about those fingerprints?"

"We must have champagne for dinner," said Lupin, and kissing Grizel, she succeeded at length in tearing herself away.

"I am sorry to have kept you," she explained to Miss Popham, handing her the letter of confirmation. "But the police wanted to take my fingerprints and that delayed things a little."

Miss Popham gazed unperturbed at the letter. "That is correct," she said. "We shall arrive about four o'clock on Friday, and boiled fish, not fried. I forget if I mentioned that."

"I should rather have it fried," said Miss Witham.

CHAPTER 24

"THE great thing," said Lupin to Diana, as she was saying good night to her, "is for you to have a good night's rest and not to worry about anything at all. I dare say nothing will happen tonight. I mean they would hardly set the house on fire two nights running, would they? And if anyone is going to be murdered, it will be Miss Dyson-Drake, not you. You see, it was her car that was tampered with, nothing to do with you at all. What a pity you and Colonel James aren't married, because then he could sleep in your room and you would feel more secure. Talking of marriage, the Smythe-Mydleton one is going very well. We all sat together at dinner and drank champagne and Mrs. M. called Arthur, 'Arthur, dear,' and Mrs. Smythe was telling Grizel about the girls' guild for good girls and they were all very loving. What was I saying? Oh, yes, I will sleep in your room if you like, though I don't really expect anything will happen tonight, but do say if you would like me to."

"I should simply hate it, as things always seem to happen where you are. I shall feel much safer alone. Thank you very much all the same. As a matter of fact, I feel very sleepy, so I shan't know if anything does happen. Don't wake me up until my bed is actually on fire, there is a good girl."

"But it will be so difficult to get you out once it is alight. I mean, we should all catch alight, too. You have no idea how inflammatory fire is."

"Please, my lady," interrupted Nanny, "I think Miss Turner ought to go to sleep now, and Colonel James said would you very kindly go into the office if you can spare the time?"

"What is left of it," replied Lupin. "I am sorry about your armchair, Diana, and I do hope you don't mind my being closeted with your betrothed, but I expect all the police force will be there, too."

"You can do what you like with my betrothed, if only you will leave me to get a bit of sleep."

"Right you are. Good night." Lupin walked down to the office and took her seat on rather a hard chair. "It would be the only comfortable one that got burned, wouldn't it?" she remarked thoughtfully. As she had guessed, a police inspector was there, also Mr. Borden.

"Did you notice a smell of paraffin when you were putting out the fire last night, Lady Lupin?" inquired Mr. Borden.

"Putting out the fire is good. I can't say I did much toward that. I didn't notice the paraffin, but what with the smoke and everything there was a lot of smell, but I didn't pick out any particular bits of it, if you know what I mean. Do you think someone did it on purpose then, with paraffin?"

The superintendent of the fire brigade thought he detected a smell of paraffin, and Miss Nunn, who discovered the fire, said she smelled it when she first went into the room.

"Well, it looks to me as if there were a lunatic in the house," said Lupin. "First they take a lot of things that no one can want and hide them in the summerhouse, then they loosen a nut on Miss Dyson-Drake's car, then they set the house on fire. Of course, Miss Dyson-Drake is the obvious person. I mean, she is the only one who is quite dotty, but would even she loosen a nut on her own car just before she went out in it? Unless, of course, she wanted to commit suicide! She was rather disappointed about the fire being put out, now I come to think of it. Perhaps when she found she had not killed herself in the car she decided she would set the house on fire and be burned to death. I wonder what she will do tonight?"

"She certainly is the most apparently unbalanced person in the place."

"And that is saying a good deal. The Rennies are both very unbalanced, but I think they are usually too busy quarreling with each other and making it up again to do anything else, and anyway, they could not have started the fire. Besides, I don't think they are really dotty, except just on top. I have a suspicion that Ruth really knows all about how much fish ought to cost at what times of year, and what to do with the cold mutton and things like that, underneath being romantic and misunderstood. Then Grizel is a bit queer, but that is only because her mother leads her such a life and being married to Arthur and not wanting people to know, and the same goes for Arthur, I mean being frightened of his mother and married to Grizel. Mrs. Smythe is the most normal person here, not counting us, of course, so I expect it will turn out to be her. It is usually the most unlikely person, though I can't imagine her painting those pictures."

"You think the person who painted the pictures must be the one involved?"

"No, I don't really, because I think Miss Dyson-Drake is at the bottom of it all, and I am sure she couldn't have painted those pictures. After all, anybody might have found the summerhouse and hidden the things there. I could have done it myself."

"So you could." The inspector had listened to this conversation carefully. Once or twice he was slightly bewildered, but though Lady Lupin talked rather wildly, she seemed to have summed up the other guests pretty well and there was very likely more in what she said than appeared on the surface. "That young chap would have led us up the garden path with his talk of Shirley Walker and Ferguson if you hadn't found the pearls yesterday afternoon," he said to Mr. Borden.

"Oh, then, you don't think it was them?" exclaimed Lupin.

"No. It seems that they've been going together for some time and the girl Shirley's father didn't like it. Ferguson, as he calls himself, is really Albert Miggs and a thoroughly bad hat, I should say, if all we hear is true. But we can't put our hands on anything actually illegal. He's a rolling stone and has a bad name with women. It seems, if you'll forgive me mentioning it, that he'd got Shirley into trouble and she persuaded him to marry her. They were married yesterday at noon at a registry office near Charing Cross."

"Everyone seems to be running away to get married, aren't they? I wonder who will be the next, Miss Popham or Miss Witham, perhaps. Are you married, inspector?"

"Yes, your ladyship," was the somewhat nervous reply.

"So am I. So it won't be us. But about Shirley and Ferguson—if they stole the things they would hardly have left them in the summerhouse, would they? I mean, Shirley might easily have stolen them and pawned them, not that they would have fetched much, not Aunt Jemima's brooch, and Miss Dyson-Drake's manuscript, anyway, and then bribed Ferguson to marry her with the proceeds. But as the things were in the summerhouse, she couldn't have done, could she?"

"No. They may have taken the notecase, of course. That has not turned up and it would be a more likely thing for them to have taken than any of the other articles. But there is really no way of proving it as we don't know the number of the notes and they would probably take the precaution of burning the case."

"But if they were only going to get married I don't see why they had to run away in that surreptitious manner," complained Lupin. "I mean, getting married is perfectly respectable, and if Shirley were in a spot of trouble, Miss Turner would have helped her and fixed things up."

"Girls like Shirley Walker don't want to be helped, and she knew her father would try to prevent her marrying the man Miggs. He has changed his name more than once, I understand."

"Well, you can hardly blame him for that if his real name is Miggs. I suppose he is good-looking in an oily kind of way. I never cared for him, he is quite a different type from John, who is a dear. I am afraid from what you say Shirley won't be very happy as Mrs. Miggs."

"She has made her bed and she will have to lie on it," replied the inspector. "But as I was saying, I am satisfied that neither of them had anything to do with the tampering with the motorcar, the theft of the pearls, brooches, or manuscript, or the starting of the fire. But," he added to Mr. Borden, "if you hadn't found the things, we might have suspected them."

"It was Lady Lupin who led me to them."

"And I wouldn't have done that if I'd stolen them myself, would I? Unless, of course, I was frightfully clever, which I am not. As a matter of fact, I shouldn't be surprised if that detective hadn't stolen all the things himself—the other detective, I mean. He was the most ghastly young man, wasn't he? I am sure he had had his hair permanently waved."

"That doesn't necessarily prove that he is a thief," murmured Borden.

"I would rather be a thief than have my hair permanently waved," remarked Lupin. "If I were a man, I mean."

"I am inclined to agree with you," said Colonel James. "But stealing is an incidental part of this affair to me. It is the tampering, with the motorcar with which I am most concerned. Diana might have been killed."

"The brute," exclaimed Lupin. "I don't mean Diana. I mean the murderer. He could have stolen Aunt Jemima's brooch three times over and I wouldn't have said a word, but when it comes to murdering Diana, it is a different matter."

"But," said Borden, "we have no reason for thinking they were trying to murder Miss Turner. It was Miss Dyson-Drake's car that was tampered with, and so far as we can tell the criminal did not know that Miss Turner would be in it."

"That does make a difference, doesn't it?" said Lupin.

"Murder is murder," said the inspector, "whoever the victim may be."

"Oh, absolutely," agreed Lupin. "But one can imagine someone having a reason for murdering Miss Dyson-Drake."

"Who do you think might have had a reason for wanting to murder Miss Dyson-Drake?"

"Almost everyone, I should think."

"What makes you say that?" demanded the inspector.

"Haven't you seen her?" replied Lupin.

"This is a serious matter, your ladyship."

"Oh, yes, I know. I really am most awfully serious about it all. But she is a bit of a menace, you know. For instance, she saw Miss Mydleton coming out of Arthur Smythe's bedroom and instead of looking the other way she drew everyone's attention to it. Of course, they were married all the time, as it turned out, so why on earth couldn't she keep quiet? I mean, it's not the sort of thing one draws attention to, is it?"

"She is a person of one idea," explained Colonel James. "Her only thought when she saw Grizel coming out of Arthur's room was that it had something to do with her manuscript."

"When did Miss Dyson-Drake see Miss Mydleton—I should say Mrs. Smythe—coming out of her husband's room?"

"Last night after the fire, just when I had cheered Mrs. Mydleton up, so it couldn't have been that. I mean it was some time after the car had been tampered with, so I am sure it wasn't them. Besides, it was Arthur who told me about the car in the first place, which he wouldn't have done if he had done it."

"You say that Mr. Smythe reported the matter of the loose nut to you?" said the inspector.

"Yes, you see he couldn't have done it, because no one would have known anything about it if he hadn't told me. He was certain it was all right when he delivered it here the night before, so it couldn't have been Mr. Gower, either."

"Who is Mr. Gower?" asked the inspector, scanning the list of the people in the hotel.

"Rosie's father, you know, the one Miss Dyson-Drake ran over. Of course, he had a motive and I thought of him at once and begged him to leave the country, but he only laughed and in any case, if the car was all right when it left the garage, he could hardly have got in in the night and tampered with it. Besides, I am sure he didn't, and if he had done I shouldn't have blamed him."

"Both Mr. Smythe and Mr. Gower might have had a motive," said the inspector.

"If the child had been badly hurt, Mr. Gower might have had a motive," interposed Borden. "But she seems to be perfectly well again, so I think we might wipe him off. As for Smythe, it doesn't seem very likely. He went up to London to get married the day of the accident. Miss Dyson-Drake might have guessed what he was going to do, though I find it hard to believe, as she was too absorbed in herself and her manuscript to bother about other people's affairs. Even if she had guessed it would not have been a sufficient motive for murder. There was no reason why Smythe and Miss Mydleton should not get married, and although they very foolishly kept it a secret, I can't believe they would have committed murder to prevent it coming to light."

"I am quite sure they would do nothing of the sort," said Colonel James. "I know Grizel has been rather unbalanced lately, but her mother has got badly on her nerves. She felt sure she would try to stop her marrying Arthur, and I think she would have done. That is why I abetted them in getting married privately, but I begged them to tell their mothers as soon as they got back. It was very foolish of them to make a mystery of it."

"Of course," said Lupin. "Arthur had gone up to London the day of the accident. I never connected it with Grizel and the dentist, how silly of me! But what with Diana being in the hospital, and then Arthur's story about the nut, and wondering how to get Mr. Gower out of .the country, I was pretty occupied. As a matter of fact, I did wonder if you and Grizel were getting married secretly, so I wasn't far out. Why on earth they couldn't come back and say 'we are married,' straightaway, instead of slinking about as if they had broken every commandment under the sun, I can't think. But I am sure Grizel never loosened any nuts. She would not have the least idea of how to do it and would probably have jammed it on so tight that the thing wouldn't have moved at all, or else would have blown the horn while she was doing it and everyone would have come out to see what she was doing."

"Taking the tampering with the car first," said the inspector, "who would be most likely to understand the mechanism of a car?"

"Arthur Smythe," said Lupin. "But we have just proved it wasn't him. Charles Rennie is a scientist and he drives a car, so he may know something about it. I dare say he does, he is very clever, I believe. But I don't see why he should have done it unless, of course, he mistook the car and thought it was Paul Ramsden's."

"Why should he wish to tamper with Paul Ramsden's car?"

"He thought he'd eloped with his wife and he said he would break every bone in his body."

"That is interesting," said Mr. Borden.

"You did not mention this before, your ladyship," said the inspector, rather reproachfully.

"I had forgotten about it for the time being, so many things seem to have happened since then. And running this hotel isn't easy, but I have secured you two more guests," she added to Colonel James.

"Tell us about Rennie," begged Borden.

"Well, there isn't much to tell really. He is quite nice, but rather bad-tempered, and his wife thought he didn't love her any more, so she ran away to her mother. At least, I imagine that's where she ran, so he went after her and brought her back again."

"But where does Paul Ramsden come in?"

"Oh. Charles thought at first she'd run away with him, because she was carrying on with him rather, but I don't think there was anything in it, any more than there was with you," she added to Colonel James.

"Thanks," said Colonel James. "I don't think there was anything between her and Paul Ramsden, but I think his talk rather went to her head. As a matter of fact, my motives in what you vulgarly call carrying on were altogether pure. I thought if I took her out occasionally it would keep her from making a little idiot of herself."

"It didn't, not much," put in Lupin.

"I talked to her like a father. It was Diana's idea that I should try to din a little sense into her."

"If Mr. Rennie really thought there was anything between his wife and Mr. Ramsden, might he have tampered with his car, or what he thought was his car?"

"But it wasn't there," said Lupin. "That was the whole point. It was because Paul's car had gone out of the garage that he was going to break every bone in his body. Though, as I pointed out, his had gone, too, and it wasn't likely they would have eloped in two cars, was it? I mean, one doesn't, does one?"

"I have never tried," said Colonel James.

"Nor have I," said Borden, "but that is beside the point. He might have done it the day before, if he knew they were having an affair, then when he realized that his wife had gone in it, too, it would have added to his alarm. You say that he was very much upset."

"Frightfully! Yet in a way he was enjoying it all, too, feeling frightfully melodramatic and all that, you know."

"Then," said Borden, "if he had tampered by mistake with Miss Dyson-Drake's car, thinking it was Paul Ramsden's, he would not have realized that Ramsden's had gone. No, that won't do. No, I don't think much of Rennie. What about Ramsden himself? What sort of man is he?"

"Rather queer in a way,"said Lupin. "Not a bit arty to look at, except perhaps in his dressing gown. But frightfully cynical and that sort of thing, you know. He was made to do engineering when he was young instead of painting, and it has warped him a bit, I think. He paints very queer pictures, clever but depressing. I don't think he is in love with Ruth Rennie. He likes talking to people about themselves and some people like being talked about. He is bosoms with Miss Dyson-Drake, though of course she is old enough to be his grandmother."

"Is she any relation?"

"Not that I know of. That would make her Diana's relation, too, and she would have told me. No, on second thought she might have kept it quiet. I should if she were my relation. I expect she was afraid you would find out and refuse to marry her," she added to Colonel James.

"She could be Ramsden's relation without being Diana's," he returned, "but I don't think she is. Diana would have mentioned it, I think."

"Is Miss Dyson-Drake very much attached to him?" asked Borden.

"Well, I don't want to be unkind, and I may have misjudged her, but she doesn't strike me as being very much attached to anyone but herself. I mean, she is awfully interested in herself. I dare say it is because of her genius, but if she does like anyone, I suppose it is Paul. They are usually together, except when he escapes with Ruth Rennie. I dare say he finds her a nice change."

"You say that Mr. Ramsden started life as an engineer?"

"Yes, for ten years and he hated every minute. Just the opposite to Arthur Smythe, who was always being pressed to write poetry when he was longing to decarbonize the magneto or something."

Borden and the inspector exchanged glances. "I think we had better see Miss Dyson-Drake," said Borden.

"There is no accounting for tastes," remarked Lupin. "Personally, I feel I'd better not."

"Just as you like, of course, but could you send someone to fetch her?"

"Oh, well, it's a pity to miss anything. Do you mind ringing the bell? I think I'll stay."

Miss Dyson-Drake was duly summoned and came eagerly into the room. "Well," she said, "have you found out anything?"

"We hope we are on the track," replied Borden.

"On the track? What is the good of being on the track? That won't bring me back my manuscript. How much longer am I to go on with half of me maimed?"

"Not much longer. But will you very kindly answer just a few questions?"

"I am sick of answering questions. I have told everything over and over again. I have nothing to conceal. I was in my room before dinner, working, so I know that my manuscript was there then."

"As a matter of fact, we are trying to get at the motor accident first."

"Motor accident! Oh, that was nothing. They tried to keep me in the hospital, but I told them my body was perfectly well, it was my mind—"

"Can you minister to a mind diseased?" broke in Lupin triumphantly. "Sorry, I don't know what I was thinking of. I never learned much at school, but the things I did learn seem to have stuck rather, and come out at the most inopportune moments."

"You forget, Miss Dyson-Drake," said Borden, "that Miss Turner had a broken arm and a concussion. She might have been killed."

"Well, it would have been her own fault if she had been. She insisted on driving."

"Did you offer to take her out in your car?"

"No. She asked me to drop her at a shop or something sordid of that sort, as I happened to remark that I was going for a motor drive to see if Nature, the great healer, could do anything for me. I felt as if there were a band of iron round my head, for I had not slept since my loss. Within there was a dull, aching pain as if I had given birth to a stillborn child."

"Indeed," remarked Colonel James, while the inspector went rather red and blew his nose loudly.

"Fresh air is good, isn't it?" agreed Lupin. "For a headache, I mean," she explained hastily. "Especially if it really is fresh."

"So Miss Turner asked you to drop her at one of the shops?" went on Borden unperturbed.

"Yes, and then she said, 'Would you like me to drive?' I suppose her idea was to spare me, though not really a writer herself—"

"Do have some whisky and soda, Colonel James," begged Lupin nervously.

"She has some gropings in that direction," went on Miss Dyson-Drake. "And she had some faint glimmerings of what my loss meant to me. I think she really meant to be kind, but actually I prefer driving myself. It seems to loosen something within me and to throw off some of the clouds that oppress me."

"But you did not dispute her suggestion about driving?"

"Dispute? No, I was in no mood for disputing anything. I simply acquiesced. In my present mood I don't really notice whether I am driving or not."

"It is better not to drive under those circumstances, madam," pointed out the inspector severely. "Did you go together to the garage, or did you bring the car to the house and pick up Miss Turner here?"

"I wonder," mused Miss Dyson-Drake. "I longed for rapid movement and I said to Paul Ramsden, 'I must go out, I must breathe,' and he said he would fetch me my car."

Lupin put the burning end of her cigarette into her mouth and exclaimed, while Colonel James swallowed his whisky down the wrong way and choked.

"Mr. Ramsden fetched your car from the garage and brought it round to the house for you?" asked Mr. Borden.

"Yes, he wished to come with me, but I told him he must not neglect his message to the world."

"What message?" demanded the inspector.

"Beauty!"

The inspector looked rather nonplussed, but Mr. Borden explained, "Mr. Ramsden is an artist."

"Oh, you mean his pictures. He stayed behind to paint his pictures, did he?"

"Did he ask if he might accompany you?" inquired Borden.

"Not in words. He knew I wouldn't permit it. His working hours are as sacred to him as mine are to me."

"How long was he fetching the car?"

"I have no idea, time is nothing to me. Once I worked for fourteen hours at a stretch with neither food nor drink. I thought it was but half an hour and wondered why the light was fading. At other times five minutes may seem a month."

"Well, thank you, Miss Dyson-Drake. There is just one other thing I should like to ask you, if you don't mind. Suppose that accident had been fatal. Who would have inherited your money?"

"What is money? I have never cared for money, I do not write for money. I write to enrich the world."

"Quite! You have never made a will?"

"Yes, I made a will. My lawyer worried me about it last time I met him. It seems I have a good deal of what this world calls riches, but as I say, riches mean nothing to me. While I have enough to eat and drink to enable me to bear my torch, it does not matter to me where my money goes after I am dead. But he pestered me—these men have no souls—so I made a will, leaving all my worldly goods to Paul Ramsden, knowing that he would follow in my footsteps. I told him what I had done and he promised that if he survives me, he will carry on my message of beauty to the world."

CHAPTER 25

MISS DYSON-DRAKE left the office and the others looked at each other. "Motive, opportunity, and special knowledge," said the inspector.

"Yes," agreed Borden. "It looks rather black against Mr. Ramsden, although if everyone who had a motive and an opportunity for murder were condemned, there would not be many of us who could plead 'not guilty'."

"I don't see quite why he should murder her for her money," said Lupin. "He has got plenty of his own. His aunt left him practically all of hers, and Diana got the house. I think Diana would really rather have had the money."

"If it were Mr. Ramsden who tampered with the car, I should say it was someone else who stole the things," said the inspector.

"You mean," said Mr. Borden, "that if it were money he was after, he would have made a better collection."

"Yes," agreed the inspector. "None of the things, with the exception of Mrs. Mydleton's pearls, were worth anything much. Oh, and there was ten pounds in the notecase, of course."

"Well, Paul Ramsden can't have stolen his own notecase," pointed out Lupin. "And, as you say, if he were stealing things he wouldn't have chosen such a dud lot. But what about all those fingerprints you took this afternoon?"

"They are not much help. There were no fingerprints on any of the stolen things, except a few of Miss Dyson-Drake's and Mr. Ramsden's on some pages of the manuscript, which was only natural. Whoever took the things must have wiped them carefully."

"And the car?"

"They were blurred, but there were some of Miss Dyson-Drake's, Mr. Ramsden's, Miss Turner's, Mr. Smythe's, George, the porter's, and others."

"I see," said Lupin. "Well, I think I'll go along to bed, not that it is likely to be for long. I shouldn't be surprised if there were a flood tonight. As Miss Dyson-Drake did not succeed in killing herself in a motor accident, or in the fire, she may try drowning. I shouldn't mind if she just did it to herself, but she is one of those unselfish people who like others to share her experiences."

When Lupin reached the hall she found quite a merry party in progress. The Smythes and Rennies were grouped round Mrs. Mydleton, who was very mellow after her champagne and seemed to think that she had arranged her daughter's marriage herself and was delighted with it. "And here is our little hotelkeeper," she said kindly, as she saw Lupin approaching. "Now do come and sit down quietly for a moment. You work so hard, looking after us all. I am sure I don't know what we should do without you. Arthur dear, what about a little whisky and soda for Lupin. It will do her good after all her hard work."

"Or would you rather have a cup of cocoa?" suggested Mrs. Smythe, who was enjoying a cup of that rather revolting beverage herself. "It will help you to sleep."

"I shall sleep all right," said Lupin, "if I am not woken up to put out a fire, catch a burglar, or rescue the drowning."

"Why the drowning?" asked Charles Rennie with interest.

"Well, it was fire last night. I feel whoever it may be will probably do something with water tonight. Just a premonition, you know."

George walked through the hall. "Hallo, everyone," he said. "Drinking the bridesh health?"

Lupin started. Whatever had come over the invaluable George? "Good night, George," she said rather firmly.

"I know shum as will have better nightsh than poor old George," he said. "Itsh dull shleeping alone, ishn't it?" he added to Mrs. Smythe.

Arthur appeared with Lupin's drink. "Another little drink won't do ush any harm," went on George, and he winked at Mrs. Mydleton.

"Be quiet, George," said Arthur.

"Oh, I'll be quiet all right. I never told anyone when I shaw your mishus slipping into your room at night, if she was your mishus. Live and let live shay I. I won't give any of you away," and he grinned first at Mrs. Smythe and then at Mrs. Mydleton in a knowing manner.

Arthur took hold of his arm and Charles Rennie got up to help him, but George slipped his arm, advanced to Mrs. Mydleton, and kissed her soundly on the cheek. "Kish for the bride," he explained.

"What a terrible thing drink is," said Mrs. Smythe, taking another sip of her cocoa, as Arthur and Charles took hold of George and marched him away.

"Isn't it," agreed Lupin, gulping her whisky and soda.

Grizel hovered over her mother with smelling salts, while Mrs. Smythe rubbed her assaulted cheek with a clean pocket handkerchief. Lupin caught Ruth's eye and began to choke, while Ruth said in a quivering voice, "I think perhaps I'll go to bed, unless there is anything I can do, of course."

"Shall I go and find Barker?" suggested Lupin hoarsely.

"Yes, please, dear, and ask her to bring some eau-de-cologne. What a good thing we had dear Arthur with us."

Lupin and Ruth collapsed on a couch on the landing. "Mrs. Mydleton's face!" sobbed Ruth.

"Mrs. Smythe's!" gurgled Lupin.

"I thought Charles was going to laugh."

"Be an angel and go and find Barker. I must go and tell Colonel James about it," and Lupin went back to the office.

The three men looked up gravely as she came in. "Oh, I thought perhaps I'd better come and tell you," she said. "George is drunk and has just kissed Mrs. Mydleton," and she collapsed once more into unseemly mirth.

"That is interesting," said Borden thoughtfully.

"It certainly is," agreed Colonel James.

"I have been rather interested in George all along," went on Borden. "No one seems to know much about him. Mr. Ramsden came across him at his club and persuaded Miss Turner to engage him. He has, hitherto, I understand, proved a good servant."

"Hitherto," agreed Lupin.

"His fingerprints were on Miss Dyson-Drake's car. Not that that was peculiar as he would probably open the door of it for her and may even have sometimes brought the car round from the garage. I gather he doesn't mind what he does."

"He doesn't, does he?" and Lupin began to laugh once more. She was really feeling very exhausted after her long day and felt that she would never able to stop laughing again.

"There were also his fingerprints on the door of the summerhouse," said the inspector, "and in several other places there."

"That might merely mean that part of his duties were to keep it clean," said Borden. "There is no real reason for suspecting him, but I should like to know a little more about him."

"Well, Mr. Ramsden would probably know all about him,"Lupin

said. "I have always liked him awfully myself. It is a pity about him drinking. Of course, he may have taken the things while he was drunk. They were just the sort of things one would take if one were drunk, weren't they?"

"But Mrs. Mydleton's pearls were taken before breakfast," pointed out Borden. "That is not the sort of time anyone would be drunk. And Miss Dyson-Drake's manuscript was taken during dinnertime. Surely if he had been drunk then someone would have noticed it. He is always on duty in the hall and people would be walking backwards and forwards at that time."

"Unless it were his afternoon off," said Lupin.

"Well, that can be found out. Of course, the setting of the place on fire might easily have been the work of a drunkard. And it would account for the two telephone calls. He suddenly realized what he had done and rang up the fire brigade."

"And the smell of paraffin might have been whisky," put in Lupin. "Or he may drink paraffin or methylated spirits or something."

"But it doesn't account for the nut on the car," said Borden. "Someone sober must have done that—at least, that is probable."

"Perhaps Miss Dyson-Drake knew that he drank and he was afraid she would tell Diana."

"The first thing," said the inspector, "is to find out what we can about George—his past history and so on."

"Looks rather as if Mr. Ramsden tampered with the car and George took the things," said Colonel James. "And set the house on fire."

"And Shirley and Ferguson stole the notecase," added Lupin.

"We must not jump to conclusions," said Borden.

"No, nor we must," agreed Lupin. "Well, I'll go to bed. One good thing is that Arthur is absolutely it with Mrs. Mydleton now. She is so thankful to have a man to protect her. The only trouble is whether they won't find that they have both got two mothers now, instead of one apiece, so the last is worse than the first, if you know what I mean. Good night." She put her head in at the door again. "I was wrong about the water," she said. "It wasn't water that George had been drinking."

CHAPTER 26

MR. BORDEN was up early the next morning. He walked out into the garden. There had been rain in the night and the air was full of the scent of spring flowers. In the borders were old-fashioned wallflowers, not the neat annual variety, but huge bunches of tawny yellow blossoms, forming a background to golden tulips and daffodils. He found his way to the orchard where the cherry blossom had not yet started to drop, although it could not last at the height of its beauty much longer, as the apple and plum were already on their way. Borden wondered why he did not get up early more often. Surely this was the best time of day, as it was the best time of year. Paradise must be rather like this place, and yet there was some evil spirit at work here. He stood on the threshold of the orchard taking deep breaths of fresh morning air, noticing the raindrops glistening on the leaves and a spider's delicate web on the bough near him, when he caught sight of a figure farther on. Picking his way carefully through the daffodils, he discovered Paul Ramsden sitting in a little clearing in the middle of the orchard with an easel before him, and on it the unfinished picture of the orchard that Borden had seen in the summerhouse the other day.

He studied Paul's face. It was looking quite different from usual. The expression of good-humored mockery was gone and in its place was the look Borden had seen on some men's faces in church, or when looking at some particular woman, a look of worship. But just as he was thinking about this, Paul glanced up and saw him and the transfigured expression left his face as suddenly as if it had been wiped off with a sponge. The usual cynical mask took its place as he remarked in a slightly amused voice, "Hallo, you up early, too, to enjoy the dew on the grass?"

"This is a lovely time of day," said Borden. "And this is a lovely place."

"I suppose so," agreed Paul, "but it is not much in my line. I am not really an early riser by nature."

"Perhaps you find it worthwhile if you can catch this moment, when the orchard is looking like this."

Paul shrugged his shoulders. "One has to do potboilers occasionally," he said.

"It must be rather a bore for you to have to paint pictures which are not congenial to you," replied Borden sympathetically.

"Oh, well, one has to live," said Paul. "The majority of the public are not educated to modern art yet."

"I am afraid I am one of the majority," confessed Borden. "And I like this," and he looked at the picture on the easel.

"Do you?" said Paul, rather bored.

"I should like to live in a place like this, but I suppose it is so familiar to you that it does not strike you in the same way as it strikes a stranger?"

Was it his imagination, or was there rather a wary look in Paul's eye as he looked at him for a moment before replying? Slowly he lit a cigarette. "When you have known a place all your life, you can't go into ecstasies about it," he said. "The place is pretty enough, but I am not a sentimental person and I must admit I am glad my aunt left me the money and Diana the house instead of the other way round. Vulgar of me, I suppose, but there it is. The house by itself would have been rather a white elephant. It is sporting of Diana to have turned it into a hotel."

"You have helped her a good deal, she tells me."

"Oh, I've done what I could. I felt a bit mean having nearly all the money while she was left with a place she couldn't afford to live in."

"Several of the guests are friends of yours, I believe?"

"Miss Dyson-Drake is a friend of mine, but I am afraid my cousin finds her a bit of a trial. She is rather eccentric, but she does understand my views about art, which is more than most people do. It is a nuisance about her manuscript being lost. It has made her a little trying to everyone, but the poor soul lives for her work."

"I don't expect she approves of you painting potboilers," suggested Borden.

"I have never confessed it to her," laughed Paul. "It would break her heart. The dear soul has made a will leaving me all her money because she thinks I will carry on her message of art for art's sake. Well, so I will if I ever inherit the money. I shan't need to paint potboilers then. However, I hope the day is far distant, as I should miss Lavinia. She is one of the few consistent people I know. Most people flounder about without knowing what they want, instead of keeping to their own pattern. My cousin's friend, Lady Lupin, is a case in point. She is a lovely little fool and would fulfill a useful place in the world if she would be content to look beautiful and to talk agreeable nonsense, but she must needs run about trying to do things. She doesn't do them well and she upsets the general balance."

"I wonder," said Borden reflectively. "But tell me something about the Rennies. They are friends of yours, aren't they?"

"I only knew Rennie slightly, but he was talking about where he should go for his holiday and I naturally suggested this place, hoping to do Di a good turn. I had only met Ruth once or twice before they came here. She is another person who tries to be something that she was not intended to be."

"What was she intended to be?"

"A good wife and mother, but she will try to talk about art, of which she knows nothing, or about the problems of the universe, about which she knows less. She ought to go to church on Sunday with her husband and six children, then go home and eat roast beef and Yorkshire pudding. Her only problems should be the girl giving notice, little Johnny's new tooth, and whether her husband remembered to take his muffler when he went out."

Borden laughed. "You know that is rather the same conclusion that Lady Lupin came to about her."

"Is it?" Paul looked surprised. "I should never have thought she would have seen through her."

"I think her instincts about people are rather sound. By the way, did you hear of last night's excitement?"

"No, not another fire, I hope! Or was it a burglary?"

"Neither, only George kissing Mrs. Mydleton."

Paul put back his head and laughed. "Naughty old George! He is at it again, then. He got fired from the club because he drank. He was down and out, but he promised me he would amend, so I got Diana to give him another chance."

"Did you tell her that he drank?"

"No, it would have been a case of giving a dog a bad name and hanging him. I thought he really would pull up. He is a very good chap apart from the drink."

"Rather bad luck on Miss Turner if he didn't. He might have lost her all her guests if he started running amuck."

"I suppose it was a bit of a risk, but I knew I was going to be here myself for some time, so I thought I should be able to keep an eye on him. He must have given me the slip last night. Of course, the fire the night before may have upset him, sort of delayed shock or something But I am afraid he can hardly expect Diana to keep him after this. I do wish I had seen Mrs. Mydleton's face."

Mr. Borden walked thoughtfully back to the house. Of one thing he was convinced. That picture of the orchard was not a potboiler. It was a picture lovingly painted of a scene the painter loved.

George stood on the steps. He did not look at all abashed. "Good morning, sir, a nice morning."

"Good morning, George. What are the trains to London from Ryeport?"

"Eight thirty-six, nine thirty-six, and ten thirty-six, sir."

Borden glanced at his watch. It was ten minutes past eight. "Could you get me a car to catch the nine thirty-six?"

"Certainly, sir, we usually allow half an hour. I will order one for nine o'clock if that will suit you."

"Thank you, George. Oh, by the way, you know the summerhouse in the garden, do you attend to that?"

"Yes, sir. Mr. Ramsden uses it as a studio and I keep it clean for him. I am always glad to do anything for Mr. Ramsden. He has been very kind to me. It was he who got me this place, but I am afraid I shan't be here much longer. I went one over the eight last night and forgot myself."

"So I heard."

George gave a grin. "I can't think how I came to do such a thing, sir. I'd promised Mr. Ramsden that I'd keep off the drink, but last night he came into the studio when I was clearing up and he said, 'Well, George, so we are celebrating a wedding this evening, Mr. Arthur Smythe and Miss Mydleton as was,' and he said, 'you must drink their health, it won't hurt you just this once, you have been a trump since you've been here,' and he offered me a glass of whisky, sir. And then, to tell you the truth, sir, after he'd left me to clean up, I did have another glass or maybe two and I suppose, not being used to it, for I've had nothing but a glass of beer since I've been here, it went right to my head like, and when I went back to the house I didn't rightly know what I was doing, and well, as a matter of fact, I believe I went and kissed one of the ladies."

"That was a pity. I am afraid it may be a little awkward for Miss Turner to keep you here after that."

"You are right, sir. I wouldn't expect it. Not that I can help laughing when I think of myself doing such a thing, but I wouldn't have had it happen for anything. I am very sorry about it. Miss Turner is a real lady and I am sorry if I have given her trouble just when she is ill and all, and I've gone and let Mr. Ramsden down, too, after all his kindness. Oh, well, there it is, sir. I have no one but myself to blame. Proper fool I was. I'll order your taxi, sir."

Borden leaned back in the railway carriage, thinking over the various people at Orchard House. They were an interesting collection, ordinary enough on the surface, but full of surprises underneath. Borden found that that was the case with most people. He met a great many varieties in the course of his profession, but he had never met a really dull person yet. Mrs. Mydleton was a foolish, selfish woman, but she was not so stupid that she did not see where her own interest lay. Once she realized that her daughter was married and that nothing could unmarry her, she came round and made herself as pleasant as possible both to her and to her son-in-law, hoping to enslave him and to have two people in her toils instead of one.

Arthur Smythe appeared a feeble, weak-chinned young man. But he was quite an exceptional engineer and now that he had the job he had always wanted would probably make a success of life. Borden had learned to discount features in summing up characters. He had known men with jutting chins who were utterly lacking in strength of purpose.

The Rennies appeared a modern hardboiled young couple. But they were really extremely old-fashioned and one might easily have found them in different clothes in Edwardian days.

Lady Lupin talked like a fool but out of her silly chatter came unexpectedly shrewd remarks. For instance, she had noted Ruth Rennie's conventionality under her posings, and it was she who had said that the pictures in the summerhouse had been painted by someone who loved the place.

That brought Borden to Paul Ramsden. Ramsden undoubtedly loved Orchard House and he was bitterly disappointed that he had not inherited it. He, too, was not what he seemed. Borden had seen his cartoons and although clever, they had struck him as being painted with the idea of fooling people. He had also seen a picture he had painted of the mammoth cinema at Ryeport and there he could detect his savage hatred of the monstrosity. He was a man who loved beauty and on whom everything ugly jarred. The years in an engineering works had embittered him and made him grow a protective shell so that no one should know what he ready, felt. Had he tried to murder Miss Dyson-Drake for her money? Borden found this hard to believe. He had had motive, opportunity and the knowledge needed for the crime. Yet he had spoken quite naturally about her and about her money eventually coming to him. Would he have done so if he were guilty?

Was it his cousin whom he wanted dead, not Miss Dyson-Drake? Did he know that she was going in the car with Miss Dyson-Drake that morning? Borden had not been able to interview Miss Turner yet, but he would like to know to whom she had left Orchard House.

Another thing that had struck Borden was that Paul had shown surprise on hearing that George had got drunk last night. That must have been put on, for according to George, Paul had offered him a glass of whisky and then left him in the summerhouse with the bottle. If one were trying to help a man to get the better of his craving for drink one would hardly do that. He might have offered him a glass of beer, but he would not have offered him spirits if he were really interested in curing him. Did he want George to get drunk, had he brought George to Orchard House with the idea of getting him drunk one night so that he would insult the guests?

Had he made friends with Miss Dyson-Drake and brought her here hoping that her eccentricities would drive people away? And what about the Rennies? He evidently did not know much about them, but had probably thought they were the sort of couple that might prove awkward. Had he started the fire so as to frighten everyone and rung up the fire brigade just beforehand so as to ensure them arriving in plenty of time to prevent any damage? Had he committed all the thefts? It would have been tiresome for him if he had been caught in Mrs. Mydleton's bedroom, but he probably took the things as occasion offered. He might have been walking down the passage, and caught sight of the pearls lying on the dressing table and just slipped in and out. He could have done the same with Mrs. Smythe's brooch, but he must have actually had to unlock Lupin's jewel case and if Staines had come in, it would have been awkward for him. He may have forgotten all about her, and known that he could satisfy Lupin, who was never surprised about anything.

Yes, it was a good theory. He wanted the guests to leave Orchard House so that Diana would give up the idea of a guest house, so he kept on thinking of one thing after another to drive them away. Of course, George may have been in it with him or he may have merely been an unconscious tool. The unfortunate thing was, that clear as the case now seemed, Borden had no proof.

CHAPTER 27

MR. BORDEN went to Somerset House and found that Ramsden's aunt had left forty thousand pounds to him and Orchard House and ten thousand pounds to Diana. There was no mention of the house reverting to the family after Diana's death. It was left to her absolutely. Of course, the income on forty thousand pounds was not a great deal nowadays, not for anyone with extravagant tastes. Paul may have wanted more money. But Borden did not really think that money was his motive. He felt convinced of his love for Orchard House.

On his return he sought out Diana. She was sitting in her office looking pale and tired. "I am terribly sorry to bother you just now," he said, "but I know you would like to have things cleared up as soon as possible. Do you mind very much telling me to whom Orchard House would go if you died?"

"To my goddaughter, June Scott. At least, that is how my will stands at the moment, but as you know, I am getting married quite soon and I haven't decided whether to sell this house or not. Robert has a place in Somerset, so I don't expect we will keep this on as well."

"Has your cousin, Paul Ramsden, ever offered to buy the house from you?"

"Yes, now you mention it, he did. It was right at the beginning, just after our aunt died. He said, 'Would you care to sell me the house?' and I was tempted because the money would have been very useful to me. I knew I should never be able to live here myself without taking guests, and that really is rather a bore. Unfortunately, I felt pretty sure that if he did buy it, he would modernize it in some way. I had seen his pictures and heard him talk and that is why my aunt left the place to me because she knew I should keep it just as it was. So it would have been rather a mean trick on my part to sell it to him. If I have to get rid of it I shall find someone who appreciates it as it is."

"I think your cousin loves it as it is," said Borden. And he told her the story of the pictures and of his impressions from the talk he had had that morning with Paul in the orchard.

Diana looked at him intently, "What a fool I have been!" she exclaimed. "Paul did love this place as a child. I remember how upset he was when his parents came back from India and he had to live with them. I thought he was rather unnatural at the time, but I suppose to some men places are more important than people. I don't believe that is ever so with women. I didn't see Paul for a long time after he grew up. I know his people persuaded him to take up engineering and I believe he loathed it. He was quite a different person when I did see him again. He had been such a dear little boy. I see now that he put on that pose about despising beauty or only finding beauty in ugliness. Poor old Paul!"

"Do you think it is possible that Ramsden engineered all the mysteries of the last week?"

Diana suddenly sat up quite straight. "I have just remembered something," she said. "It is funny how things suddenly come back to one. It was during the summer holidays, and Paul's people had arrived back from India and had taken a house at the seaside for a month. They came down here to see him and then had to go away for a few days and Paul was to join them at the sea for the rest of the holidays. He didn't say anything. Everyone thought he was looking forward to it, but somehow I guessed he did not want to go and on the last afternoon I found him in the little spinney. He was lying with his head pressed up against a beech tree, crying. He was about twelve at the time and would not have liked to have been found crying, so I slipped away. When he came in to tea he was quite normal and said what fun it would be at the sea. But in the night he woke up violently ill with diarrhea and sickness. The doctor came and looked very grave and everyone was upset. It was a fortnight before he was able to go to the seaside, but I found that a practically new bottle of Epsom salts of mine had nearly all gone. He must have just quietly taken them, knowing they would upset him and prevent his having to go away so soon. His mind works differently from other people's, in a secretive kind of way. Of course, he was never with his parents for long, and although Aunt Lucy was fond of us in her way, she never took much notice of us, so I suppose this place became human to him and all his affection was centered on it. But why on earth didn't he explain all that to me instead of staging burglaries and fires and—no, I can't believe that."

"It doesn't really fit in with the rest, the other things are more in the manner of practical jokes and yet—" Borden paused. Then he went on, "By the way, what about George?"

"Oh, he came to see me this morning and apologized. He said he quite understood that I wouldn't be able to keep him here after what had happened. I was sorry, he really is a good sort. Of course, I couldn't keep him on very well, but I hope Robert and I may be able to find him something. I think it was only a lapse."

"I am afraid that lapse was your cousin's fault," and Borden told her about the whisky in the summerhouse.

"It was rather bad luck on George," said Diana. "But I do wish I had seen Mrs. Mydleton's face."

Colonel James came in and Borden left him with Diana, who was looking really ill now. He wished he had not had to distress her, but he had not been able to help it. He walked through the grounds to the summerhouse. It was locked but he had had a duplicate key made and he let himself in.

On the easel was a picture of Orchard House, but it was Orchard House disfigured. There was a large glass portico in place of the front door and there was a row of petrol pumps beside it. Borden stood looking at it with interest. It was a very clever picture, but why had Paul painted it?

"Well, how do you like it?" Ramsden had come in noiselessly.

"Not at all," said Borden. "Is that what would have become of the house if it had been yours?"

"Probably, but you see, it isn't mine."

"No, it isn't, and you were very much disappointed. You asked your cousin to sell it to you, but unfortunately you had given her to understand that your tastes were opposed to hers and to those of your aunt, and she felt that it would be wrong to let you have it as you might do that to it," and he waved his hand towards the picture on the easel. "Instead of telling her plainly that you loved every stone of the place and would die rather than have anything altered, you acquiesced in her decision and planned in your own mind to get it away from her in some other way. When you found that she would have to run it as a guest house, you decided to drive away the guests so that she would be unable to afford to live here any longer, and would be glad to sell it to you. You had come across Miss Dyson-Drake somewhere and you knew that she was eccentric enough to be considered mad by most people, and that she would be very likely enough in herself to drive any normal people away from her vicinity, so you persuaded her to come here. When you found that in spite of her extraordinary conversation and behavior the guests still stayed on, you took her manuscript, knowing that she would make everyone's life a burden till she got it back."

Borden paused a moment but Paul did not speak; he was looking at him with wonder tinged with admiration. Borden went on, "In the same way you imported the Rennies, who seemed to you a promising couple to upset a conventional circle of people, but when you found they were not so unconventional as you thought, you started to flirt with the wife, hoping to start some sort of flare-up. Nothing however, would move the guests, who found the hotel extremely comfortable, so one day when passing Mrs. Mydleton's room and seeing her pearls lying on the dressing table, you slipped in and pocketed them. This was so easily done that you played the same trick on Mrs. Smythe, as regards her brooch. Then you had the bright idea of pretending that your notecase had been stolen, and finally you went into Lady Lupin Hastings' room, unlocked her jewel case and took out the least valuable thing you could find. Now you had thoroughly persuaded everyone that there was a burglar in the house, and given an uneasy feeling to all the inmates, but still they stayed. You felt desperate and one day when you could bear thins no longer you heard your cousin say that she was going out in Miss Dyson-Drake's car, and you offered to bring it round. Before doing so, you loosened a nut on the steering-gear."

"That is not true," said Paul.

"What is not true?" asked Borden.

"That I loosened the nut on the steering-gear."

"Is the rest true?"

"Yes. I should have given the things back eventually, but the people had got to go first and nothing on earth would budge them. Do you think I could bear seeing this place as a hotel? To see people like Mrs. Mydleton and Mrs. Smythe walking about as if they owned it, calling our hall the lounge and criticizing the bedrooms! Diana is very capable. As the place got more and more successful it would have become more and more like an ordinary hotel, till it became like this," and he pointed to the picture.

"You misunderstood your cousin just as she misunderstood you. She had kept this house out of loyalty to her aunt and she would never have altered it. She did not like taking in guests and she would gladly have got rid of the place if she could have been certain that it would not have been defaced. Why didn't you let her know that you cared for it?"

"I learned to keep things to myself when I was quite young. If you let people know what you are thinking they either sneer at you or else try to be sympathetic, which is worse. I never minded the boys laughing at me at school, they were quite good-natured. It was the ones who tried to be friends that I hated, those who said they were fond of art, too, and that sort of thing, trying to break into one's private places and trampling on one's private thoughts. There was one master who encouraged me to talk about pictures and lent me books to read. I did not want to share what I felt with anyone.

"When I went to Oxford I deliberately joined a set who admired all the things I hated. I rather enjoyed living my own private life while pretending to belong to them, affecting to despise all the things I really cared for and to admire the things I despised. I was able to laugh up my sleeve at them all the time, and they never knew. Then my father died and there was practically no money. An uncle put me into his engineering firm. There was nothing else I could do. I simply loathed it; I had no time to paint or to think about the things I cared for, but my mother had only enough for herself and I couldn't earn my living by painting. I lived for the moment I should inherit this place and then, well, I didn't!" He laughed. "So now you know," he said. "How you guessed all this, I can't imagine."

"You will be surprised to hear that it was Lady Lupin Hastings who gave me the idea. She found this studio, and she brought me to see the pictures. She said, 'Whoever painted these loved this place very much.' "

"I told her that her business in life was to sit quiet and look lovely. It is a pity she did not take my advice."

"From your point of view it is, certainly."

"Yes, well, there it is. It was rather fun while I was doing it."

"You rang up the fire brigade before you set light to the chair, I gather?"

"Yes, and I sent George for the stirrup-pump. Unfortunately, he had taken it out to hose a car with and he was a few minutes finding it. Still, perhaps it was as well. It would have been awkward if he'd arrived before the chair was alight."

"Did George help you in any of your transgressions?"

Paul stared at him. "Goodness, no, I work by myself. Poor old George! The only thing I regret is making him drunk the other evening, though it must have been a frightfully funny scene. When I brought him here, knowing his reputation, I thought he was bound to break out sometime. But not a bit of it, he was determined to get over it, so it was rather a dirty trick to push him back on to it again."

"Yes, it was a dirty trick, but not so dirty as trying to murder your cousin."

"I never tried to murder my cousin," said Paul.

CHAPTER 28

LUPIN walked through the garden to the garage. It was the next afternoon and it was not a nice afternoon and it had not been a nice morning. Spring seemed to have gone away and winter returned. It was cold and gray with a fine drizzle, and the blossom was dropping off the cherry trees and lying about on the ground like confetti when the wedding is over. Indoors everything was depressing, too. Poor Diana was very unhappy, for Paul had confessed to the burglaries and to the attempted fire and to having made George drunk, but he would not confess to the attempted murder. Who else could have done it? Diana would not believe it, but it must have been Paul. Naturally the whole thing had been a terrible shock to her because she was fond of him. Lupin did not want to believe it either. She had rather a liking for Paul in spite of his disgraceful behavior, and no one really bad could have painted those pictures of the house and orchard. Nor did she really believe anyone very bad would enjoy reading *The Cock House at Felsgarth* and *The Speckled Band.* But who else could it be?

She picked her way through the wet grass in her gum-boots and pondered the question. Arthur? No, it couldn't possibly be Arthur, they had proved that again and again. Nor could it possibly be Mr. Gower, or had he got in in the night and tampered with the car? But surely he would not take all that trouble, when Rosie was quite all right again. Charles Rennie? No, they had gone over that, too. If he had mistaken Miss Dyson-Drake's car for Paul Ramsden's, he would not have realized that Paul's was not there that morning and suspected him of having eloped with Ruth. Colonel James? Why should he? Oh, dear, I am afraid it is Paul. Poor Diana, she is so fond of him.

Lupin reached the garage. She was going into Ryeport to get some things for Diana. Miss Dyson-Drake in blue drill overalls was washing her car. She had a smear of grease on her cheek and her hair was escaping from under an orange handkerchief. She wore a pair of long Oriental earrings which completed the bizarre effect of her attire. "Oh, hallo," said Lupin. "I didn't know you went in for that sort of thing."

"No manual work is degrading," explained Miss Dyson-Drake, absentmindedly directing the hose on to Lupin, who skipped agilely out of the way. "I find it inspiring. Once I scrubbed out my bathroom and polished the taps, then sat down and wrote magnificently for six hours. I often oil and grease my own car. I find it helps to release something."

"I am afraid I am frightfully bad at insides," said Lupin. "I can drive all right, but if anything goes wrong with the innards, I just sit still and scream for a man."

"What a man can do, a woman can do," announced Miss Dyson-Drake. "Not all women, but those of us who are gifted beyond the rest of our sex."

"I don't think I am," said Lupin, reflectively.

"No, you are not," replied Miss Dyson-Drake. "I decided one day that I should like to understand the workings of a car. As a matter of fact I was writing a very strong chapter at the time about the workings of the human body."

"Oh, dear," ejaculated Lupin.

"So I got Paul Ramsden to show me. He worked as an engineer when young, a soul-destroying job for an artist. All the same, a certain amount of manual work is good for the brain. I often say to him, 'those years may have helped your art in the long run, little as you would expect it.' "

"Do you mean that you know what all the different nuts are about?" asked Lupin breathlessly.

"Yes," said Miss Dyson-Drake. "I understand the whole thing. I have a marvelous grasp of any subject that I may happen to take up. This nut, for instance, is the one that affects the steering. The other day I thought the steering was rather tight, so I loosened it and it made a great difference."

"Was that the morning you took Diana out in the car and had the accident?" said Lupin.

"Let me think," and Miss Dyson-Drake pondered for a moment, holding a greasy hand to her forehead and making another black mark. "Yes, I think it was. Paul Ramsden brought the car round, and I went out into the drive. As I did so I remembered that the steering had been constrained the day before. I needed more scope, so I loosened the nut. Then I got into the car and Miss Turner came out and said would I drop her at a shop. She offered to drive. I dare say she likes a tighter steering gear, and that is why she had the accident. If I had thought of it I would have warned her, but my mind was otherwise occupied."

Lupin was laughing hysterically, but Miss Dyson-Drake did not notice. She was thinking of her manuscript, which had been restored to her, and of the wonderful work she was going to do when she had stimulated her brain by this manual exercise. Lupin had a wild desire to embrace her but was put off by the greasy marks on her face. With an inarticulate cry of thanks, she turned and ran back to the house, running faster than she had ever run before.

In her headlong rush through the hall she collided with Mr. Borden. "Come quick," she said. "Everything is all right. Diana will be so thankful and poor Paul, too! I never really thought he had done it, and they won't do anything frightful to him now, will they? I mean about the other things? What a pity we ever told the police, we might have hushed it up. But I dare say they will put him in a home for a bit, and then he will be able to come and live here and be happy ever after. He would have been welcome to Great-aunt Jemima's brooch."

"Do you mean by all this that you know who it was that loosened the nut on the car?" asked Mr. Borden.

"Absolutely, and I always said it was from the beginning. Oh, there is Robert. He said I was to call him Robert. I say, what have you done with Diana? Just tell her that I haven't gone to Ryeport, after all, so there won't be any salmon for dinner, but never mind, I will gladly eat cod. It isn't Paul, I don't mean the cod, but the murderer. It was Miss Dyson-Drake all the time. Oh, there you are, Di. It wasn't Paul, it was the Dyson. She wanted more scope for her steering so she loosened the nut. She thinks that may be why you had the accident and she would have told you if she had thought of it. I really don't feel I can go to the fishmonger's till I've told everyone—what? What did you say? Why didn't you tell me? Andrew?" and sure enough there was Andrew following Diana down the stairs.

"You have not given anybody much time to tell you anything so far," remarked her husband when at length he had disentangled himself. "I came to see what you were up to. From your letters you did not seem to be exactly having a rest cure. And I gather you are just finishing your career here by solving a murder."

"Well, one thing led to another. What with burgling and fires and Diana being nearly killed, it has been pretty hectic. Oh, here is Mrs. Mydleton, and Mrs. Smythe and Mrs. Arthur Smythe. This is my husband and Miss Dyson-Drake loosened the nut by mistake, so that's all right." Two women she could not place stood near the door. She seemed to know their faces, then suddenly she remembered Miss Popham and Miss Witham. She darted across to them. "Oh, I am so sorry, but we are all feeling rather excited as a murder has just been cleared up."

"We have arrived," announced Miss Popham. "Will you please send the porter to take our luggage out of the car?"

"Well, I would if he were here, but he had to go, he got so drunk," explained Lupin. "Oh, here is Mr. Rennie," as Charles rushed up to the car and started to haul out two trunks, two hatboxes, two dressing-cases, a bundle of mackintoshes and umbrellas and a basket full of bottles. Lupin looked with interest at this last, but was disappointed to find that they were mostly bottles of Agerol.

"Please be careful with those bottles," said Miss Popham. "They are very necessary to my friend's comfort."

"This is Mr. Rennie," explained Lupin, "and by the way, the one I was kissing was my husband. You can imagine how thrilled I was at seeing him again. I had no idea he was coming, but when he heard about all the queer things that had been happening here, he thought he had better come and investigate. He is a clergyman, you, know."

"We should like some tea, straightaway," said Miss Popham. "China tea, please."

"I like Indian tea best," said Miss Witham.

THE END

About The Rue Morgue Press

The Rue Morgue vintage mystery line is designed to bring back into print those books that were favorites of readers between the turn of the century and the 1960s. The editors welcome suggests for reprints. To receive our catalog or make suggestions, write The Rue Morgue Press, P.O. Box 4119, Boulder, Colorado (1-800-699-6214). The Rue Morgue Press tries to keep all of its titles in print, though some books may go temporarily out of print for up to six months.

Catalog of Rue Morgue Press titles January 2003

Titles are listed by author. All books are quality trade paperbacks measuring 9 by 6 inches, usually with full-color covers and printed on paper designed not to yellow or deteriorate. These are permanent books.

Joanna Cannan. The books by this English writer are among our most popular titles. Modern reviewers favorably compared our two Cannan reprints with the best books of the Golden Age of detective fiction. "Worthy of being discussed in the same breath with an Agatha Christie or a Josephine Tey."—Sally Fellows, Mystery News. "First-rate Golden Age detection with a likeable detective, a complex and believable murderer, and a level of style and craft that bears comparison with Sayers, Allingham, and Marsh."—Jon L. Breen, *Ellery Queen's Mystery Magazine*. Set in the late 1930s in a village that was a fictionalized version of Oxfordshire, both titles feature young Scotland Yard inspector Guy Northeast. *They Rang Up the Police* (0-915230-27-5, 156 pages, $14.00) and *Death at The Dog* (0-915230-23-2, 156 pages, $14.00).

Glyn Carr. The author is really Showell Styles, one of the foremost English mountain climbers of his era as well as one of that sport's most celebrated historians. Carr turned to crime fiction when he realized that mountains provided a ideal setting for committing murders. The 15 books featuring Shakespearean actor Abercrombie "Filthy" Lewker are set on peaks scattered around the globe, although the author returned again and again to his favorite climbs in Wales, where his first mystery, published in 1951, *Death on Milestone Buttress* (0-915230-29-1, 187 pages, $14.00), is set. Lewker is a marvelous Falstaffian character whose exploits have been praised by such discerning critics as Jacques Barzun and Wendell Hertig Taylor in *A Catalogue of Crime*.

Torrey Chanslor. *Our First Murder* (0-915230-50-X .$14.95) When a headless corpse is discovered in a Manhattan theatrical lodging house, who better to call in than the Beagle sisters? Sixty-five-year-old Amanda employs good old East Biddicutt common sense to run the agency, while her younger sister Lutie prowls the streets and nightclubs of 1940 Manhattan looking for clues. It's their first murder case since inheriting the Beagle Private Detective Agency from their older brother, but you'd never know the sisters had spent all of their lives knitting and tending to their garden in a small, sleepy upstate New York town. Lutie is a real charmer, who learned her craft by reading scores of lurid detective novels borrowed from the East Biddicut Circulating Library. With her younger cousin Marthy in tow, Lutie is totally at ease as she questions suspects and orders vintage champagne. Of course, if trouble pops up, there's always that pearl-handled revolver tucked away in her purse. *Our First Murder* is a charming hybrid of the private eye, traditional, and cozy mystery, written in 1940 by a woman who earned two Caldecott nominations for her illustrations of children's books.

Clyde B. Clason. Clason has been praised not only for his elaborate plots and skillful use of the locked room gambit but also for his scholarship. He may be one of the few mystery authors—and no doubt the first—to provide a full bibliography of his sources. *The Man from Tibet* (0-915230-17-8, 220 pages, $14.00) is one of his best (selected in 2001 in *The History of Mystery* as one of the 25 great amateur detective novels of all time) and highly recommended by the dean of locked room mystery scholars, Robert Adey, as "highly original." It's also one of the first popular novels to make use of Tibetan culture.

Joan Coggin. *Who Killed the Curate?* Meet Lady Lupin Lorrimer Hastings, the young, lovely, scatterbrained and kindhearted newlywed wife to the vicar of St. Marks Parish in Glanville, Sussex. When it comes to matters clerical, she literally doesn't know Jews from Jesuits and she's hopelessly at sea at the meetings of the Mothers' Union, Girl Guides, or Temperance Society but she's determined to make husband Andrew proud of her—or, at least, not to embarass him too badly. So when Andrew's curate is poisoned, Lady Lupin enlists the help of her old society pals, Duds and Tommy Lethbridge, as well as Andrew's nephew, a British secret service agent, to get at the truth. Lupin refuses to believe Diane Lloyd, the 38-year-old author of children's and detective stories could have done the deed, and casts her net out over the other parishioners. All the suspects seem so nice, much more so than the victim, and Lupin announces she'll help the killer escape if only he or she confesses. Set at Christmas 1937 and first published in England in 1944, this is the first American appearance of *Who Killed the Curate?* "Marvelous."—*Deadly Pleasures* (0-915230-44-5, $14.00).

Manning Coles. The two English writers who collaborated as Coles are best known for those witty spy novels featuring Tommy Hambledon, but they also wrote four delightful—and funny—ghost novels. *The Far Traveller* (0-915230-35-6, 154 pages, $14.00) is a stand-alone novel in which a film company unknowingly hires the ghost of a long-dead German graf to play himself in a movie. "I laughed until I hurt. I liked it so much, I went back to page 1 and read it a second time."—Peggy Itzen, *Cozies, Capers & Crimes*. The other three books feature two cousins, one English, one American, and their spectral pet monkey who got a little drunk and tried to stop—futilely and fatally—a German advance outside a small French village during the 1870 Franco-Prussian War. Flash forward to the 1950s where this comic trio of friendly ghosts rematerialize to aid relatives in danger in *Brief Candles* (0-915230-24-0, 156 pages, $14.00), *Happy Returns* (0-915230-31-3, 156 pages, $14.00) and *Come and Go* (0-915230-34-8, 155 pages, $14.00).

Norbert Davis. There have been a lot of dogs in mystery fiction, from Baynard Kendrick's guide dog to Virginia Lanier's bloodhounds, but there's never been one quite like Carstairs. Doan, a short, chubby Los Angeles private eye, won Carstairs in a crap game, but there never is any question as to who the boss is in this relationship. Carstairs isn't just any Great Dane. He is so big that Doan figures he really ought to be considered another species. He scorns baby talk and belly rubs—unless administered by a pretty girl—and growls whenever Doan has a drink. His full name is Dougal's Laird Carstairs and as a sleuth he rarely barks up the wrong tree. He's down in Mexico with Doan, ostensibly to convince a missing fugitive that he would do well to stay put, in *The Mouse in the Mountain* (0-915230-41-0, 151 pages, $14.00), first published in 1943 and followed by two other Doan and Carstairs novels. *Staff pick* at The Sleuth of Baker Street in Toronto, Murder by the Book in Houston and The Poisoned Pen in Scotsdale. Four star review in *Romantic Times*. "A laugh a minute romp...hilarious dialogue and descriptions...utterly engaging, downright fun read...fetch this one! Highly recommended."—Michele A. Reed, *I Love a Mystery*. "Deft, charming...unique...one of my top ten all time favorite novels."—Ed Gorman, *Mystery Scene*. The second book, *Sally's in the Alley* (0-915230-46-1, $14.00), was equally well-received. *Publishers Weekly*: "Norbert Davis committed suicide in 1949, but his incomparable crime-fighting duo, Doan, the tippling private eye, and Carstairs, the huge and preternaturally clever Great Dane, march on in a re-release of the 1943 *Sally's in the Alley*. Doan's on a government-sponsored mission to find an ore deposit in the Mojave Desert...in an old-fashioned romp that matches its bloody crimes with belly laughs." The editor of *Mystery Scene* chimed in: "I love Craig Rice. Davis is her equal." "The funniest P.I. novel ever written."—*The Drood Review*.

Elizabeth Dean. Dean wrote only three mysteries, but in Emma Marsh she created one of the first independent female sleuths in the genre. Written in the screwball style of the 1930s, *Murder is a Collector's Item* (0-915230-19-4, $14.00) is described in a review in *Deadly Pleasures* by award-winning mystery writer Sujata Massey as a story that "froths over with the same effervescent humor as the best Hepburn-Grant films." Like the second book in the trilogy, *Murder is a Serious Business* (0-915230-28-3, 254 pages, $14.95), it's set in a Boston antique store just as the Great Depression is drawing to a close. *Murder a Mile High* (0-915230-39-9, 188 pages, $14.00), moves to the Central City Opera House in the Colorado mountains, where Emma has been summoned by am old chum, the opera's reigning diva. Emma not only has to find a murderer, she may also have to catch a Nazi spy. "Fascinating."—*Romantic Times*.

Constance & Gwenyth Little. These two Australian-born sisters from New Jersey have developed almost a cult following among mystery readers. Critic Diane Plumley, writing in *Dastardly Deeds*, called their 21 mysteries "celluloid comedy written on paper." Each book, published between 1938 and 1953, was a standalone, but there was no mistaking a Little heroine. She hated housework, wasn't averse to a little gold-digging (so long as she called the shots), and couldn't help antagonizing cops and potential beaux. The Rue Morgue Press intends to reprint all of their books. Currently available: *The Black Thumb* (O-915230-48-8,155 pages, $14.00), *The Black Coat* (0-915230-40-2, 155 pages, $14.00), *Black Corridors* (0-915230-33-X, 155 pages, $14.00), *The Black Gloves* (0-915230-20-8,

185 pages, $14.00), *Black-Headed Pins* (0-915230-25-9, 155 pages, $14.00), *The Black Honeymoon* (0-915230-21-6, 187 pages, $14.00), *The Black Paw* (0-915230-37-2, 156 pages, $14.00), *The Black Stocking* (0-915230-30-5, 154 pages, $14.00), *Great Black Kanba* (0-915230-22-4, 156 pages, $14.00), and *The Grey Mist Murders* (0-915230-26-7, 153 pages, $14.00), *The Black Eye* (0-915230-45-3, 154 pages, $14.00), and *The Black Shrouds* (0-915230-52-6, 155 pages, $14.00).

Marlys Millhiser. Our only non-vintage mystery, *The Mirror* (0-915230-15-1, 303 pages, $17.95) is our all-time bestselling book, now in a sixth printing. How could you not be intrigued by a novel in which "you find the main character marrying her own grandfather and giving birth to her own mother," as one reviewer put it of this supernatural, time-travel (sort-of) piece of wonderful make-believe set both in the mountains above Boulder, Colorado, at the turn of the century and in the city itself in 1978. Internet book services list scores of rave reviews from readers who often call it the "best book I've ever read."

James Norman. The marvelously titled *Murder, Chop Chop* (0-915230-16-X, 189 pages, $13.00) is a wonderful example of the eccentric detective novel. "The book has the butter-wouldn't-melt-in-his-mouth cool of Rick in *Casablanca*."—*The Rocky Mountain News*. "Amuses the reader no end."—*Mystery News*. "This long out-of-print masterpiece is intricately plotted, full of eccentric characters and very humorous indeed. Highly recommended."—*Mysteries by Mail*. Meet Gimiendo Hernandez Quinto, a gigantic Mexican who once rode with Pancho Villa and who now trains *guerrilleros* for the Nationalist Chinese government when he isn't solving murders. At his side is a beautiful Eurasian known as Mountain of Virtue, a woman as dangerous to men as she is irresistible. First published in 1942.

Sheila Pim. *Ellery Queen's Mystery Magazine* said of these wonderful Irish village mysteries that Pim "depicts with style and humor everyday life." *Booklist* said they were in "the best tradition of Agatha Christie." *Common or Garden Crime* (0-915230-36-4, 157 pages, $14.00) is set in neutral Ireland during World War II when Lucy Bex must use her knowledge of gardening to keep the wrong person from going to the gallows. Beekeeper Edward Gildea uses his knowledge of bees and plants to do the same thing in *A Hive of Suspects* (0-915230-38-0, 155 pages, $14.00). *Creeping Venom* (0-915230-42-9, 155 pages, $14.00) mixes politics and religion into a deadly mixture. *A Brush with Death* (0-915230-49-6 grafts a clever art scam onto the stem of a gardening mystery.

Craig Rice. *Home Sweet Homicide*. This marvelous funny and utterly charming tale (set in 1942 and first published in 1944) of three children who "help" their widowed mystery writer mother solve a real-life murder and nab a handsome cop boyfriend along the way made just about every list of the best mysteries for the first half of the 20th century, including: The Haycraft-Queen Cornerstone list, probably the most prestigious honor role in the history of crime fiction, James Sandoe's Reader's Guide to Crime, and Mevlyn Barnes' *Murder in Print*. Rice was of course best known for her screwball mystery comedies featuring Chicago criminal attorney John J. Malone. *Home Sweet Homicide* is a delightful cozy mystery partially based on Rice's own home life. It was filmed in 1946 with Peggy Ann Garner (who earned a special Oscar that year for her work as a juvenile lead), Randolph Scott, and Dean Stockwell, whose performance as Archie, the young son of mystery writer Marian Carstairs, captivated the hearts of the movie-going public. Negotiations are underway for a possible remake of this classic movie. Rice, the first mystery writer to appear on the cover of *Time*, died in 1957 at the age of 49. For more information on the author see the introduction to *Home Sweet Homicide.* Rice and her real-life office provided the inspiration for the cover to this new edition of *Home Sweet Homicide.* 0-915230-53-4, $14.95

Charlotte Murray Russell. Spinster sleuth Jane Amanda Edwards tangles with a murderer and Nazi spies in *The Message of the Mute Dog* (0-915230-43-7, 156 pages, $14.00), a culinary cozy set just before Pearl Harbor. "Perhaps the mother of today's cozy."—*The Mystery Reader*. Our earlier title, *Cook Up a Crime*, is currently out of print.

Juanita Sheridan. Sheridan was one of the most colorful figures in the history of detective fiction, as you can see from Tom and Enid Schantz's introduction to *The Chinese Chop* (0-915230-32-1, 155 pages, $14.00). Her books are equally colorful, as well as showing how mysteries with female protagonists began changing after World War II. The postwar housing crunch finds Janice Cameron, newly arrived in New York City from Hawaii, without a place to live until she answers an ad for a roommate. It turns out the advertiser is an acquaintance from Hawaii, Lily Wu, whom critic Anthony Boucher (for whom Bouchercon, the World Mystery Convention, is named) described as an "exquisitely blended product of Eastern and Western cultures" and the only female sleuth that he "was devotedly in love with," citing "that odd mixture of respect for her professional skills and delight in her personal charms." First published in 1949, this ground-breaking book was the first of four to feature Lily and be told by her Watson, Janice, a first-time novelist. "Highly recommended."—*I Love a Mystery*. "This well-written. . .enjoyable variant of the boarding house whodunit and a vivid portrait of the post WWII New York City housing shortage, puts to lie the common misconception that strong, self-reliant, non-spinster-or-comic sleuths didn't appear on the scene until the 1970s. Chinese-American Lily Wu and her novelist Watson, Janice Cameron, are young and feminine but not dependent on men."—*Ellery Queen's Mystery Magazine.* The first book in the series to be set in Hawaii is *The Kahuna Killer* (0-915230-47-X, 154 pages, $14.00). "Janice Cameron's return to Hawaii is 'the signal to set off a chain of events which [bring] discord and catastrophe,' as well as murder. Originally published five decades ago (thought it doesn't feel like it), this detective story featuring charming Chinese sleuth Lily Wu has the friends and foster sisters investigating mysterious events—blood on an ancient altar, pagan rights, and the appearance of a kahuna (a witch doctor)—and the death of a sultry hula girl in 1950s Oahu."—*Publishers Weekly*. Third in the series is *The Mamo Murders* (0915230-51-8, $14.00), set on a Maui cattle ranch.